# TOILS AND SNARES

## A DESERTED LANDS NOVEL

# ROBERT L. SLATER

ROCKET
TEARS
PRESS

BELLINGHAM, WA

2017 Rocket Tears Press

Copyright © 2017 by Robert L. Slater

www.RocketTears.com

Printed in the United States of America

ISBN 978-1-942096-09-2 (paperback)

First Paperback Edition

First Electronic Publication - 28 February 2015

Editor: Amanda Hagarty, Spencer Ellsworth
Copy Editors: Jesikah Sundin, Elena A. Bianco,
        Colleen A. Slater

Cover design: Pintado. www.pintado.weebly.com
Interior design: Random Max
        Text:, Calibri & Arial Narrow

# OTHER WORKS
# BY ROBERT L. SLATER

*All Is Silence* - Deserted Lands I
*Straight Into Darkness* - Deserted Lands II
*No Man's Land* - Deserted Lands III

*Outward Bound* - Science Fiction and
Poetry Collection

Some of the Parts - *Rob Slater*
*(original music album)*

*To all the grandparents, born and chosen.*
*And for the special ones who taught the lessons in the story.*

# CHAPTER ONE

SAMUEL HERMAN FELT MOVEMENT IN his wife Anna's pregnant belly. "Everything will be okay." He nestled his chin in the curve of her neck.

"Sam," Anna said. "We need to leave now." Her voice rose, still a whisper, but audible to their children down the hall. "Leave Portland. Go into the wilderness, like Moses. Go where there aren't any people."

"How many times, Anna?" he said, softening his voice, hoping she would do the same. Noah was too young to understand anything except the tension in their voices, but Abigail was six and sharp as a tack.

"If we don't leave Portland and one of my kids gets the plague..." She spun, eyes stabbing, voice still rising. "What then?"

My kids too. "Honey, shhhh... Let's not scare the kids any more than they are already." Samuel placed his hands on her shoulders. Then slowly he started working on her knotted muscles. "It's not the plague."

"I don't care what it's called. They might get infected. The hospitals are closing. There's no reason to stay—"

"No reason?"

For a moment, she looked chastised and guilty as her eyes fell from his. But it only took a moment for her eyes to glaze with anger again. She spoke, no longer even attempting to be quiet. "None of us have it yet. People are looking at us funny."

Samuel couldn't imagine that anyone had even seen them. "Who is looking at us funny?" He'd been in the office crunching numbers until two days ago when the emergency order had been issued. Anna had only been out for groceries once and people had been staying inside. Those that weren't already dead and dying.

"People." Anna grabbed his face, in order to hold his gaze. Had the stress kicked her back into mental health watch mode? He needed her here, not catatonic. "When Maria gets here. Then we'll go."

"Maria may not even be on the way. Your daughter—"

"Maria is our daughter." His face flushed hot. "When you married me, she was part of the package. I know you two don't get along, but she is ours."

She pursed her lips and nodded.

Samuel choked down his frustration. "We can go to your grandpa's place up at Lake Quinault. That's the middle of nowhere."

"Yes. That's perfect." A slight smile snuck past Anna's guard. "Thanks for not thinking I'm losing it again."

"Honey, I never-"

"If you don't find Maria—"

"I will find her." Sweat broke out on Samuel's forehead as his anger surged back. He spoke deliberately, "If you can't wait, you take the younger kids and I'll come when I can."

Samuel watched her reassessing, closing him off.

"Okay," Anna agreed. "Go see Brad. Please."

"I called him four times."

"He's not going to call you back. Go see if he and Pam are—Ask him for help. Ask them to come with us. I would go with them."

Samuel sighed and stood. "Okay, I'll go talk to Brad." He paused at the door, facing away from her as he spoke. "If Maria hasn't called by tomorrow, you can leave with them while I head east to find her." The last thing he wanted to do was leave his pregnant wife alone; how could a man choose between his daughter and his wife?

"Go to Brad's," she said. "Go now." Her jaw clamped down. "Be careful. I love you."

"I love you, too."

She wanted to say something else.

"What is it?"

"If they—if Pam and the kids are—" Anna couldn't say the word.

Samuel kissed her forehead, then held her at arm's length, memorizing her worried scowl, even angry she was an amazing beauty. "This is Brad and his family we're talking about, honey. He's been preparing for this his whole life. They are probably the safest people in the city." No new reports of looters in weeks, but the level of lawlessness they represented made Samuel nervous.

"Lock the deadbolt."

Samuel climbed into his truck, turned the heater on against the October chill and flipped the radio to the Oldies station. Bill Haley told him the time as he rocked around the clock backing out of the driveway.

Tonight was Halloween. This morning he'd pulled a box of oatmeal out of the emergency supplies pantry cabinet and spotted the candy stash. It felt wrong that his children were going stir crazy instead of squealing with excitement at their choice of costumes; arguing over whose was the best, and would get the most treats.

Deserted streets should be full of kids—zombies and ghosts. Some of the pandemic survivors looked like zombies, but they didn't eat flesh. Samuel searched the fading twilight. He didn't want to run into any cops asking questions about why he'd broken the curfew.

Samuel's phone buzzed. He pulled it out of his pocket, feeling guilty for checking it while driving. An alert flashed on the screen. Samuel pressed the play icon and a recorded announcement overrode the music.

"Update for October 31st 2019. There are reports of a secondary wave of the virus. It is unknown if survivors are immune to this strain. Stay in your homes. Portland area hospitals will not be accepting new patients. This message will be repeated and rebroadcast through bluetruth networks and all other emergency systems. Stay in your homes. May God save us. Goodnight."

Samuel glanced up as he rolled through a flashing red light. "Shit." He jammed on the brakes; his chest tightened. The CDC said the thirty percent survival rate had stabilized. How deadly would this new strain be? The intersection was deserted; he let the car roll forward again.

Maybe Anna was right and God had taken enough of their children. Maybe miscarriages and losing a baby to SIDS gave them some sort of pass. But despite his decades of Catholic guilt, Samuel couldn't believe in the God that carried Anna through. If He was watching over every human action, why would He let innocents die? Why did He stand by while others inflicted suffering on so many?

Let Anna believe in that God. It had saved her sanity. Let her believe that one day she'd see all her children again. Adopting Abigail and giving birth to Noah had further cemented her faith. But if God was rewarding her for her faith, would Samuel get that same reward with his lack?

He slid his thumb over his phone. "Call Maria." He had hardly heard from his oldest daughter since she started her second year of video-game production courses at Eastern Oregon University in September. Facebook posts and a text here and there. Then the pandemic hit. "Dad, you know the media is always making things out as worse than they are. Fear mongers. You taught me that."

When the University closed a week ago, she said she was going to find her boyfriend James on the Warm Springs Reservation and head to Portland. Then the cells went down except for local point-to-point bluetruth networks. They worked again now in Portland, but what about where Maria was? The phone finally started ringing her number as he counted to five.

When the line connected Maria said, "Yeah?"

He took a breath to speak, then hated her voice-mail. Her voice sounded so real that every time he heard it, his heart thought she was there.

But her voice on the other end continued. "Leave a message if you want to, but I won't promise to call you back. Send me a text."

He'd tried texting, too, with no more luck. Samuel spoke.

"Ria. It's Dad. It's Halloween. We're leaving town. Call me now."

He ended the call. Was she still alive?

Samuel shook himself out of those thoughts. He hated being held hostage to his fear. There were riots in L.A., New York City, New Orleans, D.C. But there had been little violence here in Portland. Not yet. Some people thought the government was holding out on them, convinced that the cure was out there, or that a government project had gone wrong.

An old drunk, one of the secondary casualties lost in his head, stumbled down the middle of the empty street. If Samuel lost his family, give it a week and he would look just as bad. But his family was alive, against all odds. Anna was right. He had to get them out.

Part of Samuel did not want to check on Brad, his oldest friend. It had been more than two years since he'd seen him. As Brad had become angrier and more paranoid, Samuel found reasons to not be around him. But he'd be a good man to have around if things got even worse.

Samuel pulled into the driveway of the 1970s era split level and sat in his truck surveying the house. The lawn was high, and the lights were out. Pam's Trans-Am was the only car in the driveway. Had they gotten out? That's why no one had answered his calls. He didn't know what he expected to find, but there might be extra survival gear even if they were gone.

He opened the truck door and stepped down. The flimsy veil of street lights held back the dark of night. Most of the other houses were dark, too. When he reached the door, he knocked, waited a moment, then knocked again. Peering through the curtains didn't help; the inside looked black. He reached under the porch, hoping the key would still be there on the nail. Yes. He pulled the key off and slid it right into the lock; the telltale drip showed that Brad had applied WD-40 anticipating the coming winter. Brad was a fanatic about electrical and mechanical things. The cold knob turned silently, and he pushed the door open.

Samuel reached for the light, but the click of a handgun's hammer froze his finger on the switch.

* * *

Maria Herman slipped into the quiet house in Warm Springs as the sun set over the flat-top hills. She'd found the door swinging free and closed it behind her. All the lights were on. James' truck was parked out front of his family's house. He had to be here.

"James?" she called softly. Her breathing quickened.

Inside the house was a mess. Very unlike the usually neat company-ready home his mother kept. Scents of smoke and mold permeated the house. The table held the remains of a meal; casserole dishes, salmon bones, glasses. Bottles littered the counter. Candles and tokens of affection—remnants of a memorial service—surrounded a photo of James' mother and his sister, Karaya.

Down the hall, she opened each door. "Mr. Johnson? I'm looking for James." She had to know if he was still alive. She wasn't sure if she loved James, and she still wasn't going to marry him, but none of that mattered anymore.

At the last door at the end of the hall she paused—James' father's room. The door had never been opened when she visited. Maria knocked softly. She heard a sound. With a deep breath she turned the knob. A cloth draped over a lamp shade gave off soft reddish light. There was a body in the bed and another on the floor. As her eyes readjusted, she recognized James' bulky body on the floor curled inward at his father's deathbed. *Oh, God! Not you too.* She knelt to kiss him, her movements stiff as tears spilled. Her lips touched his forehead. Not cold. Her hand felt for his heartbeat.

James eyes snapped wide open and locked onto her face as they focused. "Ria?" He stared as if he didn't believe she was real.

"Ria?"

"You were sleeping." She touched his face. "I'm here."

James sat up and glanced around, still confused. His eyes took in the body on the bed. "Dad and I were walking down by the..."

Maria saw the realization dawn as the confusion turned to grief and a moan escaped his mouth.

"No," he whispered, collapsing back to the floor, his body in the fetal position.

Maria wrapped her arms around him. "James." Her heart pounded in shared pain. She held him as he sobbed, her face on his. She knew the pain of losing a parent. Her mother had died in a car accident a few years after her parents' divorce. But she didn't know what it felt like to lose her entire family. "I thought you were..."

He rolled to his back and opened up his arms to her. She laid her face on his chest, happy to listen to his pounding heart. "I'm sorry about your dad."

His big arms held her tight, clinging to her. His teeth ground together. After a few moments, he spoke a strangled, "Thanks."

Silence stretched between them once more. What could she say? As if sensing her discomfort, James took another shuddering breath and whispered, "I'm glad you're alive."

"You didn't answer your phone."

James stared at her blankly and patted his pockets. "Huh. I

don't know where it is."

"It doesn't matter now. I don't have service here anyway." Maria slid off his chest and rested herself on her elbow, her small hand nestled in his. "I need you to come with me. Back to Portland. I'm scared. I think we're safer there."

"I don't think anywhere is safe anymore." James sat up, not letting go of Maria's hand.

Maria's mind raced. How should she tell him? Her heart pounded and her tongue stuck to the roof of her mouth. She knelt in front of James and held his face in her hands. "I'm scared," she said, soft and gentle, "because I don't know what's going to happen to our baby." She watched James process the information.

"Oh, god." James' eyes closed. He turned away from her. After a moment he returned to face her. "If you were... But, I... I didn't—" His jaw tightened as he glanced at his father's body on the bed. "I don't know if I can handle it, Ria."

Maria's stomach churned. "We're gonna be fine." Her hands returned to his face. "I'm here. You're here. We'll handle it. Together."

"Yeah." His features softened. "We're gonna have a baby?"

"Yeah."

James stared at her. His eyes lit up, and he jumped to his feet, dragging Maria gently to hers. "We're gonna have a baby." He wrapped his arms around her and lifted her off her feet. "Can we name him after my father?"

"Who says we're having a boy?" Maria laughed. Her heart warmed. She couldn't remember the last time she had laughed.

James kissed her. She closed her eyes, tasting salt on his rough lips.

He set her down on the floor. "When?"

"I'm not sure. Near as I can figure, in about seven and a half months. Must have been that last time. Before you quit school."

"I'm sorry I didn't stay with you, Maria."

"No." She pressed her fingers to his lips. "Your mother was dying." She shrugged, though part of her was still angry. It wasn't right to be angry about a thing like that. Not now.

"She's dead."

"I'm sorry."

"They all are." James knelt by his father.

Maria knelt beside him and took his hand.

"Goodbye, Father. If you can hear me, take care of Mama and Raya." He looked upward. "Mama, I'm sorry you didn't get to be a grandma. Watch over my *oha'a*, I will teach him what you taught me. Take care of Father." He brushed the hair back from his father's, craggy face.

Maria marveled that even in death he seemed calm. She had seen him getting chewed out by James' mom and always that hint of a twinkle in his eyes, patiently waited for a moment to escape. She loved that about James, too.

"I suppose I should do something, but there is no one— hardly anyone left." He glanced sideways at Maria. "No survivors to sings songs or give gifts to." His voice faded out.

"I'll sing with you." She felt a calmness that scared her.

His voice started softly, a low rumble, and his hands beat a rhythm on his thighs. After a few cracks and stumbles, his voice rose in confidence. No words, or if there were, Maria could not understand them, but she could follow the music as it repeated. She held onto him as they sang. When the song stopped, the calm remained. He kissed his father's brow and stood.

"I'll get some things and then we can go."

"Take all the time you need."

"No. It is time to go. Only death lives here now." He strode from the room.

Maria followed him out. He stepped into a room and closed the door behind him. What did he need and why shut the door? Moments later the door reopened and James, a mild smile on his face, held something behind his back. "I have a gift for you. For us. For the baby." He pulled a pretty, beaded frame of leather and woven reeds from behind him. "It's my *hoob*, my baby basket," he said. "My mother made it for me. Then my sister used it." His Adam's apple bobbed as he held the basket out to her.

"She would want you to have it."

Maria accepted it gently, caressing the multicolored bead-work. "It's lovely." Would she need to use it? And how? "Thank you."

He brushed past her into his old room, emerging with a duffle-bag he'd brought home from the university. With a thump, he set it by the front door and dug in his pocket. "Can you drive? I'm not sure I am up for it right now."

"Sure," Maria took the keys from James' hand and fingered the little laser pointer still attached to his key chain. She'd bought it for his big dumb dog, who apparently liked pouncing on a moving speck of light as much as any cat. "Where's Dozer?"

James' jaw tightened. "Got hit by a car. My cousin was drinking and dying."

"Jesus, James," Maria said. "That's a horrible thing to say."

She wrapped her arms around him and squeezed.

After a moment of stiff hesitation, he hugged her back. "Hey, if you can't join 'em, make a joke about it. Could you take this out to my truck?" he asked, handing her the bag before she could say anything else. "And the baby-basket? I'll grab some food and stuff and we can go."

The little junker she'd borrowed had barely made it here from Eastern in La Grande; would it make it all the way to Portland? She was glad to swap it for James' more sturdy truck. By the time James came out lugging a heavy cooler, Maria had all the gear from her dorm room transferred into the idling truck. Seemed stupid to bring the posters and other junk, but she hadn't wanted to leave it a mess.

Once on the road, Maria gripped the wheel tight. It had been a while since she'd driven James' truck, but it felt good.

James spoke, "Father wasn't sick."

James' voice startled Maria from her melancholy.

"But when mother and Raya died... He stopped eating, I wanted him to stay; I needed him." His body shuddered, and he took a deep breath. "But I didn't tell him. Not until it was too late. It was like he decided to die and then he did."

"He loved you."

"Not as much as he loved Mama and Karaya." Only a hint of bitterness sounded through James' sadness.

"I'm sorry."

The silence resumed, each of them lost in their own worries.

The phone at her hip buzzed, startling her. It had been a week since her phone had done anything other than run out of power. She pulled it out. Missed call. When she pressed the callback icon, the out of service notice popped up.

"Who is it?" he mumbled.

"Damn. I must have had signal, but not any more. Missed a call from my dad."

"Hand it to me," James said, sitting up straight. "I'll keep trying."

# CHAPTER TWO

"FLIP THE SWITCH, SAM," BRAD'S gruff voice echoed in the darkness.

Samuel let the air out of his lungs and breathed. "Brad." He flipped the switch. His friend Brad sat reclining in an armchair, his pistol pointed at Samuel. "Thank god it's you."

"Not sure you should be," Brad said.

Brad's once dark, now salt-and-peppered beard was several days past stubble. His crew cut had grown long enough to look shaggy. The gray at his temples had expanded and big bags hung under his eyes. He glared at Samuel. "I got your messages."

"Why didn't you—"

"Didn't really want to talk."

"Oh." Sweat slipped down inside Samuel's shirt despite the cold. He took in the state of affairs in the living room. A microwave dinner tray with the corn still in it sat on the coffee table. Where were Pam and the girls?

"I'm ready to talk now." Brad gestured with the handgun. "Have a seat."

"You mind putting that thing down, or at least releasing the hammer?" Samuel sat on the couch facing Brad.

"I do mind." The handgun stayed fixed on Samuel. "How's your wife? The kids?"

"They're fine." Samuel's hands shook. He clasped them together. Had Brad gone off the deep end? "Yours?"

"Remember Y2K, Samuel?"

"What about it?" Samuel's pulse pounded.

"Still got the bug-out-bag I gave you?"

Samuel laughed, nervous and hollow. "Yeah. But I never updated it, except to put in the water and MRE leftovers you gave me." He glanced sideways into the kitchen. The table looked like the morning after a college party. There were liquor bottles, some on their sides, most empty, without caps or corks.

A raspy chuckle escaped Brad's throat; the sound scared

Samuel.

"I gave you those leftovers ten years ago. I hope you don't have to eat them. I switched to freeze dried. Lasts longer." He stopped laughing and stared at Samuel. "Wondered if you'd make it over."

Samuel didn't like the gleam in Brad's eyes.

The pistol dropped, now aimed more toward Samuel's gut. "You thought you could get my stuff. Didn't you? All of it. Right here. A regular one-stop survival shopping spot."

"Jesus, Brad. I came to see if you wanted to go with us. We're heading to Quinault. The wilderness area up there should be pretty deserted."

Brad's head gestured upward. "Pam and the girls are upstairs."

A chill ran through Samuel. He hadn't heard a sound from upstairs. "Look, Brad. I'm not going to take your stuff."

"Damn straight you're not." Brad's bloodshot eyes narrowed.

A bead of sweat roll down Samuel's face. "Brad. I thought—" He held his shaking hands up.

Brad pulled a flask from his pocket, spun the lid open and drained whatever was left down his throat. One eye never left Samuel as he tossed the flask onto the couch.

"Brad," Samuel said, keeping his voice calm and soothing. He needed to get the hell out of here. He started to stand. "I should get back to Anna and the kids."

"Stay there." The handgun rose again, pointing at Samuel's head. "Your family's still alive?"

"Yeah, they are." Samuel swallowed, his tongue thick in his dry mouth. "Brad. We're friends. Way back. Twenty years. What do you want?"

"I want your life." Brad stood, stepping forward, bearing down, the handgun inches from Samuel's face. His eyes were red-rimmed. "She's gone. They all are. They were so sick."

"Brad—" Samuel leaned forward in his seat, reaching for his friend.

Brad's face hardened again. "Stand up, Sam."

Samuel stood, slowly. His hip vibrated and his phone began to sing Schubert's Ave Maria.

"Answer it," Brad growled, resting the barrel of the gun against Samuel's chest.

Samuel pulled out the phone and slid the screen. "Ria? Where are you?" His chest constricted in relief and fear all at once.

"We're driving through the thriving metropolis of Boring, Oregon, turning onto 212. Sorry, I didn't answer your call. I was out on the rez."

Samuel eyed Brad and thumbed the speakerphone icon. "Warm Springs?"

"Yeah. Looking for James." The voice scratched out of the small speaker.

*What does she see in him?* "Did you find him?"

"Yeah. He's here with me. You leaving Portland?"

"I hope so." Samuel stared at Brad, begging the question with his eyes. "I'm at Uncle Brad's house."

"How is he?"

Brad glared at Samuel. "I'm fine, Ria," he growled. "How you doin'?"

"Well, being pregnant at the end of the world isn't all it's cracked up to be, but at least I found my boyfriend alive."

Samuel sank into the soft couch, again. A million thoughts spun through his head. Then he refocused on Brad and the gun. Brad glanced away and spoke. "Ria." His voice softened. "Can I finish up with your dad? I promise he'll call you back in a few."

"Sure. Thanks, Uncle Brad. Talk to you soon, Dad."

Brad's hand dug into his pocket and pulled out a ring of keys. "Here. Take 'em." He tossed the keys onto the carpet at Samuel's feet. "Suburban's out in the alley. Trailer's attached. Ready to go. I was going to take Pam and the girls — I wanted—" His jaw clenched.

Samuel scooped the keys up off the floor and stood to face his friend. "Come with us, Brad."

Brad shook his head. "No, I can't. Not now." He shoved the pistol in the waist of his pants. He offered Samuel his hand and then jerked it back. "Go. Now. Before I change my mind."

Samuel nodded. "We're heading to Anna's grandpa's place."

North Shore. Lake Quinault. Where we camped the summer before we all had kids? Join us if you change your mind."

Brad turned away. "Take care of the kids."

Samuel wanted to give him a hug or at least touch his shoulder, give him some comfort. But if the disease had struck this house—

Samuel crossed to the front door and opened it instead.

"Go with God," Brad said softly behind him.

"Thanks. You, too." Samuel didn't turn back; he stepped outside and closed the door. Behind him, he heard the deadbolt slip into place.

He jogged down the steps and around the house. The Suburban and its full trailer were there as Brad had promised—all prepped for his family.

Samuel pushed the unlock button, and the lights flashed on inside the Suburban. He opened the icy door and stuck the keys in the ignition.

What about his truck? Was there anything he couldn't do without? Samuel turned back around. A loud sound exploded inside the house. Terror gripped him. He forgot his truck, jumped in the SUV, fired up the engine, and shoved it in gear. The behemoth lurched forward.

A few minutes later his phone sang Ria's song. Samuel answered it with a jab at the screen. "Yeah?" he panted.

"You okay, Dad?" Ria asked.

"Fine."

"You still at Brad's?"

"No." Samuel swallowed, his jaw tight. He softened his tone. "Congratulations, Ria. To you and James."

"Thanks, Dad." She paused. "Didn't want to tell you until I was sure. Not exactly the best timing, I guess."

Samuel forced a smile. They say you can hear the smile. "Anytime is both the best and the worst time to have a baby. You're coming with us, right?"

"If you'll have us," Maria's voice was aloof, and he knew the "you" she meant was Anna.

Would the two of them ever get over their issues?" Of course. When are you due?"

"Mid-May. Where are we going?"

"North. Into the wilderness. Grandpa's place at Quinault. When can you and James meet me at home? We need to leave as soon as possible."

After they hung up, he coasted into the driveway and sat staring at his house. Anna was holding it together. Taking them to her grandfather's place might make it worse. They'd buried their first baby, Jesse, there on the property.

He took a big breath and rehearsed what he was going to say. He had the good news of the gear and the big vehicle, but the worst news would not reach her ears. He'd take the true story of Brad's last gift to his grave.

What Anna would consider the bad news was that Ria and James were both coming along. Samuel feared he'd have to pull the head of the family card. Anna respected it because it was what she'd grown up with. But he hated it—biblical master and all that. In his family, his father had publicly been the head, but as his grandmother said, his mom was the neck.

When he finally went inside, small arms grappled him. Noah wrapped around his knees and Abigail his waist. He scooped Noah up and buried his face in the boy's soft stomach, giving it a belly-blow. Noah responded to the raspberry with a jiggling belly-laugh.

"Me, too, Daddy," Abigail begged, sniffling.

Anna appeared at the door, her arms crossed over her pregnant belly. Her pulled-back hair made her look severe, but a hint of a smile teased across her face as Samuel placed the giggling Noah in her arms.

Samuel dropped to his knees and kissed the baby bump. He twisted to give Abigail a quick belly-blow and a rib-tickle for good measure. Her laughter ended in a cough. "How you doing, little one?"

"I'b fide," Abi said, snorting snot back up her nose. "Ew. Snot."

"Snot, snot, snot," Noah chortled. Since he'd started talking, he'd been an echo of his sister.

Samuel glanced at Anna; her face mirrored his own worry.

"Well?" Anna wiped Abigail's nose and slid the back of her

hand across their adopted daughter's brow, trying to be surreptitious about checking for a temperature.

"I've got supplies. Lots of them. Brad gave us his truck. It's fully stocked. And a trailer, too."

"What about Pam and—"

He cut her off, holding up his hand. He set Noah back on the ground. "Abigail, take your little brother and help him pick out five stuffed animals to bring."

Abigail rolled her eyes. She knew when she was being excluded from big people talk. "Come on, Noah."

They marched off hand in hand.

Samuel watched them totter down the hall, grateful and saddened.

"Pam and the kids are gone." The good news about the supplies disappeared under the weight of the bad news. "Send up prayers."

"But Brad can come with us?"

"I tried to get him to, but, he wouldn't. Told me to take his stuff. For you and the kids. Ria, too. He talked to her on the phone." Samuel knew he was stretching the truth, but the intent of his words reflected Brad's conflicted state of mind and his last request to take care of the kids.

Anna glared at him. "Your daughter—"

"Our daughter, dammit. She's going to need you when she makes us grandparents." Samuel watched the emotions cascade across his wife's face. That part, he hadn't intended to say yet, but it had to come out.

Anna stared. "Ria is pregnant?" It came out like an accusation.

Samuel caught her in a hug. "Yeah." He let the smile he felt come out. "She and James are going to have a baby. We're going to be grandparents." Anna was rigid in his arms. "About five months after our baby."

"God help us." She softened into his embrace.

"He will, Anna." He lifted her chin. "He has. This is a blessing."

A slightly sad, apologetic smile graced her face. "I'm sorry," Anna said. "I will be better for her. For them."

"I know you will. They'll be here in a bit. I need to crash if I'm going to drive all night--"

"I can take a turn."

"Thanks, I may take you up on that. Let me see how the truck and trailer handles."

Samuel went to their room, slipped his jeans off, and climbed into bed, curling under the down comforter. On a normal night, with a need to sleep he'd read *Accounting Today*, but there was no point. He lay there on the only bed he'd ever bought new, knowing he would miss it when they got to Quinault. The beds at the old homestead were older than Anna. Thoughts of Brad returned. Was he lying in bed with Pam? What if that gunshot hadn't been Brad? What if it had been Brad shooting Pam? Oh, God.

# CHAPTER THREE

THE SILVER OF MOON SHONE through the bedroom window, but Samuel still hadn't slept when a car pull up outside.

Anna hollered, "Abigail, Noah. Your sister's here."

Good. Maybe this would all be fine. He got up and hurried downstairs—better to be there for the reunion. He found Anna in the kitchen as the little ones buzzed past.

"Sorry, Sam," Anna said. "Hope I didn't wake you."

"Nah. I couldn't sleep. Too much to do and too much to think about."

The kiddos squealed at the front door as their big sister and her boyfriend came in.

"Abigail and Noah!" Maria crowed happily.

When Anna saw Maria and James, the corner of her mouth tightened, but she turned it into a smile.

Maria's face had a similar progression when she saw her step-mother. "Hi, Anna." She knelt wrapping her siblings in her arms. James hung back in the doorway, eclipsing most of the street light.

"Ria and James," Anna said. "I'm so glad you're safe. Be right back." She spun on her heel and headed down the hall.

Maria raised an eyebrow in Samuel's direction.

Samuel shrugged. "Noah. Abi. Let them get inside." He shooed the little ones back. "Glad Ria found you, James."

James' face broke into an embarrassed smile. "Thanks. I'm glad she found me, too."

"Congratulations." Sam offered his hand.

James wiped his hand on his pants and shook Samuel's firmly. Then he retreated back to lean against the door.

Anna bustled from the back room carrying a nylon shopping bag overflowing with baby clothes. She dropped them on the floor by the kids and gave James a hug. "Welcome to the family, James."

James' eyes grew as he accepted the embrace. "Thanks."

Anna pulled Maria into a hug, too. "Congratulations on the

baby, Maria." She motioned to the bag. "We can share these when the babies come. I might even have old maternity clothes to fit you."

"Thanks, Anna." Maria mechanically returned the hug. Well, Samuel couldn't expect everything to be all better all at once.

"Ria, Ria." The children crowded around.

"We're going on a trip," Abigail explained. "To Lake Kinwalt."

Maria bit her lip so she didn't laugh. "It's Quinault, lil sis. I know. I'm going with you."

"You are?"

"Yes, she is, honey," Anna agreed. "And James, too."

"Are you gonna ride with me?"

"No, Abigae-nae. I'm gonna ride with James. You ride with Dad and... Mom. But I'll see you when we stop."

"Let's go."

"You're right, Abi." Samuel patted her head. "We better get out of town. Okay, James, how reliable is your truck?"

"She's great. My uncle owned it before me. He wouldn't sell her because he knew how to work on her. Taught me. The body's for shit, but—" His brown face darkened. "Sorry, I ain't been around kids much recently. The truck looks like junk, but it's solid and the engine and all the moving parts work well."

"Great," Samuel clapped him on the shoulder. "That's what counts. The stuff on the inside." He hadn't meant it to come out as a jab, but it sounded like one. "Everybody to the bathroom."

"I don't have to go," Noah whined.

"Try anyway," Samuel commanded. "James and Maria, can you help me load stuff into your truck or the Suburban?"

"Sure."

"I'll get our bags," Anna said.

"I'll take a hug, too," Samuel said, his arms open.

Maria slipped inside his embrace. Her slim body hardly seemed ready to have a child. His head rested on her bleached hair. "Love you, kiddo."

* * *

Samuel kept to the back roads, heading out of Portland—up through Milwaukee and out the truck route toward Astoria before cutting more directly north. Leaving in the middle of the night would only be a problem if they got noticed. Hopefully, they wouldn't.

The streets were still too quiet. Samuel flexed his hands, tightening and loosening them to get the tension out. It was going to be a long ride. Ahead, movement caught his eye. "You see something?"

"Huh?" Anna started, her eyes wide.

"Thought I saw," his voice trailed off. "Somethi—someone."

He slowed the truck and trailer; behind him, Ria matched his speed and pulled alongside. Yes. A lumbering shape, drunken or sick? Didn't matter. Samuel motioned a circle and pulled into the next street, keeping their pace to a crawl.

At the I-5 on-ramp heading across the Columbia River toward Washington State, he breathed a deep lungful of air and let it slip out. He accelerated. Soon they'd be over the river and through the woods to Grandfather's house they'd go. Not necessarily where Samuel wanted to be, but at least Anna might be happy. It had once been home for her.

As they merged onto I-5, red lights on the warning signs overhead flashed. BRIDGE CLOSED. "Damn." Samuel kept driving. But as he hit the on-ramp to the bridge, he saw the superstructure raised high and the barriers in place. The bridge ended abruptly, leaving only the mighty Columbia rolling on. They weren't crossing into Washington here. "Shit," he muttered.

"Sam!"

"Dammit, Anna." He shoved on the brakes. "The kids are asleep. Nobody's gonna hear me swear, and I didn't take the Lord's name in vain." The vehicle slowed to a stop and Ria pulled up. He lowered the window by Anna.

"We'll go back, cut over and cross at Longview." He motioned her to turn around in front of him. He didn't have a whole lot of experience hauling a trailer, but knew he needed the turn radius.

As the window rolled up, Anna watched him, tight-lipped. Shit. Wherever they slept tonight, there was going to be a cold space between them. He headed back up the highway and Maria slowed to let him take the lead. They were now driving the wrong way on the interstate. His instincts screamed at him that any moment a semi-truck was going to come at them head on.

He gripped tight on the steering wheel, until he got back to MLK Boulevard, the main drag of old Highway 99, and switched over to the proper lane.

The kids had always been good travelers because he and Anna had never given them a choice. There was family to see and worlds to explore and that meant going places. Every time Anna had lost a child, he'd taken her away somewhere, and those habits carried over into the present. He sighed. That was part of the reason Maria resented Anna so much. Anna had taken him away.

As they approached Longview, Anna reached over and took the hand he rested on his thigh. She squeezed it. He glanced over. As close to an apology as she gave, but it was enough. She kissed the back of his hand. God, he loved her. But she didn't make it easy. *I guess I'm not quite Prince Charming* He pulled her hand to his lips and kissed it, then continued to hold it as he drove.

James' truck's lights bounced in the rear view mirror. Probably needed new shocks.

The trucks ate up the miles, and the kids continued to sleep. Samuel was starting to feel the monotony when his phone buzzed. He slipped it from his pocket. "Yeah?"

"Mr. Herman?" James asked. "Ria needs to pee."

"Okay, I think there's a gas station not too far ahead."

"You need to go yet, Anna?" They rolled into the rest stop crossways and he left the motor running. Not like he had to worry about wasting gas. With most of the population dead, the planet's fossil fuels were no longer endangered.

Anna's eyes followed Maria toward the toilets. She shook her head. "No, you go first. I'll sit with the kids. Need to make sure Noah hasn't messed his big boy underoos."

Samuel nodded and climbed down from the big truck. With anyone other than Brad the big truck might seem like over-compensating, but Brad was a big man who did big things. He drove it into the woods to haul out rocks and trees; for him it made sense. Brad was not the shiny Escalade type.

James stepped out of his truck and lit a cigarette. He leaned on a propane tank. His eyes nervously scanned the surrounding area. Would he be of any use in the wilderness? The area around Warm Springs was a different kind of wilderness, desolate and dry.

When Samuel got back, Anna was fiddling with the car seat. Maria came out of the restrooms and Anna finished on the car seat and strode away. She exchanged a nod with Maria.

James stubbed his cigarette on the tank and sidled over as Maria came up to Samuel.

Maria spoke, "Are we going to even make it into Washington tonight?"

Samuel shrugged. "Don't see why not. The bridge at Longview can't be raised. I'd like to get as far as possible."

James nodded. "I'll take the next shift, Ria. You can take a break."

Maria shook her head. "No, I..." Something shifted in her manner. "Okay. Probably a good plan." She wrapped her arms around James, then said to Samuel, "Thanks, Dad. For waiting for us. For bringing us along."

"I wouldn't leave you behind." *Again.* Though he hadn't said it out loud, the word echoed in his head. Was she thinking it, too? "Everything's going to be fine, Ria."

Samuel watched as James lifted her off her feet. Her face glowed and Samuel felt a calmness she had not had since hitting puberty. Then the restroom door banged and James let Maria go. They walked to his truck hand in hand without acknowledging Anna's approach.

"You need me to drive?" Anna asked.

"No, I'm fine. Let's get across the river." He opened the door and offered her a hand up.

She took it, her other hand tucked under her burgeoning belly. "When we get close, I can drive. I know the country better than you."

"Sounds good. Rest now if you can."

He pulled his door shut and shoved the gearshift into drive. The gas gauge was still on F. When the vehicle was rolling, he turned the stereo on. The speakers blasted momentarily as Samuel fumbled with the controls. "Sh...."

Anna glanced back at the children as she fastened her seat

belt.

"Sorry." He punched the search button until he found a country station he figured he and Anna could both ignore. It was better than all the silence.

# CHAPTER FOUR

SAMUEL'S BRAIN FLITTED FROM THOUGHT to thought, but he kept coming back to Brad. Especially Pam and the kids; his imagination filled in the gaps of Brad's missing family. He tried to put it out of his mind—tried not seeing his own family in the same circumstances.

Behind Samuel, James followed, closer than Maria had. He would have a talk with the boy about tailgating later when they were done outrunning the apocalypse. Anna leaned the seat back and twisted away toward her door. He'd seen no cars out tonight except the police car. Even with the curfew, it surprised him.

An emergency tone cut into the song on the radio and a woman's voice came on with the familiar announcement. "Emergency restrictions are still in place in all areas." Her slight southern accent sounded strained. "Do not leave your home unless necessary to get food or medicine. Hospitals are operating with skeleton crews."

Was that intentional gallows humor from the announcer? Her voice continued. "Here is the latest from the newswire."

There was a pause and a more official voice came on—this announcer sounded like a guy who already had his family evacuated to the safety of a cabin in the woods. "The President and Congress have recessed their electronic meetings and will continue to search for solutions. The United Nations reports that every nation on the planet has been infected. That is all for now. Good night."

After another static-filled pause, the woman's voice came on. "This station will continue to broadcast emergency bulletins on the hour." He wondered if it was recorded—if she was still alive.

He envied Anna's ability to sleep in the car; he couldn't relax with anyone else driving.

The quarter moon sailed above the horizon. The Columbia River was a giant black snake following them in the darkness beside the road as they approached the bridge to cross into

Washington state at Longview.

As he drove up onto the lip of the bridge, bright spotlights stung in his eyes. He shaded his eyes as they adjusted. Halfway across the span, stacks of sandbags and orange cones left a gap only wide enough for one vehicle. Besides the blockade he noticed no signs of human activity. Then a metallic glint caught his eye.

Guns poked over the tops of the sand bags.

"Shit," he muttered and his heart dropped into his stomach. "God—" He braked and changed what he was going to say to: "Help us. Please."

Samuel shoved the truck into Park as he stopped. The crackle of a loudspeaker sounded as he opened the door and stepped down with his hands up.

"Get back in your vehicle and turn around," a male voice echoed.

"We want to get home," Samuel said, his voice sounding strange and soft compared to the amplified order.

"You've heard the news report. Stay put," Static crackled across the bridge. "Where's home?"

"Lake Quinault." Lights flashed on top of a car, but was it a police car?

There was silence. "Sorry. You'll have to go around."

"Please."

"No exceptions."

"How are we going to get across?"

A sigh filtered through the static. "I don't know. But you're not crossing here."

"Take a boat," another voice called, laughing.

"Come on," Samuel begged, "please, my family..."

"Step back."

An explosion blasted the silence of the night and the asphalt at his feet spat up black gobs, stinging his legs through his pants. Samuel stood dumbfounded for a moment as the echo of the shot died away.

Anna yelled for him to get inside. Noah howled.

The loudspeaker barked. "Who the hell did that?"

"Those are Oregon plates," a voice hollered back.

Finally, Samuel ducked for cover behind the open door.

James pulled something out of his back seat.

"No! Get back in the truck and go!" Samuel jabbed a finger back the way they'd come. Maria pulled James back inside as Samuel jumped back in the driver's seat.

"God damn it," Anna muttered under her breath.

"Stay down." He slammed the shifter into gear and jockeyed the big vehicle back and forth on the bridge, sweating profusely. He drove forward until he hit the guardrail and backed up until the trailer tapped the bridge piling. Forward again. Bump. He spun the wheel until it clicked; back—forward. He cleared the guardrail. His tires spun, and he roared past James and Maria.

Samuel knew his hands would be shaking if he released his vise-grip from the steering wheel. He wanted to go back and stand up to the bastards. He felt like a coward and that made him even more pissed off.

He tried to remember the last time he'd heard Anna swear.

Might have been when the doctor said, "These things happen."

Once they had put some distance between them and the bridge, the headlights flashed on James' pickup. Samuel pulled into a parking lot in front of a drugstore and laundromat. James rolled to a stop beside them. Maria scrambled out of the cab as Samuel opened his door. As he stepped to the ground, Maria's arms wrapped around him and she buried her head in his chest.

"Daddy, they were gonna kill you. And James got all manly. I saw you both dead in puddles of blood on that bridge."

Samuel patted her back and held her close. "Ria. It's all right. We're all okay. Some little son-S.O.B. went off half-cocked. They're just scared."

"They shot at you."

He shook his head. "No. They shot at the ground. And they hit it. And they made their point." He felt Anna's eyes upon him as she pulled the sobbing Noah from his car seat.

"God has judged them," Anna said in a low voice laced with vitriol.

"I'll judge them," Maria said. .

Anna and Ria had both gone from fear to fire in a moment. James stood helpless, staring at Samuel for guidance.

"Look." Samuel kept his voice low and calm. "We have two questions. Do we still try to get across the river into Washington? And if so, how?" There was a grateful silence as they all thought about it.

Samuel looked in on Abi, still asleep. Damn, that kid could sleep through anything. He touched her forehead, sweaty, but not feverish. He hoped that meant that the coughs and sniffles were just a cold.

After a moment when the only sound was Anna patting Noah, she spoke, "What about Astoria?"

"It's the only way over the Columbia River other than going halfway across the state."

"Why didn't we go out to I-205?" Anna asked. "We could have crossed the river there."

"We were headed west," Samuel answered, gritting his teeth. He didn't have a good answer. Truth was, he hadn't thought about it. They could still go back and try, but they would have to deal with Portland all over again. Right now, he wanted to be as far away from the rest of humanity as possible. "We're still heading west."

"What about a boat?" James asked softly behind him.

Samuel spun, realizing he was excluding Ria and James. They were adults and soon-to-be parents. They deserved a voice. He stepped back to let them into the conversation.

"We'd lose the trucks," Ria countered.

"Trucks we can replace." Anna bounced Noah in the crook of her arm, running her fingers through his hair.

"There might still be people with guns on the other side—" Samuel said. "There's plenty of wilderness around here. What if we stay on this side of the river and find somewhere other than Grandpa's cabin to hole up?"

"We could go to the rez," James offered.

"We're going to Quinault," Anna said in her one who will be obeyed voice.

Samuel held his frustration in. "Astoria first, but we come up on it slow." No response. "If we have trouble there, we make another plan. We don't have to go to Quinault." He stared into Anna's eyes. She said nothing out loud, but the set of her jaw told him exactly what she thought of his attempt at an ultimatum. Noah's eyes were active. He knew everyone was on edge. Abi still snored. Oblivious. It was starting to worry him. Samuel smoothed a stray curl on her warm forehead.

Back on the road, Anna refused to look at him; Samuel recognized the posture. He concentrated on driving once it became clear that she wasn't talking. At least the adrenaline kept him wired. When the headlights behind him flashed him again, Samuel realized he'd been zoning, Anna's head lolled, her mouth open. Maybe she would wake up not pissed off at him.

A sign flashed by: Welcome to Astoria. Population: 9,529. "None-thousand," Samuel muttered to himself. He slowed and rubbed his eyes as James pulled up beside him.

Ria rolled her window down, "Well?" she asked.

Samuel sighed. "Looks quiet. Maybe it's best if we drive on through."

"Okay," Maria nodded with a glance to James. He nodded, too. "Let's do it."

"Turn off the lights and drive slow." He glanced down at the buildings, the city demarcated by the street lights. There were dark sections. "We don't stop for anything. We can't afford to."

Samuel let the beast of a vehicle and its trailer roll forward, picking up speed as they descended into Astoria. Samuel let it cruise faster where lights were out. Astoria was pretty small. He didn't see anyone but his nerves prickled the back of his neck. His family was being watched. There were people here; but they were not showing themselves.

Darkness swallowed them. Samuel flipped the lights back on. James' headlights came on a second later. He wondered if Ria and James were freaking out as much as he was or just following his lead. Anna continued to sleep peacefully as they crossed the bridge.

A wave of dizziness hit as Samuel realized he had been holding his breath. The truck rolled down the incline as they passed the middle of the bridge. He wondered if Ria was holding her breath too. When Ria was little, before he met Anna, he and Ria would hold their breath over the water or through tunnels.

He rolled his window down. Up ahead, he saw headlights, but

no sandbags, broken bridges or armed men. Cones blocked part of the lane. He drove past them. The headlights of a police car stared at him. A body, head slumped against the window, was the only thing guarding this Columbia River crossing. He let the air escape again and sucked in another grateful breath. If the headlights were still on, he must have died recently.

Samuel had gotten lucky. Which made him feel guilty because a man was dead. But he'd gotten his family across safe and sound—that was what mattered now.

Everyone in his car still slept. He chuckled, a strange euphoria bubbling up in his chest. He pumped his fist out the window for Maria and James. Their lights flashed in response.

They were across but this route promised twisting back roads. He had gone this way with Anna once, stopping at a little hick bar in the middle of nowhere. The people were friendly, but even back then you couldn't help thinking that if they wanted to go Deliverance on your ass, they could and would, and no one would be the wiser. Maybe he should go the long way. Highway 101 North was also winding, but it seemed less likely to be blocked by folks like the ones who had shot at him earlier.

Abi coughed and started to whine, unintelligibly, as she woke from her long sleep. Samuel tried to tell her to go back to sleep with a gentle voice, but her coughs woke Anna, too. She flipped her seat back and spun around to comfort Abi, automatically jumping into mother-mode.

When Abi slipped back into sleep, Anna glanced at the side of the road. "We're in Washington?"

"Yeah. Crossed the bridge at Astoria. Didn't see anyone."

Anna nodded, calmer than he'd seen her in days. He grasped her hand, she put it to her lips, smiling as she reclined on her side in the seat.

A few minutes later, Samuel heard her light snore. But it didn't last. Abi woke more and more often. Every time she fussed, Anna woke too. Anna's manner became more and more manic. There was definitely something going on with Abi. He prayed it was just a cold.

Samuel reached over, flicked the radio on to distract himself from the possibility that Abi was sick and they had all been exposed. He scanned with the volume on low, searching for something that wasn't just a canned broadcast. When the low band NPR stations came in, he stopped and listened. The messages were the same as they'd been for the last few weeks. He listened anyway. There might be something new.

The announcements droned on. The drowsiness returned and Samuel hit the search button, stopping on a heavy metal station. After a bit, he opened his window a crack. The cold would help him stay awake.

But it didn't. He woke when his wheels crossed the rumble-strip. He gripped the steering wheel as Anna jerked up to a sitting position.

He urged the Suburban back inside the white line. The trailer complained at the rough treatment. His eyes were wide with the new dose of adrenaline he'd given himself by almost sending his family careening off the road. "Shit."

"Where are we?" Anna glanced around, but all that was visible were the lines going down the road and the evergreen trees lining the ditches.

"Almost to Raymond."

"Why didn't you wake me? You just about drove off the road."

"Yeah, I'm aware of that." He might kill them before the pandemic got the chance.

"Stop in Aberdeen. See if there's a motel or something. It's too late for either of us to be driving, I can't imagine how James and Ria are keeping awake."

He wanted to push on and keep going, but she was right. A sign for Artie RV Park made up his mind for him. He turned down through the arch. "Let's go here. Bathrooms. Showers in the morning. Looks empty too."

The power was on, but the emptiness of the camp made Samuel remember the apparent emptiness in Astoria and horror movie reels started to play in his mind. At any moment a guy with a hockey mask and an ax might walk out of the woods.

# CHAPTER FIVE

SAMUEL WOKE TO A COUGHING Abigail. She started to fuss when the cough wouldn't stop.

"Hey, Honey. Everything's okay," He undid her from the seat belt, lifted her from her booster seat and pulled her into his chest, resting her head underneath his chin and rubbing her back to soothe the coughing fit.

Her arms, surprisingly strong, squeezed him tight as her body shook. When her cough diminished, she spoke, "I love you, Daddy," Her voice trailed off in a cute little fry.

"I love you, too, Abi." The dawn was sneaking down through the trees. "Do you feel achy, honey?"

She shook her head and then nuzzled it against his chest. He closed his eyes, enjoying the warmth of his daughter on his chest. Aches in the joints were one of the biggest symptoms of the virus. The relief of hearing she was ache-free allowed sleep to return a little more easily.

He woke when the sun shone in his eyes. Anna slept in the passenger side with the seat reclined. They were going to need breakfast. He reached for the buck knife tucked in the side pocket beside his seat and Abi stirred and came awake. Her shining smile made everything okay.

"Breakfast, Daddy?" Her voice rattled.

It was a great sign if she was hungry. At least he hoped the saying was true.

When they camped he was the cook. Most of the rest of the time Anna made food. He had no idea what sort of food they had.

"I'll find you something, pumpkin," he whispered, opening the SUV's door as gently as possible. "Shhh…" If everyone else stayed asleep he might wake them with food.

Abi nodded, and he gestured with his head as he settled her down to the ground. Ouch. Sleeping all night in limited quarters with a kid on your chest was nice until you tried to move again the next morning.

"Are you all right, Daddy?"

Samuel grimaced. He must have groaned out loud. With his feet on the ground, he glanced back to see if Anna was still asleep. Nope, her eyes were sleepy slits. He blew her a kiss and motioned to her to stay asleep.

He put his foot up on the tailgate and froze. Boot prints overlay the muddy tracks of the truck. Someone had been looking in their windows.

"I have to go potty."

Samuel sighed and took her hand as they walked toward the main buildings. His eyes flitted from the stacks of firewood to the leaning broken fence choked out by tall grass, all of them likely hiding place. They passed the empty alcove under the edge of the pub's roof on the way to the restrooms. Everything looked dark and quiet. He helped Abi to the restrooms and waited right outside while she talked about the smells. The pub looked charming, with decorative windows and planters that would be full of begonia's in the spring. He had always wondered about it when they drove by on the way to Grandpa's.

When Abi finished, he picked her up and they walked into the pub. "Hello?" The silence remained. He found most of a dozen eggs in the fridge. He took the eggs and left the last couple bucks out of his wallet, not really sure if food for paper was a fair trade anymore. But his family needed to eat and nobody was around to make an issue of it. If they were going to skulk in the shadows and spy in his windows while he slept instead of greeting them like a normal person, then they didn't get to have an opinion on the matter. Still, he felt guilty.

He picked up a newspaper off a stack. October 12th, 2018, Aberdeen Daily World. It was a single sheet. PANDEMIC in all-caps and then National Disaster Declared - Washington State Follows Suit underneath it. Where was the government now?

Samuel went outside and got an armload of firewood, dropping it by the wood stove. He put the paper down on the floor, pulled out the buck knife, and shaved off strips of the cedar to use for fire-starter. Abi watched intently as the pile on the newspaper grew.

"Can you build a pyramid with the sticks, Abi?" He crumpled

up a sheet of the older newspaper and shoved it into the ashes on the bottom of the stove. He changed the direction the shavings flew so she could work. Her hands deftly built a teepee-like frame by leaning the little sticks together. She beamed at him, but coughed and knocked them over. Her eyes teared up as her hands struggled to rebuild it, but the persistent coughs wracked her little body until it fell again. She sobbed as she kept coughing. Samuel pulled her into his arms and patted her back, whispering soothing words as she shook.

With a long raspy throat clearing, Abi clung to him, her arms holding him tight. "I'm sorry, Daddy. The pyramid fell down."

"It's all right, Abi. We can rebuild it."

After a while of gentle sobbing, Abi sniffed and cleared her throat again. "Can I have some orange juice, Daddy?"

"I don't have any, Hon."

"There's some in the fridge."

Samuel carried her back to the fridge. Sure enough. OJ. in a sealed container. Abi gulped it down.

He helped Abi make a new pyramid. He lit it with a match and a receipt from his pocket. When it was roaring, he closed the door. Abi stared at the flame.

Samuel returned to the kitchen and flipped the gas grill on. When it was hot, he made scrambled eggs. One eye on the door and the other out the window on their vehicles.

The eggs were ready by the time everyone else came in stretching stiff muscles. The mood was palpable. Everyone was nervous but excited. James kept giving him meaningful looks and staring out the window. He had probably seen the footprints too. He gave James a look that he hoped was interpreted keep it to yourself. They'd escaped Portland, home for so many years, now a cemetery for the dead, and a trap for the living. Most of the people left alive were either insane or senseless with grief and shock. If they didn't leave, then they may have turned into crazies themselves.

After breakfast, Abi played for a bit with Noah, running around the RV park, but then she slumped against him and asked to get back in her car seat. She was fast asleep by the time they were packed up to leave.

When they were ready, Samuel took a last look around, giving the residents one last chance to come out and say hello— and hoping they wouldn't at the same time. But as they drove toward the entrance, a large man in camouflage stepped out from behind the Artic Park sign. He had a bushy gray beard, a couple large dogs on leashes, and a shotgun.

Anna let out a shriek. "Go. Drive over him if he won't move."

The man held up his hand, letting the shotgun droop. He stepped aside.

Samuel eased forward, staring, ready for a quick move, but the man's eyes were calm, so he slowed the truck.

"Sam, what are you doing?" Anna grabbed his arm.

"He's fine." Samuel rolled to a stop and rolled down the window.

"SAM!"

The man's brows knitted in concern. He stepped back. "You folks okay?" His voice had a rumbly timber to it.

"You've been watching us," Samuel said.

The man nodded his head slowly. "I'm sorry. You don't have to go so soon, it's just me here."

Samuel felt Anna's nails digging into his arm. "We better move on. We ate some eggs, I left some money."

The man chuckled. "Not sure where I am gonna spend it. Guess I can use it as fire-starter."

Samuel couldn't help a sheepish smile. Anna's grip on his arm stayed firm.

"It's not my place anyway, I'm John Brooks," he said as if that explained it. The man's brow creased. "What's it like out there? Where are you coming from?"

"Not good," Samuel said. "We came from Portland. It's not as deserted as this place. Some of those that are left, you wouldn't want to meet alone in a dark street."

The old man sighed and shook his head. "You sure you don't want to stay a few days?"

Samuel saw pain wash across John's face. "Sorry. We've got a place to go."

John nodded sadly. "Good luck."

Samuel's chest twisted. He nodded. "You, too." He stepped on the gas and rolled up the window. John stared after them until they turned the corner out of sight.

\* \* \*

Maria drove James' truck, following the big Suburban and trailer up Highway 101 from their morning camp. She flicked a smile at James as he set the radio on a station playing hip-hop and bobbed his head, grinning.

Evergreens, bare alders, and salmonberry bushes bordered the two lane highway. Maria remembered wandering in the woods with Anna's Grandpa—the only grandparent she'd ever known. He'd taught her which of the berries were edible and the names of some of the plants: oxalis, trillium and fiddle-head fern.

They snaked through long curves, tree farms and boarded up houses as they came to Cosmopolis, more sad than the greatness of the name implied. Maria was struck by how much more beaten down the properties looked since she was here last. As they entered Aberdeen over the Chehalis River bridge, she spotted someone tottering toward them—a wild-haired person she wasn't sure was man or woman.

"Step on it," she muttered.

"Infected?" James asked.

The big SUV in front of them lurched forward, making it to the corner before the suspect did.

Maria accelerated, too, hugging the curb as the person stumbled in their direction. "I don't know. I mean, this is a virus, not the zombie apocalypse, right? Maybe they lost their mind, or they're drunk or drugged." Maria watched the person as they passed, their dead eyes following slowly. This wasn't the first person she had seen like this since she first hit the road in search of James.

The person, a long-haired male she thought now, wore an Iron Maiden concert T-shirt; his arms were drug-skinny. Sure enough, there were needle tracks in the inside of the elbows—a self-induced zombie.

Maria shuddered at the glazed-over eyes. "We don't stop for anything. We can't afford to."

James nodded, his eyes searching ahead. He pointed as the

street curved—another person meandered down the side street. Maria's phone rang. She hit the speak button. "Yeah?"

"We're gonna stop at a drug store," her father's voice rattled in the truck. "Anna knows where one is."

"Are you sure that's safe, Dad? Do you seem them?"

"Yes. But we can't miss a chance to stock up on supplies before we get to the woods. We may need cold medicine or something to lower a fever."

Maria didn't argue. She knew he was worried about Abby.

She followed the trailer, bouncing into the non-thriving metropolis of Hoquiam. Still, things seemed in better repair than Aberdeen's south-side. They rolled into a parking lot. No weird empty-eyed people hung around. That was a relief. None of them seemed to have an inclination for brains, but Maria had seen too many movies to get out of her car near a shambling, half-dead looking person. Or maybe it was just common sense, reinforced by movies.

Across the door of the Harbor Drug pharmacy someone had scrawled a hasty message in what looked like red lipstick. "No more Flu meds. Try the hospital. Sorry."

Her father pushed on the door. He looked surprised when it gave way; a bell hanging on a pretty green cord jingled a welcome and a warning. "Hello?" he called.

No one answered. Maria followed him in. The lights were on in the drug store as if it was a work day.  Her gaze roamed over the merchandise: lovely trinkets, cheesy tourist gifts, charms and fancy pottery mixed with bedpans and fine art jewelry.

Maria slid a waiting chair up to the Rx counter and launched herself over. "What do we need?"

"How should I know?" Her father called. "Epinephrine?"

"For what?" Anna asked. "None of us are allergic."

"Not that we know of," he answered.

"I'm going to check out the back room," James said. "See what supplies might be out of reach."

Maria scanned the shelves. She really had no idea what she was looking for. "I bet the narcotics are under lock and key."

"Yeah. If there are any left."

"We don't need narcotics," Anna said, flipping the

countertop up and coming into the pharmacy area.

Maria gritted her teeth. She hadn't meant it like Anna implied. Did she enjoy twisting Maria's words to make her seem like an evil step-daughter?

"Should I grab anything that seems useful?" James hollered from the main floor. "I got band-aids. There are splints. What if someone breaks a leg?"

"Grab it," Anna ordered. "Aberdeen is a hell of a drive from Quinault."

*Like we'd drive to Aberdeen to go to the hospital. If someone really got hurt, they would be screwed.* Maria shivered at the thought. She set aside her petty issues with Anna and concentrated on finding as many useful medical supplies as possible.

The shelves of medicines meant nothing to Maria. "I don't know what the hell I'm looking for." Anna glanced sharply at her across the aisle. "I'm going to get over-the-counters: cough medicine, ibuprofen, acetaminophen. Shi—shit stuff that I recognize." Maria's face twitched into a smile and she ducked under Anna's next glare. As she worked her way around the medications, she heard James talking strangely. Like he was talking to a baby.

"James?"

"Maria," he whispered. "Come here. Quietly."

She left her bag of loot on the floor and followed his voice out the back door. James was kneeling on the floor, bending over something. Maria looked over his shoulder and saw a dead mama cat in a basket with several week-old kittens cuddled up around her.

James sniffled and swiped his sleeve across his face. "They're all dead except a little one. Crawled back in under the water heater." Little paw prints showed in the dust under the platform.

"I'm too big."

Maria slid down and reached in. "Go get me something he'd want to eat."

"Right," James hustled out the front of the store.

"Here, kitty, kitty," Maria cooed.

Wait. She had the Laser Monster. She extricated James' keys from her jeans. She wiggled the red laser in the wall between them, making sure to not point it directly at the kitten. The kitten moved forward a step. She slid backward as the kitty came forward. The kitten shoved her head into Maria's hand, seeking the warmth of her body. James was there. He set a little semi-circular plastic dish with white liquid in the bottom near the edge of the heater.

She twisted her head and whispered to James, "Milk?"

"Evaporated," James mouthed.

The cute little nose peeked out from under the heater platform, twitching. Maria flashed the laser over by the milk. When the kitty reached the dish, it dipped its head, and its tongue came out.

In a few minutes the kitten had lapped up all the milk and was purring loudly.

"More?" Maria asked.

"No. Too much will make him sick. I'll get some water." James slid the bowl toward himself and stood slowly. The kitty looked like it was going to run back under, but it didn't.

When James left the room, the kitten padded after him. Maria scooped him up. He squirmed a bit and cried in weak protest.

Her father and Anna stared at the kitten in her hands.

"Can I keep him, Daddy?" Maria said in her best baby girl voice.

"I found him," James said.

The door jingled and there stood Abi, bleary-eyed. When she spotted the kitten she squealed in delight, her small hands outstretched.

Maria hated her little sister's squeals, but at least this time it wasn't about something stupid. "Come meet the kitten James found."

"For me?" Abigail crowed, then coughed deeply.

Maria hated these sounds even more.

James shrugged and smiled faintly. "Of course, for you, silly. You've got to get him fat and happy."

Abi took the kitten from Maria, cradling it in her arms.

"That cat's lucky to be alive," Anna said, a happy smile creasing her face. "We better get cat food. And stock up on canned goods for ourselves. There's a grocery store a few blocks away, the only big one between here and Quinault."

"Anything else we need here?" Maria asked, glancing around the store.

Her father grinned. "Reading material." He snagged a book from the shelf marked *Local Authors*.

"I think I went to school with that guy," Anna said. "Let me see that."

Her father grabbed another copy of the book and tossed it in his shopping bag. "I like the cover. I'll take this stuff out and check if Noah's still sleeping."

"Oh, no." Abi's smile fell and her eyes went wide. "I forgot. He's not. He's crying. I'm sorry."

"No worries, little one," her father said, patting her on the head as he hurried to the door. "We're ready to go."

Maria gently removed the kitty from Abi's arms and placed it in James' big hands. "I think the kitten should ride with us today, Abi."

Tears welled up in Abi's eyes.

"You can take care of it when we get to Kinwalt, 'kay?" She knew she should say it the right way for Abi's sake, but she couldn't help herself.

Abi sniffled and nodded.

"Good girl." Maria headed for the door.

"Shouldn't we pay?" Anna asked.

Maria rolled her eyes at James and headed for the door.

"Only if you want. It's the end of the world, Anna." She shoved the jingle bell door open, not waiting to hear Anna's response.

She felt the heat of her glare on her back.

James followed her out. "Is it a good idea to antagonize her?"

"No," Maria said. "But sometimes I can't help it."

"Why do you hate her so much?" James pulled open the passenger door and climbed inside.

"You want to know what the shrink figured out?"

"I want to know what you think."

"I can't tell you 'cause I don't know." Maria turned the key and the engine started.

James nodded.

She pulled out of the parking lot following the Suburban with

Anna at the wheel. "The counselor," she noted the bitterness she'd placed on the word, "says I hate her because she took my father away."

"But you said your father met Anna after the divorce."

"But the next year he went on a mission trip around Central America with Anna for a month." Maria's face flushed. "My mom died in a car accident while they were gone."

"I'm sorry," James put his hand to her cheek. "I was always curious."

"No worries. Don't really want to talk about it." Maria gritted her teeth and continued her story. "They got sick after they came back, some third world nasty bug. Grandpa and Grandma took care of Anna and I took care of Dad—he almost died. When they got well, I didn't talk to Anna for a year."

# CHAPTER SIX

SAMUEL DROVE HIGHWAY 101 AS it rolled on into the low hills, at times twisting and turning, but often cutting a straight swath through the underbrush of a once noble forest. Tree farms now lined the empty road. Anna's midday drop in energy had sidelined her as a driver. Samuel had been glad to take over, but he felt like napping, too.

He came around a long curve; his feet hit the brakes, pumping. His eyes tried to make sense of the mess in the road. As the giant vehicle skidded, and the trailer whipped out sideways, the truck bounced on branches.

A jagged, broken branch aimed straight for the cab.

Anna screeched and came awake, bracing her hands on the dashboard.

The seat-belts locked. Brush scraped metal as the truck ground to a halt.

"What the—?" The branch bobbed, head height pointing at Anna's wide eyes.

"Shit." In the rear-view mirror Samuel watched as James' truck slowed down safely behind the mess.

Anna pursed her lips, but didn't comment on his profanity.

"Well," Samuel said. Noah yowled and Abi whimpered.

He shoved open the door, scratching boughs and branches against it, setting his teeth on edge. Tree debris littered the road. He stomped around the truck. None of the limbs had pierced a sidewall.

There were at least three trees down. A big storm must have blown down the biggest and taken out all the smaller ones in between it and the highway. And, of course, no road crews to clean things up. Samuel groaned. He was too tired for this.

He heard a whistle from behind him. Turning, he found Maria grinning. "Nice save, Dad."

"If I'd been paying attention…"

"Hey, we're all okay. No harm, no foul."

"Got some wood to cut, huh?" James came up behind Maria and wrapped his arms around her. "Are we close enough for this to be firewood?"

James seemed to love his daughter. Still Samuel felt a twinge of resentment. Instead of acknowledging it, he agreed. "Yeah, maybe. Wish I had a chain saw."

"Any other way around?"

"You kidding?" Samuel said. His tone was harsh; James recoiled. "Nope," he continued, softer. "This is it. The roads that go off of 101 dead-end or double back." He jerked the rear of the Suburban open. "Find tools." He gestured at the trailer. "Saws, machete, axes. Anything like that."

After a few minutes of digging, Samuel found a hatchet, a collapsible triangle saw and a machete under the back cargo area with the travel safety kit. Thanks, Brad. I hope you're at peace, old friend.

"Hey," James hollered, his voice joyful. "Check this out." He brought over a red plastic case with a Milwaukee logo on the side and popped it open in front of Samuel. "A cute little circular saw."

"Hope the battery's charged."

James popped the battery in and pulled the trigger. The blade whined and spun. "Looks brand new."

"All right, let's take turns with the tools. The electric saw gets saved for bigger limbs. Use these to clear the small limbs and toss them aside." Samuel handed James the hatchet. He flipped the blade around and locked the triangular saw in place before handing it to Maria. "We'll take turns with the hand tools."

A few smaller alders were tangled up with the big evergreens. He sighed and rolled up his sleeves. When was the last time he'd gotten a workout? Too long. Despite his exhaustion, it would feel good to do something he could finish.

Samuel glanced around to make sure no one was within swinging distance and started swinging the machete. He lopped a wrist-sized branch off the trunk. Nice—sharper than the one in his garage and the handle was wrapped like a tennis racket. Blisters on his soft hands would take longer. He kept whacking. Limbs flew off in a pleasant rhythm.

A swish pulled his attention. The butt of a branch flipped toward him. Samuel spun. The branch slammed into his left forearm as he swept it aside. A lucky deflection.

James stared, hatchet in his hand and a shocked look on his face. "Sorry."

Samuel embedded the machete deep in the bark of the tree. He took a moment, letting James feel his glare. "Watch where the limbs are going to fly before you swing. That could have been my face."

James' jaw worked. He slammed the hatchet down into the bark. "I said I was sorry."

"You okay, dad?" Maria asked, reaching for his arm.

White skin peeled up, exposing some tiny drips of seeping blood and a lump. He would have a bruise and a scab, but nothing serious. "Be aware of where everyone else is," he said slowly. "And where you're stepping and swinging."

"Yeah, I got it," James said. He jerked the hatchet from the trunk of the tree and stomped away to attack the smaller tree on the other side of the road.

God, he hated confrontation.

Maria gave him a shrug that said he wasn't out of line and returned to sawing at a branch.

Samuel pointed his machete at her cut. "Be careful near the end that it doesn't crack and kick up at you."

"Thanks, Dad. I'll be careful."

The sound of an engine in the distance made him turn. Maria and James looked up, too. A panel truck came around the corner. It stopped a long way off; its lights stared at them.

"Who is it?" Anna asked from the passenger seat.

"I don't know." Samuel turned away from the vehicle and whacked more branches off. "Keep working."

A door slid open and shut.

"Someone's coming," Maria said.

"Yeah." Samuel looked through the Suburban's window.

A harmless-looking blond kid with a scruffy beard strolled toward them. "What's the trouble?" he called in a pleasant masculine voice. "Tree down?"

You're brilliant. Samuel sighed and turned toward them. "Yup," he hollered back.

"How long before you're done?"

"Depends on whether you help or not." Samuel settled the machete in his hand.

"Well, I'm not interested in getting close enough to help. Seems like that would be close enough to get infected. Suppose you don't really want us that close either."

Samuel wanted to say something about not wanting the kids' lazy, paranoid ass near his family, but he decided not to answer. Instead he flipped the machete and whacked off another small limb.

It fell at the kid's feet. He stepped back. "Where you headed once you're through?"

"Forks." Samuel called. "Hoping we still have family up there."

Maria stared at him, her eyes wide. She knew he was full of shit and she knew he thought these punks were bad news.

Another man stepped from the panel truck. He stood near the vehicle and crossed his arms.

What did they have hidden in that windowless back

compartment of the panel truck?

The kid said, "We're just driving. Nothin' else to do," then walked back up the hill to his friend.

Brad must have a gun in here somewhere. It would be nice to have a piece strapped to his side. Warn them off. The young men, a couple of wanna-be mountain men too young to grow full beards, stood by their panel truck talking, but he couldn't hear what they said.

Out here there never was much law. Now, there was none. Maybe they weren't trouble, just harmless kids, as scared as they were, but Samuel remained on guard.

"Why don't you go behind the Suburban?" Samuel said to Maria.

"Paranoid much?"

"Not sure what's up, but I got a funny feeling. Why a panel truck? What are they doing heading out into the wilderness?"

Maria shrugged. "Always some bad apples."

"Keep an eye on them." Samuel's nerves were in high gear. Having somebody volunteering to do nothing pissed him off. The helplessness of getting shot at on the bridge had not left him.

He rubbed his forearm where the branch had hit. The bruise there would be pretty, darkening into a purple, yellow mess. Like the day. He saw James looked away and go back to work on the trees. Samuel slashed off the next branch, taking his frustration and helplessness out on the brush.

By the time the sun neared the horizon, they had cleared enough that Samuel figured they could move it with the truck. The panel truck duo had gotten out lawn chairs and beers at some point. Assholes du jour.

"Hey, James. You want lay out the rope? We'll use your truck to pull this one out of the way."

James nodded agreement, but his face remained impassive.

Samuel heard the last of the battery power winding down on

the saw.

"Dad?" Maria called. "It's dead."

James laid out the rope while Samuel patiently got to work with the triangle saw, finishing off the last couple inches on the log Maria was cutting.

When he finished the cut, Samuel double wrapped the rope around the butt of the smaller tree and tied it off with a timber hitch.

He walked over to James truck as James flipped a bowline loop onto the hitch. "Nice knot." Brad had taught Sam the knot several times, but it had never stuck.

James face softened as he turned away. "I'll start the truck."

"Okay!" Samuel called. "Everybody back off. Get in the Suburban and keep your heads down. Don't need anybody else getting hit by flying branches."

James moved the truck ahead slowly. The tree creaked and cracked as he tugged, then finally split and pulled away, shedding everything but the bark revealing a blackened center. James' truck lurched forward,, but he braked quickly. The road was clear enough to drive through and they had all survived with only a few minor scrapes and bruises.

A cheer rose from Maria, Anna and the kids. The dweebs from the panel truck joined in and raised their beers at him. He ignored the boys even as he recognized their cans: PBR. Piss Beer Redux.

Samuel released the rope carefully, not certain that the tree wouldn't swing back toward its earlier position, but it settled with a thud onto the road.

The panel truck roared to life and the driver ground the gears. It sputtered toward them and Samuel waved his family aside.

He glared at the men. They nodded, hollered thanks and the passenger again raised his jumbo can of Pabst. Samuel liked his beer—hoppy or heavy, amber or dark. Not wimpy.

After the panel truck passed them, Samuel went through the rest of the boxes in the Suburban and the trailer. In a few minutes he found what he was looking for. Brad's back-ups: a semi-auto shotgun, a black powder rifle and two revolvers with a gun belt. He also found a compound bow and a Pulaski. The fireman's ax would have been more appropriate for fighting zombies. When he glanced up, everyone's eyes were watching him.

"Anyone know how to shoot any of these?"

"I can hit the broadside of a barn with all of them," James said, a flash of anger and danger as he turned away. "Something smaller? Like a panel truck? Maybe."

Kid wasn't the pushover he seemed to be. "Brad gave me some pointers, but it's been years... Let's hope a threat is all we need."

"Can I carry the old rifle?" Anna asked, pointing at the working replica. "It looks pretty burly!"

Samuel remembered Anna competing against her grandfather at target practice. "Yeah. Keep one of the revolvers close." He handed them to her. "Maria and James, you take the shotgun. Whoever is not driving keeps it close at hand."

The sun had dropped nearly to the tall topped hills. He stared down the highway toward the lake. He'd seen ancient photographs when the road had been narrow, even more impressive with the old growth so close to the road that the trees formed a vertical canyon pointing to the sky. Now they had added turn lanes and a shoulder to pull off on and of course cut all the trees a couple of times.

"Let's go." Sam took the wheel and continued driving. A new clear cut, piles of limbs and brush, with all those lovely trees torn away, revealed Lake Quinault. At least this had been a tree farm, but the devastation still hurt.

Anna put her hand on his arm. "Can we stop at the spot?"

Samuel nodded. It had been tradition. Whether it was raining, snowing, sun-shining or black of night. They always stopped at the viewpoint to get out and look at the lake and the sky.

His whole body ached as he stepped out into the gray light. The tension of the last 24 hours had set in as muscle pain. He tried to stretch and relax, but it didn't help.

Anna came around to his side and wrapped her arms around him, then turned to look at the lake.

"From here," Anna said, "it's like nothing has changed."

"Maybe nothing has. Not from the world's point of view. Has it even noticed the lack of human beings?"

Maria snorted behind him. "I think mother earth has noticed in no uncertain terms."

"It is as God wills it," Anna said softly enough for only Samuel to hear.

Maria laughed.

Samuel turned. James was tickling Ria. Ah, to be young and in love. A strange parade of emotions crossed Anna's face—anger skewering Maria as Anna thought she'd been laughed at, then softening as she realized the reason for the laughter, followed finally by her guilt betrayed for the glare. At least Maria had not seen it. Anna looked away, but her arms clung tight to him.

He caressed her baby bump as he stared out into the twilight over the lake. God's country. Just gazing off into this wonder made him feel better. Glancing around at his family, it seemed to be affecting them too. "I love you, lady." He closed his eyes as he held her, still comforted by the warmth of her body next to his.

A cough from the Suburban pulled them from the moment. Samuel pulled open the door and plastered a smile on his face. "Hey, Abi. You remember Grandpa's lake?"

Her eyes brightened as the cough faded and she wiped the snot from her nose down the length of her sleeve. "Lake"

Kinwalt?"

"Yeah." Samuel undid her seatbelt and picked her up. "Lake Quinault."

Samuel held Abi close as he returned to Anna's arms. Anna took Abi and guided his arms around both of them. Then another sound interrupted, Noah's whine. Samuel extricated himself. "I'll get the little guy."

After a bit of wandering and helping Noah take a pee-pee, they all climbed back in the vehicles.

As they headed down the hill into the dusk, headlights came toward them.

"Panel truck guys, part two."

He heard Anna's intake of breath and she reached behind the seat for the rifle. Samuel set his pistol on the dashboard as the two vehicles neared each other. Both men were waving at them.

When they stopped, Samuel waited.

"Hey, thanks for clearing out the mess back there."

Samuel nodded. "Yeah."

"You know if there's any place to spend the night around here?"

Samuel motioned back the way they had come. "Take the next left. There's a really nice resort. Old-timey log cabin kind."

"Thanks and good luck," the driver said and drove off.

"You think they're dangerous?"

"Not likely. Young and stupid. Lazy. Let's get to Grandpa's place. We're far enough off the road there that they won't find us." But his eyes kept straying to the rear-view mirror, hoping they had turned onto the South Shore Road instead of coming back and following him and his family.

As he drove the twisting road through moss-coated vine maples and red-barked cedars, the sense of peace the forest usually instilled failed to come over him. How could he be stressed out here?

He coasted in the last mile or so to minimize the engine noise from carrying across the lake. He turned down into the rutted, leaf-covered drive.

When they pulled up to the cabin, it was clear that no one had been here recently. Not in or out. No fresh logs had been added to the firewood stack in some time. Leaves had gathered in the porch. It wasn't like Grandpa to let things like that go.

Anna sighed, and Samuel couldn't tell if it was from relief or regret. "He's dead."

# CHAPTER SEVEN

MARIA PULLED JAMES' TRUCK IN behind the trailer, grateful to be able to stop driving and feel safe. Her father stepped out of the Suburban shaking his head. Maria pushed the door open and stepped out into the wilderness twilight. As a child this had always been the end of the earth or nearly so. If you drove a couple more hours northwest you'd hit the real end of the earth, Cape Flattery, where you could crawl to the edge and watch the ocean eating away at the earth. Her father came toward, relief in his face. "Any sign of Grandpa?"

He shook his head, "Nope, Anna's going to go in first. Looks deserted."

James came up behind her and wrapped his arms around her. "It's pretty."

Her father nodded and pushed through the tall grasses by the side of the house.

"Yeah," Maria sighed, breathing deep of the soft, wet air.

"Come on, James. Let's go across the crick and see if we can see any sign of Grandpa. Maybe his truck's by the barn."

"The crick?" James spun her around, a quizzical look on his face. "What's a crick?"

"Cogan Creek. Sorry. I grew up hearing it called The Crick. Later, I'll show you Canoe Crick."

James shook his head in wonder, "What about the kitten?"

"Let him run."

"Didn't you say there were cougars and bears in the area?"

"All right, leave 'him' in the truck, we'll take him inside when we get back."

She scampered down the driveway, feeling energized by the great outdoors.

The old half log bridge hadn't been used recently. The handrail from her childhood had fallen down leaving only moss covered stakes placed at regular intervals. Weeds and grass had sprung up among the moss. A fern had spread its fronds across the close end as if to say this is no longer a bridge. Maria held it gently to the side as she stepped over it. "Grandpa Tom?" she called into the woods.

"Should we keep it quiet?"

"I don't think anyone is within earshot. But you're right. Sound carries across the lake." She took his hand and pulled him through the brush. She could duck under, but he had to duck and push the stickers out of the way.

"My little brother, Jesse is buried here," she said, her voice hushed. "Just a ways ahead. Under an apple tree." The grass under the apple tree was laid down, like something had been here. Maria noted a path down to the creek. Deer probably, here to eat the apples and get a drink. The small simple cross with Jesse's name cut into it still stood in the shade of the tree. James came behind her and again wrapped her in his arms. They stood there for a moment in softness of the evening, the gurgle of the creek and wind in the trees, the only sounds besides their breath.

"Let's check out the barn." She followed the deer trail down into what remained of the field, now dotted with small to medium-sized alders. The old barn was empty, but the rutted tire tracks that went up to the road showed some use in the last months. Someone had been here recently.

James was checking out the electric fence controller and an old multi-band radio. He twisted the knob and static erupted. "Grandpa must be nearly deaf," he said as he turned it back off. "Last time I saw him he only didn't hear what he didn't want to hear."

James chuckled. "Kinda like my dad."

Maria slipped inside his arms, put her face up and kissed him gently on the lips. "Yeah." If Grandpa was dead, she really didn't want to face it yet. "Let's go see what they've found at the house."

The sky had darkened and a few stars dotted the space between the trees.

She found her father at Grandpa's gun cabinet, trying to remember the code.

"House is empty. Nothing in the fridge except some baking soda."

"I think I remember the code."

"Be my guest."

Maria typed in Grandma's birth date and the lock shifted. She pulled open the door. It held half a dozen rifles, a couple ancient shotguns and a few handguns. The center position in the cabinet was empty. "What goes here?"

Her father shrugged. "Anna might know."

"What might Anna know?" She came around the corner.

"Beds are made, but no sign of him."

"Good," her father said.

"Good?" Anna's voice judged him.

"You'd rather find him dead in bed?"

"No. Spose not." She looked inside the gun case. "The thirty ought six is missing. Good sign that he left here under his own motivation."

Giggles echoed down the hall. And the patter of little feet. Abi and Noah shuffled into the already full room.

Abi had the kitten in her arms squirming to get free. "What's his name, James?"

"Dunno. Have to get to know him first."

"I want to call him Simba."

Maria laughed. "We'll see."

\* \* \*

Anna demanded that Samuel check on their new "friends." So he found grandpa's old spotting scope and drove back down the road to look across at the Lodge. Through the drizzle of the rain and the dingy eyepiece, he saw three shapes in front of a roaring bonfire.

Sam heart sped up as he wiped off the lenses with the cleaning cloth and focused the scope. No. Only two.

Tonight it was wet and gray enough that the bonfire felt like celebration. He wanted a fire like that. He glanced back at Grandpa's place. The window shades kept the sun out and also did a decent job of keeping the light in. When he got back, he'd better make sure he couldn't see the bonfire from the house.

When he pulled into the driveway, he noticed some slivers of light escaping the windows on this side. The rain had started to fall more thickly, and the wind was picking up. Before going back inside, he walked the path around the house one more time to make certain they were hidden. There were lots of trees between them and the resort. The panel truck boys would have trouble finding them unless they were looking carefully from the road.

They'd better get that tightened down.

Inside it was quiet other than the whispering of the wind and Anna's voice reading bedtime stories to the little ones.

Samuel carried an armload of wood to the fireplace before tossing his coat aside. In a few minutes the fire popped and sizzled. The wind whistled over the top of the chimney.

As big as it was, the house could hardly contain the tempers of the two women he loved most. On the road from Portland they had worked as a team, somewhat dysfunctional, but a team. Now everyone had slipped away, James and Maria to their room and Anna with the kids. Maybe that was okay.

He closed his eyes and listened to the wind and the snap of the fire. A door closed down the hall and he reopened them.

Anna emerged walking slowly—the 'waddle' as she called it. As she labored toward him, her face transformed from exhaustion to the face he'd fallen in love with. He realized with a warm clench of his heart that the transformation was for him.

"All asleep?" Samuel patted the old couch next to him and dust puffed out. He sneezed. "That was a mistake."

Anna settled in beside him with her head on his chest, tucking her feet up, and adjusting her belly to rest on his thigh.

"Need to go furniture shopping," she said, yawning.

Samuel watched her heartbeat pounding in her neck. "You okay?" When Noah was born she had issues with blood pressure.

"I am." Her arms squeezed him. "Thanks for the fire. Cozy."

Samuel stared into the flames. They helped to put a distance from the rest of the world and its chaos.

Outside the storm threw rain sideways past the chimney cap, and the old house shook as the wind caught it.

"Remember our first time on this couch?" Anna twisted her head to look in his eyes.

There was a twinkle there he had not seen in months. Samuel nodded with a smile. Yes, he remembered. This couch had been downstairs in front of the lower fireplace. They were newlyweds. Jesse had likely been conceived on this old couch in front of a similar fire in another winter storm. "How's Abi?" his voice came out in a hoarse whisper.

"Sniffly." Anna tensed. "I'm scared."

Samuel held her close. "Yea, though I walk," She relaxed back into his arms as he continued, "through the valley of the shadow…"

"I know, Let go, Let God." Anna closed her eyes.

"Yes." If she could let it be out of her power, let God take it on instead of her, she'd be all right. That was how she had come to peace with the miscarriages, at least as much as anyone ever could. Her muscles softened even further. Good. But Samuel's mind raced. The words did not ease his burden like they did hers. There was too much to do, and he didn't think God was going to come and help chop wood. "I'm going to kiss the kids goodnight." You want to head to bed?" Anna shifted up for him.

"No, The fire is nice." He stood. "Be right back." He kissed the top of her head and trudged down the hall. When he reached the bedroom, Noah's toddler bed was empty, covers thrown aside. He'd crawled in bed with Abi to sleep, her arms wrapped around him. Samuel sighed. If Abi was sick, they were all exposed. It didn't matter. A sharp pang gripped his heart again. He knelt and brushed Abi's curls aside, kissing her warm, but not quite feverish forehead.

Noah stirred and Abi's slim arms tightened around him, protecting him from whatever danger he dreamed. He kissed Noah's rat's nest of hair, feeling his heat as well. He told himself not to worry—the kids always slept hot. He needed to be the glue that kept them together. Anna's grip was tenuous now, and sick children would only make things worse.

\* \* \*

Maria sat on the macramé blanket-covered bed, staring dumbstruck at James. How could he ask her right now? Too many other things to think about.

Now the wind and rain outside buffeted the windows already cloudy with moisture between their double-panes. If this was going to be their room, it really need some paint on the drywall and some curtains.

"But you love me. And I love you." James gripped her left hand tightly in his.

She forced herself to not jerk her hand away. "Now I do. Now you do. But what if that changes? What's the point? It's a legal definition. Society is gone. We've got no minister, no church, no courthouse. But we've got each other."

"We don't need a church."

"Either we're partners or not. Doesn't matter whether anyone else approve."

"I want someone else to approve. I want your dad to approve for one. I want to be part of your family. Not just your kid's dad."

"You are in my family." Maria sighed. "But I haven't seen marriage work out so well. And what if you change your mind? What if you run off?"

"I won't."

"Will getting married keep you from doing that even if you feel like it? Forever is a long time."

"I want to promise to love you as long as I live. I want to do it in front of witnesses."

"How will that change anything?"

"Maria." James looked more serious than she ever remembered seeing him. "I've got a history of doing things half-assed. Good enough. I don't want to do *good enough* anymore!"

With her free right hand, Maria touched the spot where his worry lines knotted in his brow. "Let's not rush into it. I'm not totally against it. Especially if it really means that much to you. But I don't see the point." Under her fingertips she felt his forehead relax.

"I want you to be my wife."

"I want to be your partner." She let her hand fall, brushing his cheek.

"Then marry me. It's the same thing!" James was getting exasperated.

"It's not. The whole wedding idea is about inheritance and parentage. It was never about love. We know we're the parents and we're now the meek who get to inherit the earth. What do we need to get married for?"

"We don't!" James let go her hand and flopped down on the bed facing away. "Don't have to do anything except die."

Maria put her arm on his shoulder. "James, I don't mean to make you mad." She sighed and wrapped her arms around him. He didn't respond. "I'm not saying no. Maybe the idea'll grow on me."

"Maybe," James muttered.

"You did. You grew on me."

"Yeah, cause I'm a fungi."

Maria forced a giggle as she stuck her finger in his ribs. "That's for the pun." Then she kissed him softly on the lips. "That's for caring. And putting up with me."

He kissed her back. "I don't want to fight."

"Then let's not get married."

"Yeah. I guess you're right." His arms wrapped back around her.

Safety. Love? Why wasn't this enough?

\* \* \*

Samuel ran his fingers across Anna's back as she faded in and out of sleep with little jerks of her limbs. A big gust of wind pushed at the windows like the house breathed in and held it. If they survived the winter, maybe he could convince her to find a newer, better insulated house. Outside, lightning flashed. Then thunder followed. The windows rattled.

His eyes were drawn to motion outside. Thunder blasted as another explosion of lightning split the darkness in the big Alder tree across the driveway. It cracked before his eyes. *God, no!*

It twisted as it fell. Crack. The floor shuddered like it was an earthquake. Glass shattered. Then a strange quiet as if the house was taking a breath to brace for the next onslaught. For a moment even the wind abated.

Samuel slid from under Anna, as she came fully awake, eyes wild and frantic. He rushed down the hallway, sliding to a stop at the children's room, jerking the door open.

The children, nestled together, still sleeping undisturbed. The windows were whole, but branches pressed up against them.

"Samuel?" Anna's tremulous voice called.

"We're all right," Samuel answered, softly closing the kid's bedroom door.

The tree must have hit the room Anna had chosen as theirs.

She moved toward him, dream-like, but when they paused at the door, reality started up again.

"We're fine," he said, trying to keep his voice low and comforting. Then he turned the doorknob. The cold wind whipped the door out of his hand and, smacked it against the wall. A branch had pierced the broken window and rain blew in. Broken glass sparkled in the glow of the night-light.

"Dad?" Ria's voice echoed down the hall. "You all right?"

"We're fine," Samuel called. "Tree fell." His mind replayed the lightning strike and the fall. A different gust of wind and the tree could have hit either of the rooms his children slept in. Anna collapsed into him, her body shaking with soft sobs.

"The children. It might have...."

"Yes, but it didn't," Samuel pulled Anna gently, but firmly from the room and closed the door. "We'll clean up in the morning."

"But, what if another tree falls?" Anna's voice edged toward hysteria.

"It won't. It was a lightning strike. Won't happen twice." He forced his voice to carry the confidence he thought they needed. James stood there in the firelight holding Maria. They were bleary eyed, and she looked like she'd been crying.

"Go back to bed, kids. It can wait 'til tomorrow."

As Anna stumbled back toward the couch, Maria's eyes softened with concern.

"Let's go to bed, Ria," James pulled Maria close to him. "Samuel? I'll help you tomorrow."

Samuel helped Anna settle back into the couch and waved to Maria and James. Maria nodded mutely. Samuel sat next to Anna's shaking body as the door closed behind Ria and James.

Anna broke. "Sam. It could have killed them." Sobs shook her body, even as she stifled herself to keep them quiet.

"No. They're safe." He rubbed her back and ran his fingers

through her hair. "We're all safe. Look at the fire. We're home. We're together."

After a time her tension released, and the sobs faded to sniffles. Samuel pulled the big afghan off the couch and tucked it in around Anna. He shifted her into his arms as her trembling stilled.

Samuel stared at the last embers holding the middle of the top log together. It burned through and both ends fell into the center. Sparks shot up the chimney as the fire worked on the new fuel in its core. It should keep this room warm through the night before it burned out. Tomorrow would have to take care of itself.

# CHAPTER EIGHT

THE NEXT MORNING THE SUN revealed a clear blue day and the calm after the not-so-proverbial storm cast a subdued wash over everyone's spirits during breakfast. Anna and Maria were being pleasant to each other, but a silence had come between Maria and James that hadn't been there before.

He hadn't been sure how she was doing when she'd told him she was pregnant. Or how she felt about James. That made it difficult for him as her father to know what to feel. James had always seemed nice enough.

After breakfast, Anna had a manic energy that set Samuel's nerves on edge. She had already rearranged the spices and organized the junk drawer. Now she was cataloging the canned goods.

Maria set Abi and Noah up with some games and toys, relics from summers with grandpa that she'd found from some secret stash. Then she set about cleaning up the dishes, leaving Samuel and James leaning against the kitchen counter picking the remains of breakfast from the kids plates.

Samuel dreaded facing the damage to the house, but it was solid and unavoidable.

"Feel like tackling another tree James?" He crunched on a slice of bacon. "Ever used a chainsaw?"

James shook his head. "Weed-whacker's as heavy as I go."

"Well, I hope I can get Grandpa's chainsaw running or we're gonna have to break out the crosscut. I don't think the little battery powered saw will have much impact."

"Crosscut?" James asked. "What's that?"

"You better hope he gets the chainsaw running," Anna called over her shoulder from the pantry. "Crosscut saws cleared the forests, but they take two strong people and a lot of work. That's when they're sharp; Grandpa's saw hasn't been sharpened in 50 years." Her face broke into a smile.

Leaving the women to their own coping strategies, Samuel led James down the squeaky rough-hewn stairs into the unfinished basement. He pushed open the door into the dark garage, empty except for the old fiberglass canoe Anna's brothers had found adrift. A smile forced its way onto his face as he remembered canoeing on the lake. The water had been still and the moon bright, but he'd almost capsized them when he moved in to kiss her.

He'd need a ladder to get up on the roof. Grandpa's rickety old lean-up wasn't tall enough. He'd need something bigger.

They rummaged, collecting tools, a couple pairs of gloves, some rope, and a tarp that would be good to toss brush on to haul away. Maria came to join them after a while, wiping her water-wrinkled hands on her pants.

Maria picked up one of Grandpa's old hand-planes. "I remember helping Grandpa smooth the wood to replace a step back there. I think it has my initials burned into the bottom."

Samuel lifted a few long pieces of plywood to the side and set aside a stack of boxes where he thought the saw had been.

Grandpa had been cluttery, but predictable.

"What do you think happened to Grandpa?" Maria asked.

Samuel shrugged. "Who knows? I'm glad we didn't have to find him in his bed." The old man had taken to Maria much more than he had to Samuel. And from what Anna said, with more compassion and consideration than the old man had ever shown her.

Sawdust, oil, and dirt coated the old Husqvarna chainsaw, but the rubber cap on the spark plug was clean and new. That was a good sign. He checked the tank. A little fuel sloshed in the bottom, so he poured in more of the gasoline/oil mix. "Always use the chainsaw gas. It's a mix of gas and oil." James and Maria nodded.

Samuel stared at the old saw, trying to remember if there were any tricks Grandpa used to start it. Finally, he picked it up, hit the choke and jerked the starter cord up while dropping the saw. It sputtered and coughed. A couple more pulls, a couple of pops, and he got a short, loud run from the saw. He fiddled with the choke and tried again. His shoulder ached from whacking the tree limbs off the day before. He'd spent too much time in an office doing accounting and not enough time out doing real things—no use for accountants anymore. If only Brad could see him now. He took a deep breath and grimaced at his daughter. She stuck her tongue out at him.

"Want me to try?" James offered. "I got the touch with weed-whackers."

He was a big kid and in much better shape than Samuel.

"Sure. It's just particular." He handed the saw by its metal bar to James. "Grandpa always gets it by the second or third time."

James hefted it, made sure he had open space and copied Samuel's drop and pull tactic. The saw roared. Maria covered her ears and Samuel winced. James handed it back and Samuel engaged the trigger; the chain spun, but it sounded dry. He squeezed the oiling mechanism and tried again. Nice.

He motioned to the kids to open the door. It wouldn't matter if he'd yelled. The damn thing was loud enough to wake the devil. Maria pushed the latches aside and shoved the garage door up over their heads. James hauled the rest of their gear outside.

Samuel walked out of the garage with the idling saw, stepping carefully across the brush that had grown up.

Outside the storm had left the sky clean and blue. Samuel felt the beginnings of winter's chill in the air. November was here, and the frost would come soon. All the more reason to get this tree the rest of the way down and the house patched. It would be good to have a start on next years' wood too, even if it was wet alder.

Samuel let the saw rumble beside him as he surveyed the damage. The big alder had taken down a couple smaller trees. What a mess.

"Okay," he hollered. "We're gonna clean up the limbs first. Work away from each other for safety. James, you cut off the big limbs. Maria, you get the little ones with the machete."

Maria nodded and surveyed the pile of tools James had leaned up against the wall. She pulled a machete from the stack, ran her finger along the blade and grinned. She shouted, "It's sharp." She headed to the base of one of the smaller trees, pulled down by the big one and whacked at the little limbs.

Samuel turned back to James. "Okay, James. You make an undercut like this." He cut a third of the way into one of the big branches until it started to lean. Then he pulled the saw back and moved the blade to the other side. "Always keep the saw where it's not gonna get stuck if the tree shifts. That sometimes breaks your chain, bends the blade or worse." He made the back cut, and the branch fell gently to the side of the tree. "Got that?" he yelled at James.

"Yeah," James reached his hand out.

Samuel stopped short of placing the saw in his hands. "Don't screw up. We're hours from a hospital and everyone there is dead anyway."

James' face stayed dead-pan. "Love you, too, Dad." He grasped the handle next to Samuel's hand and pulled it from his grip.

Samuel's face cracked into a smile. He clapped James on the shoulder. "I'm going to check out the roof," he yelled pointing at the damage to the house.

James nodded.

The tall ladder was nowhere in the garage, so he wandered down toward the creek where it looked like Grandpa had been doing some building. Grandpa had replaced the old bridge with a bunch of logs laid parallel across the creek, cabled together with some old steel rope. The gaps were filled in with dirt and gravel, wide enough for a vehicle to cross.

Behind him, the chainsaw rumbled.

Across the creek stood a new pole building, its green steel siding and roof contrasting with the crumbling remnants of the old barn. The pile of rusted parts that had once been an old Mercury coupe sat nearby, its windshield intact, though opaque.

The big three-legged ladder, handmade from three long straight alders, had the bottom legs stretched out so that the tripod was stable. He hefted it off the ground and then decided carrying it by himself would be a mistake.

He stood for a bit surveying the scene. He'd seen pictures from the 1950s when this field had been cleared of trees for grazing livestock. The garden that supplemented their diet was closer to the house, but the creek had undercut it after a major tree fall.

The Lake Quinault Rain Forest had done much to reclaim its hold on their land. Alders dotted the field. He and James could take them down for firewood and clear the land at the same time. He shook his head. Homesteading was not the dream he had for his later years. At least he was still in decent shape physically.

He headed back to the house. James, or even Maria, could help him move the heavy ladder.

The roar of the chainsaw grew as he got closer to the house. He heard a loud crack and a whoosh. Sounded like the tree had settled. He broke into a jog and crossed the log bridge. Depending on which way the tree slid that could be problematic.

As he cleared the rise, James began to cut into the tree, now canted at a more extreme angle. It had fallen on one side of the stump and was now bent like a bow tensed and ready to fly. Maria whacked at the branches on this side of the downed tree. If James cut all the way through—Oh, God.

"Stop," Samuel yelled. No use. The saw was too loud. He ran as he watched the chainsaw biting deeper, spewing sawdust. "Maria!"

He was closer, but the saw was almost through. Time slowed. Samuel saw it all in his mind, flashing forward to Maria on the ground.

"Maria!" he yelled again. This time she heard him. She turned toward him, confusion creasing her face. The tree split.

Samuel grabbed her arms and swung her away from the tree. The cracking tree slammed into his back and drove him forward into the ground at Maria's feet.

It didn't hurt. Was that a bad thing?

\* \* \*

Maria crawled around a mess of branches. *What the hell?* She stared at her father lying on his side, unable to make sense of what had happened. Had he knocked her down?

The chainsaw sputtered to a stop. James stood with the saw in his hands, his mouth agape, his eyes wide and unblinking. The tree still vibrated, the leaves swished back and forth through the air.

Her dad lay there, not moving or making any sounds. "Dad," she shouted, scrambling over the branches toward him. Her voice rose to a howl. "ANNA!"

Her scream cracked James' frozen stance. He dropped the saw on the branches and stumbled to his knees next to her.

Maria reached out and touched her father. He was still breathing. *Thank God.* She didn't see any blood. "Daddy?" Her mind swam, drowning in thoughts. She'd gotten a first aid card once. What the hell was she supposed to do besides not move him? "James. Get Anna. Now."

"Right." He nodded and pulled himself to his feet, stumbling over branches as he tried to run.

Maria crawled around to make sure he wasn't bleeding on the front. "Daddy?" She touched his face.

His eyes snapped open, wildly searching left-to-right until they settled on Maria. "Need to fix the roof." He shook his head as if to clear it, and a grimace of pain shot across his face. His eyes closed.

"Daddy," she begged. "Daddy!" She brushed the hair from his eyes.

His eyes opened again. He looked calmer. "What happened?"

"You saved me." The door behind her opened and she heard running feet. Her father's eyes followed Anna's arrival. "You're going to be fine, Daddy." At least he seemed able to track movement.

"Oh, my God." Anna knelt her hands exploring his head. "Samuel. Where does it hurt?"

"I'm going to be fine." He tried to sit up and groaned.

"Stay still, Daddy," Maria begged.

His eyes closed and he settled back into the brush. "Hurt. Lots of places," he said, letting his breath hiss out. "Mostly my side. Probably broke a rib."

"We've got to get you to a hospital."

"NO." His eyes were clear. He grasped Anna's hand. "No. That's a death sentence." He fell back against the ground, lying there, staring up at the sky. "Got the wind knocked out of me. I feel better already."

"What the hell happened?" Anna demanded.

James cleared his throat. "I was cutting." Tears pooled in his eyes. "Then he was there. It was my fault. I didn't know."

Maria's heart continued to pound. "It's okay, James. I'm all right. Daddy will be okay."

"I will. I am." Her father agreed. He tried to sit up again, but his eyes registered pain.

"Please," Anna's hand pressed on his chest, "Don't move, Sam."

James' deep brown eyes studied Maria. "I could have killed you."

Maria's hand fell to her belly. Her stomach tightened.

"But you didn't," Anna barked. "We need a way to get him inside without moving him much."

"There were some long pieces of plywood in the garage," James said.

Maria kissed her father and said, "Stay chill, Dad." She pushed herself to her feet. "Come on, James."

In the garage, Maria and James found a bowed piece of plywood. "Not sure it'll be stable enough." She glanced around looking for inspiration. She needed two-by-four lumber or something like that. Two-by-two would do in a pinch. Then her gaze caught on a short wooden ladder. "Grab that. We can strap the plywood to it." She pulled a couple bungee cords off a hook. They were extra stretchy, but they'd work. James laid the ladder down and pulled the plywood over it. Maria wrapped the bungees diagonally and across the corners to hold it steadier.

She grasped the ladder; the handles stuck out far enough. James picked up the other end. She shook it hard, back and forth, up and down.

"What the hell, Ria?"

"Seeing if they'll hold."

"You could've warned me."

"Sorry." She gritted her teeth. "Let's go."

James turned around and stepped ahead. The contraption pulled forward then banged back into her shins. When they reached her father, he smiled up at them from the ground. "Nice makeshift backboard, Ria."

"I get my makeshiftedness from my father."

They placed the board up to his side.

"Anybody know real first aid?" Anna asked.

Was fear tempering the usual bitterness in her voice? "I earned my first aid card in P.E. a few years back," Maria offered, not confident that any advice she offered would be good. "James is a life guard."

"At church camp," James said. "I know about saving someone from drowning, but not much else."

"I'm going to be fine. Why is no one listening?" His voice changed to a singsong lower tone. "Well, Samuel, they didn't listen to you before..."

Anna chuckled grimly and glanced sideways at Maria.

Maria shrugged and smiled. "Shut up, Daddy."

"Yeah, Sam. Take it easy." Anna gestured for them to put the board down. "Let's get you onto this without moving you more than we have to."

The grimace on her father's face told Maria all she feared. He was not okay.

# CHAPTER NINE

MARIA'S HEAD NODDED DOWNWARD AS she watched her father's breath, her hand absentmindedly stroking the kitten in her lap. Stay awake, sleepy head. He'd saved her life the day before yesterday. And her baby's. Maybe her young body would have bounced off the tree better than his, but then again, her body, and the baby inside might have taken the hit even worse.

A horrible bruise colored up her father's side, but nothing seemed to be sucking out wrong. They loaded him up on ibuprofen and acetaminophen and used an ice pack when he could stand it. They kept him awake all day and into the night to verify he didn't have a concussion.

He'd slept all day yesterday as they took turns watching him. Four hours on a shift. About three in the morning, Anna had awakened Maria. The old faux digital clock flipped the minute tabs over to 6:20 as she watched.

To keep her mind busy for 40 more minutes, Maria reopened the old, brown hardcover of the Hardy Boy's Mystery, The Hidden Coins. She'd read it when she first came to Quinault. It helped her stay awake, but as she neared the end, it got harder and harder.

Something fell in her lap; Maria thought it was a tree limb, leaped to her fee. The cat jumped away, taking only a little of her skin. It skittered out the small gap in the doorway as the book hit the floor. "Wide awake now," she whispered to herself. She knelt to check her father's breathing, since he hadn't woken from the sound of the falling book. To her relief he was still sleeping peacefully.

The book stared back at her from the floor, closed. She picked it up, realizing she had lost her place. Her phone buzzed.

The alarm flashed: Seven in the morning. Last night Abigail had begged for a shift, so Anna said she could do a half shift until nine while everyone else was getting up. It would give her something to focus on other than feeling icky.

Maria sighed, leaning forward and kissing his warm forehead. "I love you, Daddy." She held back the tears for Abi's sake. There had been enough tears.

She slipped quietly down the hall, opening the door, Abigail stared up at her. "You get any sleep, little sister?"

Abigail sniffled. "It's light out," she said as if that explained everything.

"Do you need to go potty before you sit with Daddy?"

"No, I—" A cough cut off Abigail's answer. She shook her head as her lips tightened in a very Anna-like structure.

Maria fought the urge to smile. Eight years old going on eighteen. "Okay. Bring a book or something to draw on, okay?"

Abigail rolled her eyes as she slipped on her backpack. "I was already ready."

Maria wished she still had the ability to believe she knew everything. "Of course, you were."

She helped her little sister get settled in. Then Maria listened to his heart and kissed him on the head.

Abigail looked on seriously. "He'll be fine, Ria."

Maria nodded to her sister, not daring to speak, and stumbled back down the hall, knocking on Anna's door. "I'm heading to bed. Abi is with Dad."

The bed she shared with James was empty. How long had he been up? Her head hit the pillow, and she pulled the covers up, not bothering to take any clothes off. I can dream something nice. But since she'd gotten pregnant her dreams were weirder and weirder, so it might be nice to sleep without dreaming.

\*   \*   \*

Despite her exhaustion, Maria only slept a few hours. When she woke to the sun streaming through the window, she felt the need to get up, even though she had been up most of the night. She wandered out to find James and Anna sitting at the kitchen table and just staring over empty bowls of soup. Maria served herself a bowl and sat next to James. He stared out at the lake, but scooted over to her when she sat down.

"How's Dad?" The soup was lukewarm, but the chunks of beef and potato tasted good.

"Grouchy. But awake." Anna stood, scooping up James' bowl with hers. "He's had oatmeal and a bowl of soup. He's already complaining about being in bed." She rinsed the bowls in the sink.

"I think he's just bruised."

"Thank God." Maria said. *But how can we know?*

"Yes," said Anna. "Thank God."

*I didn't mean it literally.* Maria looked to James for some sense of how things were going. Though his hand rested on hers, his eyes were still gone.

Abi chased Noah through the kitchen. Anna shooed them out. Maria could see the stress etched into her forehead despite her talk of god taking care of everything.

"Anna?" Maria asked. "If it's okay with you, James and I could take the kids down to the lake. It's nice out today. Might not be soon."

Anna nodded. "Might do Abi good to get out."

"You go." James shook his head, darkness clouding his eyes. "I'm gonna finish what I started. With no one around to hurt." He wadded his napkin up and threw it away into the trash as he stood. "Gotta get the tree moved so we can fix the roof." He headed outside without another look at Maria.

Her heart twisted. How long would he hold onto the guilt? It was an accident. He could scarcely kill a spider.

James turned back to Anna. "If you want to go to the lake with Ria, I'll check in on Samuel every fifteen minutes."

"Anna, you should come with us," Maria said to Anna. She didn't want to spend the afternoon with her step-mom, but if it got Anna out of the house, she might be better off. "I can help you with the chores when we get back."

"No, I—" Anna glanced toward the bedroom. "No, I shouldn't."

"Okay." Maria's relief was palpable. Had Anna noticed? As she turned away, her face burned. She hated the way she felt about Anna, and it didn't matter what either did, they both always ended up hurt. "At least I can give you a break from the kids." She took her plate to rinse it, but Anna took it from her and scrubbed it, rinsed it, and set it in the drainer. "Thanks, Noah? Abi? You wanna go to the lake?"

Abi's hoarse cheer of, "Yeah," was parroted by Noah, "Yeah, yeah, yeah."

Anna hung the dishtowel she'd been drying dishes with on the rod. "Wait, Maria? Maybe I will come with you." She straightened out the wrinkles. "I'll go check on Sam and see what he thinks."

"Okay." Maria finished the last bite of soup, watching as Anna pulled her hair back and slid her ponytail holder up.

Anna caught Maria watching her. Her grimace changed to a bemused smile. "Need to look presentable for your father."

"I'll get the kids ready." When Anna had disappeared down the hall and into the bedroom, Maria spun on James. "Thanks," she whispered. "Last thing I want to do today is spend it with her. Don't really think she wants to be with me either."

James shrugged. "Sorry. Trying to help." He kissed the top of her head.

She wrapped her arms around him and placed her ear to his chest, enjoying the steady lub-lub of his heart. "Yeah, well, stop it."

"Yes, your highness."

"James?" She twisted her head to look up at him.

"Yes?" He tried for his usual mischief, but the strain showed in the lines in his forehead and the center of his brow.

"James. Be serious with me for a minute?"

"Okay, I'll try." His smile faded.

"Are you okay?"

"Yeah." He nodded.

"Truth."

"Truth. Okay. That's it. I'm okay. Feeling pretty damn guilty right now. Almost killed you." His arms pushed her away, extending enough that he could look in her eyes, but not letting her go. "And our baby. Your dad's hurt bad. He's not paralyzed, but we don't even know if there's something wrong inside him. You can barely tolerate Anna. Nobody knows me. Abi's sick. Everybody I've ever cared for, except you and the baby, is dead."

He put his hand on her belly.

"I'm sorry." Maria pressed her hand over his. Soon there would be a baby there to touch. She squeezed back into his arms and felt him relax.

He continued, his voice a soft rumble. "Don't want you to be sorry. I'm away from home and I don't know what's going to happen next." He gave her a wry smile, a sad echo of his usual joy. "But considering what we're dealing with? Okay is the new excellent."

\* \* \*

On the way to the lake, Maria fumed that James had stayed back to finish limbing the downed tree, while she was stuck with Anna. James was treating it like penance—if he worked hard enough, he could make time go backward.

Maria felt her chest tighten and her eyes watering. Damn it. Not like her breaking down would help. There was enough shit going on.

She heard Anna and the kids' noisy progress behind her. Anna had been trying to be nicer. Maria could see it. But it still didn't seem real. Was she only making the best of a bad situation? God, she wished Grandpa was still here. He would have taken her out to the woodpile. They would have talked while he taught her to whittle or split firewood. Maybe he could have suggested something to Maria. On the other hand, he didn't seem to understand Anna either.

The brush was more overgrown than what Maria remembered. She'd walked with Grandpa on the trails, but she couldn't seem to find them today. Maybe he was too busy this year to clear them, or he... She didn't want to finish the thought, but she did anyway. Or he was dead. Reality wasn't going to change just because you ignored it.

Maria pushed aside salmonberry bushes, but they kept getting thicker. She knew the lake was off to her right, and the trail was here somewhere. "You remember where the trail to the lake is?" she called, turning back to look at Anna.

Anna shook her head. "Nah." She paused for breath. "Baby's not letting me have as much access to my lungs as I'd like."

"Where's the lake?" Noah whined.

"Not far, kid," Maria said. "How about I stumble around and see if I can find the trail and then the kids can have an easier time."

Anna acceded with a nod and bent over, blowing fog out into the cool air.

Maria maneuvered further into the underbrush. She grabbed a stick and whacked the berry stalks and prickly devil's club out of the way. Instead of going forward, she angled to the side further upstream. Then she stepped into the open and a clear path led toward the lake.

"Found it."

As she looked down, she realized she'd found something else; she was standing in deer pellets. She stepped away and checked the bottom of her shoe. Good thing they didn't stink much and weren't as sticky as other animal's droppings. "I guess it's the deer run."

"You see a deer?" Abi called, her voice a hoarse croak.

Maria couldn't help laughing. "No, Froggy. Just deer poop."

"Eww." Abi stepped through where Maria had broken the stalks of the salmonberries. "Deer poopy."

Noah followed. "I see, I see," he said, pointing and grinning.

"Poopy, poopy. Deer poopy."

Maria smiled wider than she had in months. "All right. Come see deer poopy, poopy, poopy."

An unaccustomed smile brightened Anna's face as she stepped through the brush. Maria could see in that smile why her father loved Anna.

The walk went quickly, only interrupted by more of Noah's shouts about poopy. Maria held hands with the kids as they neared the shore. A movement ahead closer to the lake caught her attention. "Shh... Listen."

A brown deer, as big as a small horse, bounded down the trail toward them. She pulled the kids close. The handsome young buck with a single point—deadly sharp—changed direction, crunching through the brush next to where they stood frozen.

"A deer," Abi said, her voice still cute-scratchy.

"A deer, a deer," Noah crowed.

The buck leaped gracefully over the brush and back onto the trail. Without a glance back, he bounced off into the trees.

Anna's face glowed. "Lovely," she said, her voice reverent. "I loved this place as a kid."

"Really?" Maria had a hard time picturing Anna out here in the woods clambering over nurse logs. "Me, too."

"Maybe we have more things in common than either of us realize," Anna said, still smiling.

"Maybe." Maria knew they were near the lake. The trees and brush diminished and the amount of driftwood littering the ground increased. Then they broke out into the clearing, only a few logs to climb over and tall and scratchy tule grass to walk through to get to the shallow beach.

"Be careful, Abi and Noah," Anna said. "Don't climb on the logs in the water. If they slip and roll, you can get stuck underneath them and drown."

Abi looked at her mother like she was stupid. "Okay."

"Kay, kay, kay," Noah parroted.

The kids wandered along the mucky shoreline, picking up sticks and tossing them into the lake. Anna sat heavily on a curved, sun-whitened drift log. Maria sat down a few feet away.

After a minute Anna spoke, "I know you're worried about your father. It wasn't your fault. Wasn't James' fault either." She stared off toward Abi and Noah.

Maria nodded, not sure she trusted herself to say anything. If Anna was saying it wasn't Maria's fault, it probably meant part of her thought it was.

Anna continued, "I know you don't — If I were you, I—" She sighed heavily. Tears ran down her face. "I'm sorry. I'll try to be a good grandmother."

Maria reached across and put her hand on Anna's shoulder. The tightness of her muscles felt like bone. She must be freaking out too, except this time she wasn't showing it. Maria stood up behind Anna, rubbing the tightness, pressing her thumbs firmly into the knots. She wanted to tell Anna something to make everything better. But nothing would do. Except one thing. "I'm sorry, too."

Anna's shoulders shook. She turned and wrapped her arms around Maria, sobbing quietly.

Maria stared down in wonder, her hands still working Anna's muscles. *This is what it is to be a mother.* Anna was strong, a lot stronger than Maria had ever given her credit for. Warmth swelled inside her. *I will be this strong for my kids.*

Anna pulled back after a moment, sniffling. She half laughed as she wiped away her tears and glanced over at the children playing on the beach. "You know, crying without freaking the kids out is a mothering skill."

"I'll remember that," Maria said. "You can always talk to me." Was she being honest? Yes. Maybe Anna was telling the truth, too. Years of pain melted into tears. She sat down beside Anna and leaned into her. Anna's arms wrapped around her again, sharing her warmth. The children skipped along, completely enthralled by the shoreline's adventures to explore.

"I'll try." Anna's hand caressed Maria's hair.

Maria felt Anna's protective arms as the little ones' laughter carried on the wind. "I never hated you, Anna. I wanted... I wanted you to love me like you loved everyone else."

"I didn't want you to think I was taking your mother's place. Or that I wanted to. I held back."

# CHAPTER TEN

MARIA WALKED ON AHEAD OF Anna and the kids on the way back up to the house. Going down to the lake and getting their feet wet had been a great relief. Anna's words had left a calm connection she had never felt before.

The crisp cold air, almost gone in the warm over the lake, reasserted itself in the shadows of the trees.

Her mind flashed back to the fight she had with James the first night at the lake. About marriage. James wanted to get married. Maria thought the idea was stupid. There was no society left to have appearances for. They were already having a baby. Maybe she shouldn't have tried to find him. Maybe she should have left him there at the rez. No. She wanted to be with him. She liked herself better when he was around. And keeping him at arm's length so he wouldn't hurt her...

As she neared the creek, she heard hollering. She hurried over the split log bridge, her ribs still aching where Dad had knocked her down. The voices grew louder.

"Get the hell away from the house," yelled a gruff male voice.

"I wouldn't fight him if I were you," another voice warned—feminine and younger.

Maria broke into a jog.

"I can't leave. There's a man, hurt really bad inside. My family--" James begged.

He stood, his hands clenched at his sides, Maria's heart pounded. She could hear the fear in his voice mixed with the same stubbornness she'd argued with.

"I don't give a tinker's damn about your family."

Tinker's damn? No. It couldn't be. A gunshot echoed off the wall of the house.

James dropped to his knees.

"NO!" Maria screamed. Oh, God, don't die.

"Don't shoot. It's my girlfriend's family's house," James hollered. He wasn't shot.

"Like hell it is!"

"Thomas, relax!" the woman's voice ordered.

Thomas? Tom? Maria yelled, "Grandpa?" The silence echoed. James waved her back. She ignored him and ran onward. Her grandfather stood there mostly hidden behind a tree, rifle lowering—a grizzled old man with his head in a ratty wool stocking cap. He stared at her as she wrapped her arms around James and the worst of the terror let go. "Grandpa Tom? It's Maria."

"Maria? Samuel's daughter?"

Maria saw recognition dawn. "Yes." She grinned at James, shrugging her shoulders as she stepped back from him. "I guess Grandpa's not dead."

Grandpa leaned his rifle against the tree and opened his arms to Maria. "Your hair's a lot darker than the bleached blonde I recollect," he muttered.

Maria rushed into his arms and he pulled her in close; she remembered this bear of a man squeezing her so she could hardly breathe. He seemed smaller, slighter now.

"I'm in college now, trying to be more adult. Thought I'd let it go back to brown," Maria said. He still smelled the same—wood smoke and old man.

A woman with long dark hair streaked with gray came around the corner of the Suburban, shotgun in her hands.

He released Maria to hold her at arm's length. "You thought I was dead?"

"Everyone else is dead," Maria said.

"Only the good die young, little girl. I've got a long time left."

"And you're bad, Tom?" The woman sized up Maria. "Are you going to introduce us?"

Grandpa nodded at the woman. "This is Holly. My new, uh, partner."

Holly snorted. "Partner?"

"Well," Grandpa demanded, "What do you want me to call you? Girlfriend sounds stupid."

"Whatever, Tom." She nodded at Maria and James. "I'm Holly, his new partner... in crime."

Maria nodded back. "That man you were gonna shoot, Grandpa, is James my... uh, partner." She glanced at James and his face was stone, belying his near death experience. "James, meet my great grandpa."

"Well, I'll be a monkey's uncle. Not sure I'm so great today," Grandpa said with a sheepish grin. He offered his hand to James, who moved to shake it. They both stopped, uncertain.

"If you're not dead yet," Holly said, "a handshake is not going to kill you two."

They shook hands.

"Actually," Maria patted her tummy, "you're gonna be a monkey's great-great-great-grandpa."

The old man whistled and hugged her again, kissing her forehead. Grandpa released Maria. "James? Congratulations are in order, I s'pose."

"Thanks." James wrapped his arms around Maria protectively.

"You didn't answer the phone," Maria accused. Her heart was pounding. Until she saw him, she hadn't realized how much she had missed him.

"Always hated the damn thing." He tugged at his beard. "Hasn't worked for weeks."

"What the hell is all the shooting about?" Anna called from the creek side.

"It's Grandpa," Maria hollered. "He's alive." She felt her face aching with her smile. "Your beard's epic, Grandpa."

The door to the house slammed.

"Epic?" He chuckled. "That's good?"

"Who's shooting who?" Anna stomped into view. "Come on, kids. It's safe. Relatively anyway."

"Nobody's shootin' nobody," Grandpa growled.

Anna had reached them now. "Where have you been, you old..." She wrapped her arms around Grandpa.

He hugged her back and kissed her cheek. "Fool?" he offered. "I moved in with Holly."

Abi reached for Maria's hand. Noah stayed partly hidden behind her. Maria realized he didn't remember Grandpa. It had been a few years, almost half of Abi's life.

"Well,"—Grandpa knelt near to Noah and Abi's level—"Who do we have here? Abigail and Noah?"

Anna and Holly studied each other.

Maria stifled a laugh. She could feel the tension. Holly looked about ten years older than Anna, young enough to be Grandpa's kid. Well, Grandpa was spry, if curmudgeonly.

Holly turned to James. "You said there's someone hurt inside?"

"My dad," Maria said, "Saved me from getting hit by that branch."

"I used to be a nurse," Holly said, handing her shotgun to Grandpa.

Anna's face softened. "My husband needs medical attention."

Holly straightened. "Okay. Take me to him."

"And this little one, too," Anna said, taking Abi's hand and scooping up Noah. "She's got a bad cold."

* * *

Maria stuck her head in the room, trying to see past Anna and Grandpa. Her grandfather had always remained aloof with her Dad, but there was a look of concern peering from underneath the bushy white brows as Holly poked and prodded. Maybe her dad and Anna were exaggerating about Grandpa's meanness and disinterest.

Her father gave soft groans of discomfort until Holly finally stopped. She stepped back, her arms crossed.

"Well?" Anna demanded, her jaw tightened.

"I'm not a doctor," Holly said. "Hell, I haven't been a nurse in damn near thirty years."

"Holly," Grandpa said, his voice gentle, but firm, "What's your best guess?"

Her jaw knotted and then she spoke. "You may have some broken ribs. That may or may not be serious. In the worst case a broken rib could lacerate a vital organ. I can't tell if that has happened or not. There are no obvious signs of internal bleeding. The only thing we can do for him out here is keep him immobile to prevent any more damage than has already been done."

"I need to be up and around." Samuel pushed himself up on his elbow. His face contorted. "Dammit!" He tried to lower himself back down, but the look of pain flashed across his face again.

"Support his back," Holly ordered. Grandpa and Anna hurried to Samuel and propped him up.

Holly pressed against his torso, her arm under his side, and pulled his elbow out from under him.

Maria watched the pain wash his face to white as they lowered him into the mattress.

"Now. Relax," Holly's nurse voice brooked no arguing.

He closed his eyes.

"And stay still," Holly said. "Everybody out."

Anna's face flashed in anger. Maria was glad that for once she was not the target of Anna's wrath.

"He needs rest," Holly continued, shifting the pillow under his head.

"I will stay with him," Anna said. "You get out."

Holly nodded, her jaw tight, then she turned and left the room.

Maria crossed to her father. She placed her hand on Anna's shoulder for a moment. Anna patted her hand without taking her eyes off her patient. "I love you, Daddy."

"I love you, too, Ria."

Maria hurried after Holly, hoping to have a word with her. Behind her, she heard Grandpa's low voice making some forceful comment and Anna responding in kind. Well, that ought to help everything.

The outside door shut behind Holly with a heavy thud.

At the sound, Abi stopped building with dominoes, but Noah continued zooming a dune buggy around the rug.

Maria ran to her room and grabbed her heavy coat and gloves to follow Holly outside.

The sun had disappeared behind the trees, but its rays colored the snow on the tips of the hills a strange golden-hued light. The clarity of the sky, evening stars poking through, hinted that a frost might be upon them soon.

She didn't catch up to Holly until she stopped at the log bridge over the creek.

Holly looked up at Maria, her eyebrows arching in the obvious question.

"Yeah. Me, too. I hate it when she does that. She's something else."

"That's a kind way of putting it," Holly's warm smile said she was trying not to take it personally. "But she's under a lot of stress."

"Yeah, but she's being all mother bear on you while you're trying to help."

"I don't want to judge," Holly said. "Walking out seemed like the safest choice. And I'm not pregnant with an injured husband."

"Well, I am pregnant, too, but you're kinder than I usually

am. And more polite than Grandpa."

"He's pretty damn fond of you."

"That goes way back. Probably why Anna's being so beastly. She's his granddaughter, I'm not even his kin."

"Kin is what it is."

"I know. Still. Did Grandpa say anything about her?"

"Nope." Holly frowned pensively. "I can take it. Like I said. I was a nurse. Now, I'm a writer. I've been rejected by millions of people."

"Probably without quite as much drama."

"You might be surprised. I can make drama in real life almost as well as I can in books." Holly's smirk implied a lot of spunk. "Congratulations on your coming arrival."

"Thanks. Scares the hell out of me."

"Well, you're young. Less likely to have complications."

"Than Anna?" Maria wasn't sure how much to share, but Holly was the only medical person around. "She's had a lot of issues around pregnancy. Lost babies. I'm glad you're here."

Holly laughed ruefully. "When I was an Emergency Room nurse, I helped deliver a baby once. 3 a.m. At the end of a long, lonely shift. Doctor disappeared on a break." Her eyes stared at Maria, but didn't seem to see anything in the present moment.

"Wow."

Holly's eyes focused on Maria. "It was a long time ago, almost another life. I felt so powerful, like I could do anything. I know better now. Not sure my experience counts for much."

"More than we had before you got here." Despite her warm coat, Maria shivered.

"I'm not a doctor. We ought to go back inside. I'll take a look at your sister." Holly smiled. "Thanks for the background on Anna. I'm pretty good at not taking things personal."

"No problem." Maria decided she liked Grandpa's choice in partners. She wasn't Grandma, but she was cool. Not that there were many other choices. He got lucky again.

Grandpa met them in the driveway. "Coming back in already?"

"Yeah. Getting cold." Holly wrapped her arm around Maria's shoulder. "Gotta keep the pregnant ones healthy."

Grandpa stared questioningly at Maria. Over his shoulder, James swung the machete at the downed tree.

Maria grinned. "That's right, great-great-grandpa."

"Wow." A smile to match hers lit up his craggy face. "Didn't think I'd make it to that. Congratulations."

"Where's your sister?" Holly opened the front door as Grandpa headed over toward James.

"Let's go see." Maria led Holly inside. Noah was still playing in the front room. But Abi was gone. . ."Hey, Abigail, Nurse Holly is going to check you out." She headed down the hall to the kid's room.

As they entered, Abi scooted to the back of the bed against the wall, eyeing Holly suspiciously.

"Hello, Abigail," Holly said, her voice dropping into a lower register. "Do you want to hear your heartbeat?" She pulled out a stethoscope and breathed on it.

Abi tilted her head to the side and smiled shyly. She reached out tentatively for the stethoscope.

Holly put it in her hand, placed the earpieces in Abi's ears. Then she placed the chestpiece on Abi's chest nearest her heart. Abi's eyes widened with her smile as Holly moved it around her chest.

Holly moved the earpieces to her own ears and continued her exploration. "You have a strong heart, little one."

Abi straightened up. Maria tousled her hair and whispered, "I love you, Abigail."

A few minutes later, Holly placed the earpieces back in Abi's ears and handed her back the chestpiece. "If you leave them in your ears too long, they'll hurt. But if you lay down, you can listen until you feel sleepy."

Abi lay down.

Holly pointed a thermometer at Abi's forehead until it beeped. The readout flashed 99.9 in red numbers.

Maria kissed her sister's still too hot head and then followed Holly back down the hall. "Well?"

"She's doing okay. Upper respiratory. I can't tell if it's a cold or something worse." Holly slipped the thermometer back in her bag. "I'll leave this here. Check her temp every few hours. If it gets over 101, let me know."

"Should we give her something for it?"

"Only if she's suffering. Let her body fight off the virus."

The Virus or the virus? "Okay. Anything else?"

"Prayer, if you believe in it."

As they passed the front door, Grandpa came in and pulled his boots off with the boot jack. He motioned them into the kitchen. Opening what seemed to be a wall revealed a plain brown bottle and a stack of shot glasses. He sat three of the glasses in front of them.

Grandpa twisted out the cork and tipped the bottle with a practiced hand, giving each glass the same precise pour. He handed them each one.

"I shouldn't," Maria said.

"Nonsense," Grandpa said. "I don't make it strong. Apple Cider Brandy. This much ain't gonna hurt you, is it Holly?"

"Not unless you make a habit of it." Holly lifted her glass.

"To being lucky..." She sipped. "Hhmmm... Nice work on the brandy, Tom."

"Cheers." Grandpa poured the contents down in one shot and peered at Holly. "Is what you said about Samuel in there everything?"

Maria took a sip. It burned. Not like the real hard stuff. And it tasted like apples. She watched Holly trying to read her silence.

Holly took another sip. "Everything that I can verify. It might be bad, it might just be a strained muscle. I don't have the training or the technology."

"Thanks," Maria said, "He saved my baby's life. Probably mine, too."

"Not a brilliant man," Grandpa said, sipping his second shot. "But he's got heart to beat the band."

"Yeah," Maria sighed. That was high praise coming from Grandpa. She gritted her teeth, biting a bit of her cheek to not start crying again.

Grandpa's eyes appraised her. Finally he glanced away outside toward the lake. "Why'd you come here?"

"I don't think we really had a plan other than getting out of Portland before things got worse." She looked at Grandpa. "We weren't sick. Not then. Now Abi..."

"She has some of the symptoms, but I really don't have any way to tell if has the Influenza virus that's been killing everyone. Might not be," Holly said. "'Tis the season for colds."

"Thanks," Maria said. "I hope you're right." She shook off her misgivings and took another sip. It was much more pleasant than any of the crap she drank with her friends.

"Your siblings were in school, right?" Holly's brows creased, and she ran her finger over the ring rim of the glass. "I thought Tom and I were lucky. But you folks are crazy lucky."

Maria nodded. "Yeah."

"So why is your whole family alive?" Holly asked.

"Grandma's dead," Maria said.

Grandpa's jaw clenched. "She died years ago."

"I mean from the pandemic. What did you all have in common?"

Grandpa shrugged as his eyes met Maria's.

"I don't know," Maria said. "Does it really matter?"

Holly shook her head. "Probably not." She closed her eyes and rubbed her temples. "But I'm a writer by trade, habit and temperament. I want to know answers. It's those kinds of questions that keep me awake at night."

Grandpa reached up and massaged her neck.

Maria glanced around the kitchen, remembering her childhood in this room. Hot summer days spent baking. "I don't get it. Why'd you move?" she asked Grandpa.

"Are you kidding?" Grandpa chuckled. "Why spend a bunch of time fixing up the old house I never finished? I have my choice of great houses here. I only found two other people alive in the area, and them, not much so. Checked on all of my friends. Most of them were already dead. I never felt a sniffle. Then I found Holly. We'd seen each other around, but never talked much. Now, we've buried most of the people we knew and a lot we didn't. Funny how things work out."

"Yeah, James is the last of his family." Maria could feel a flush on her face. "Still some people alive at the Warm Springs Reservation, he says. But not many." The brandy in the glass was gone. Grandpa filled it half full again.

The front door opened, feet stomped on the mat, followed by the thud of boots hitting the floor.

Maria lifted the bottle from Grandpa and poured the glass full. His eyebrow raised.

"For James," she explained. She and the baby didn't need it. James' feet padded along the hallway and a door closed. Her heart twisted again. She shrugged and picked up the glass, kissing Grandpa on his bald spot.

"Thanks for helping with Abi and my dad, Holly." Then she hurried to their room.

James hadn't bothered to turn the light on. He sat on the bed, staring out the hazy window away from her.

Maria set the shot glass on the nightstand and wrapped her

arms around him. He was hot and sweaty, not stinky yet, but he would be soon. "I love you," she whispered. His hand patted her arm, but he didn't return her words. She held onto him. How could he be her stability when he spent so much time isolating himself inside his own head? Grandpa's welcome seemed to have pushed him even further away.

"James, Gramps didn't know who you were. I hope you know you are welcome in the family." She wanted to say that nobody blamed him for the accident, but...

How long would he hold onto his guilt? And her dad? Helplessness overwhelmed her, the world spun and tears rose in her eyes. The tears broke free and ran down her face as she cried silently. Not just for the kids, Anna. After a moment. James' hand reached up to brush at one on the side of his neck.

He turned to her, tears in his eyes, too. "I'm sorry. How is he?"

"No worse. Holly thinks he's got broken ribs."

"I only wanted to help."

"I know. Shit happens."

"Yeah. Far too often."

# CHAPTER ELEVEN

THE FOLLOWING NIGHT MARIA SAT in her father's sick room. Her brain tried to run through her thoughts and make sense of it all. James' marriage proposal, Daddy's accident, Abi's cold. Grandpa was alive. And she and Anna were on speaking terms.

Her phone buzzed. Had it really been a whole night? She'd fallen asleep; she hoped for not more than a few minutes. No one had called to her, and Dad was still resting peacefully. She sighed and pushed herself to her feet, kissing his brow on the way out.

She stood in the hallway, a moment of quiet peace with no one needing her. She breathed a few deep breaths and then knocked on Abi and Noah's door. Abi was being a little adult demanding her shift to watch Daddy.

There was no answer to her knock.

Maria opened the door to a noxious wave of scents. Vomit. Noah's bed was empty. She rushed to Abi's. Her red-faced little sister had tossed off all her covers, and a pool of puke seeped into the bed beside her. She shook Abi. Even through the pajamas, she felt hot. She touched Abi's forehead. "Oh, God!"

Abi's eyes opened slightly. "Sorry," she whispered, "I threw up."

"Abi. Why didn't you tell me you didn't feel good?"

Abi's lip trembled. "Daddy's hurt."

"It's okay, Abigirl," Maria soothed. "You still have to take care of yourself or you can't help him."

Abi nodded. "I'm thirsty."

"I'll bet, you're burning up." Maria scooped Abi up and carried her to the bath tub. "We're going to take a bath and get this puke off you." In the hall, she paused outside the room she shared with James. She kicked the door. "I need you. Now." She heard an incoherent sound of ascent.

"I need you to go get Abi, Holly." If she got Abi in a warm bath, they could cool it down. Cooling too fast was bad. She was pretty sure about that. Grandma had done that for her one summer when she wasn't much bigger than Abigail. Maria started the tub. Spinning the hot faucet, the water was chillingly cold. It would take a while for the heat to come through the pipes. "Sit on the floor here. When the water gets warm, turn on the cold."

She returned to the hall.

James waited at the door, bleary eyed, tennis shoes in his hands. "What's up?"

"Abi's fever. It's bad. I need Holly. Now."

"Be back as soon as I can." He moved into high gear, struggling into his shoes.

"Thanks." Maria blew him a kiss and hurried to her father's room. "Anna?" she hissed through the door, then pushed it open. Anna stared at her groggily. "It's Abi. She's worse."

She hurried back to the bathroom with Anna right behind her.

Abi lay curled up in fetal position while the water ran. Anna pulled Abi into her arms.

Abi's eyes tracked Maria as she plugged the tub and reached for the cup by the sink and filled it with water. She held the cup to Abi's lips while she took little sips.

"James is getting Holly and Grandpa."

Anna nodded, taking the cup from Maria. "Get the thermometer."

Maria retrieved Holly's medical kit from the hall and flashed Abi's head. 104.1.

Anna jerked the thermometer from her hand, read it and shoved it back.

"I'm going to put you in the bath."

Maria tried to get Abi's pajamas off, but she started shaking. Her whole body shook and her head flipped backward into her mother's chest.

Anna held her. "Abi, Abi."

Her eyes rolled up in her head as her legs and arms continued to twitch violently.

"Oh, God," Anna held onto her, wrapping her arm around her sister's head. "Help me."

Maria shoved herself between them and the tub. She wrapped her arms around both of them. She pushed her own shoulder under Abi's head.

"She's not breathing."

"Make sure her mouth is clear."

Anna's fingers worked Abi's jaw. Abi made choking sounds. Then a spew of watery bile flew from her mouth.

She breathed. Short. Quick panting breaths. Her body stilled, echoes of the shakes shorted through her limbs, but more softly. Her eyes closed and she relaxed into their arms.

"You're okay, baby girl," Anna whispered into her ears. "It's over now. You're gonna be all right." She sat up. Abi wrapped in her arms.

"What was that?" Maria turned off the water in the nearly full tub.

"Fever seizure. She had one before."

Abi's eyes opened. "Water. Please."

"Okay, baby. Here's some water."

By the time Holly arrived, Maria and Anna had Abi in the tub of lukewarm water, her clothes still on. She was lethargic, but awake and had finished almost the whole glass of water. Anna leaned awkwardly over the tub cradling Abi's head in case she had another fit.

Holly slid to her knees next to her. "Hey, Abigail. Good to

see you. Can I listen to you breathe again?"

"Fever's over 104," Anna said. "She vomited and had a fever seizure."

"Has she had them before?" Holly asked.

"Once."

"Her breathing sounds okay," Holly flashed the thermometer. "103.7 is better."

Maria rose. She needed to do something instead of kneeling here feeling helpless. "I'm going to check in on Noah and dad and get the sheets in the wash."

"Thanks," Anna said.

As Maria stepped out into the hall, she heard Anna say,

"What can we do?"

"What you're doing. And we wait."

"We wait?" Anna's voice rose. "Get out. You're no help at all."

"Drink water, Abi," Holly said soothingly, "and when you feel a little cooler, you can sleep, Anna, I'll be out on the couch. If anything changes...."

"Go."

* * *

Samuel drifted in and out of consciousness. For a while, Abi had lain beside him, her warmth keeping him alert, listening to her breathe while they made up a new bed for her.

Then there were other people in the room with him—little Noah, Maria, and Anna. And Grandpa Tom, Anna's grandfather. More time passed. Anna and Tom were here now. They whispered over him, assuming him still asleep.

"Why'd you come here, Anna?"

"You don't want us here?"

"Didn't say that," the old man hissed. "Why're you always jumping to conclusions?"

"Are we playing questions?"

"Are you nuts?"

"Yes. My husband is in there badly hurt. My daughter may be dying in the next room and I'm pregnant? I think I have the right."

Samuel forced his eyes open. Abi?

"Abigail is fine. She's sleeping and her temperature's falling."

He sighed. "I'm worried, too. Can you answer my first question?"

"Why did we come?" Her voice took on an edge, cutting. "This is as close to a safe place as I've ever had. Despite your treatment—"

"My treatment? You got the same treatment as your cousins."

"They were boys."

"SO?" Grandpa's voice rose and then dropped as quickly. "Why didn't you come when your grandmother was sick?"

There was silence. Samuel could hear the two of them breathing. He wanted to open his eyes, to say something, but he knew Anna and Tom had to get through this if they were going to have any sort of relationship.

Anna sighed. "I meant to. Didn't seem like she could die so quickly. She was always so strong."

"She was," Grandpa agreed. "She kept me strong. Took care of everyone else better than she took care of herself."

"Then she was gone. And I felt guilty. I couldn't face you." There was a long pause before Anna continued. "I'm sorry. I thought by coming here I could make amends somehow. Keep her memory strong. Didn't really expect you to make it without her."

Grandpa's gravelly voice choked with emotion. "Me neither. She always thought we were here for a reason. Guess mine was to help you."

Their voices faded and Samuel slept, lulled to sleep by their strangely calm conversation.

*  *  *

Samuel woke with Abi's head rising and falling on his chest. She felt warm, but not as bad as the heat she'd put off when her fever was stoking. How many days had that been?

He was out in the front room by the roaring fire. Grandpa and James had gotten a rolling hospital bed and a wheel chair for Samuel from a nursing home in Amanda Park. Now they could roll him around the house without aggravating anything.

The front door opened and he heard a whispered interchange. Maria and James. *Are they doing okay? How can I help? I can hardly keep my eyes open.* After a minute or two of the tense voices, footsteps echoed down the hall.

Maria came into the room and stood watching him. "How are you feeling?" she asked softly.

"Like I've got the damn virus." He could feel the rattle in his chest, but at least he wasn't coughing.

"No, Daddy. It's a cold. A winter cold." Maria said the words like she'd rehearsed them. "You got it from Abi. She seems to be getting better." Did she believe that? She came over and knelt next to the bed.

"What are you and James fighting about?"

A progression of emotions—annoyance, anger, sadness, and fear—flashed across her face. "Nothing."

Samuel sighed and let his eyes fall shut.

"He thinks someone is out there. Spying on us."

Samuel opened his eyes, his heart raced. "Dammit, I can't even get out of this thing by myself. The panel truck boys?"

"I don't know of anyone else around." She shrugged. "I think they're harmless. And I think James is just catching the paranoia. Maybe."

"We're all in protection mode. Seems like there's been enough death. Ought to be enough raw materials left to share."

"Yeah. I've always agreed with your anti-fear stance, but it's like the stakes are bigger." She knelt and put her head on his chest, kissing Abi's sleeping forehead.

"Why don't you go get some sleep, Maria?" He ran his fingers through her hair, just like he used to when she was little. Sure enough, she had tangles. She winced. "Sorry," Her hand reached for his. "I can holler if I need something."

She stood up. "I love you, daddy," she said, her mouth tight.

"Keep talking, okay? I'm happy to listen." Samuel smiled at her and she left the room. Was Abi better? He could tell that she was coughing less, but she hadn't spoken since the fever peaked. He didn't have the energy to argue with Maria about it, but knew in his heart that the disease that had killed most of the rest of the human race had found them. They hadn't escaped. Abi lived, but how soon would the rest of them come down with it? He could feel it in his bones.

# CHAPTER TWELVE

MARIA FIDDLED WITH HER TOAST as she stared across the field of alders. The toast was dry before she added the butter; she forced herself to swallow the last bite of crust. She'd better learn to bake bread.

"Maria? Holly?" Grandpa's voice called from her father's room.

Maria jumped up from the breakfast table, barreled down the hall and through the door. "What is it?"

Grandpa's face was white. "Anna's having contractions. Says she's not due for six weeks."

"And you're an ass." Anna glared at him.

"I'm worried for you," Grandpa said.

Her dad glanced from one to the other. "I'm worried, too, Anna."

"Too many other things to worry about," Ann said with less intensity.

Maria rested her hand on Anna's shoulder. "How long?" she asked, trying to keep her voice soothing. Holly stepped in the room, but only just inside.

"Started last night." Anna's face tightened. "Been timing them for the last couple hours. Coming regularly..."

Holly came in, stopping inside the door frame without stepping all the way in.

"And you didn't bother telling anyone?" Maria felt sweat roll down her chest inside her shirt.

"What can anyone do?"

"How many minutes apart are they?" Maria said, glancing at Holly. "You're sure they're not Braxton-Hicks?"

"Feels like the real thing to me." Anna's eyes were wide and she gritted her teeth. "Right now." Her hands grasped Grandpa's and her father's arms.

"Breathe," Maria ordered.

Anna nodded. Her breath hissed and then puffed—in and

out. After a minute, she slowed and then went back to breathing normally. As Anna released the hold she'd had on Grandpa's arm, Maria saw the fingers impression in his skin pressed clear of blood like a handprint. He winced and rubbed it a bit with his other hand.

"How certain are you about your due date?" Holly asked.

"Very certain," Anna gritted her teeth, glaring at her. Grandpa's partner was the last person Anna wanted around right now.

Holly's eyes caught Maria's; her head moved ever so slightly left to right. No. Not time. Maria had had the same thought. Unless Anna was way off, this was early. Way too early.

Holly gestured with her head. Follow me. She slipped out.

Grandpa and Dad were there for Anna.

"Honey, it'll be fine," her dad said, his voice soft with concern.

"Yeah. It's going to be all right, Anna," Maria agreed. "I'm gonna go check on the kids." She closed the door gently behind her.

Outside Holly motioned her close. "Six weeks is too early."

Maria whispered. "What can we do to stop the labor?"

"I don't know." A wry laugh escaped. "Never had kids."

"Lucky?" Maria asked.

"No. Planned it that way. Never was the mothering type." She shook her head. "And now I'm kind of a great grandma."

"Great-great grandma, pretty soon." Maria patted her tummy. "Well, Granny, I wish we had access to the Internet."

Holly glanced quizzically at her. "I've got it. My place. It was working a week ago."

"Really?" How has this not come up? "I'll ask Grandpa to hold down the fort."

"Okay. You know," Holly offered, "it might be nerves. Might stop on its own."

"I know. I wondered." Maria grinned. "Maybe not getting enough attention," she whispered.

"Maybe." Holly's face broke into a pretty smile. "Meet you outside."

Maria felt a little bad about playing up Anna's downside, but

Anna had always been a hard one to get along with.

Fifteen minutes and a quick and bumpy ride later, Maria slid into the seat in front of Holly's computer. "May I?"

"Sure." Holly rapped the desk with her knuckles. She smiled wryly. "For luck."

Maria crossed her fingers. "Yeah." She tapped the keyboard and the screen lit up with a news feed. The top headline jumped out at her. "**The Source? No new cases in San Pedro, Honduras. Twelve days past the 28 day contagion window.**" Maria typed **preventing labor** into the URL bar and hit enter.

"Hold it," Holly said. "I want to read that article on Honduras."

Maria hit the back button and scanned the article with Holly.

"Holy shit, 60 percent of the population survived?"

"Have you been to Honduras?"

Maria snorted. "I've never been out of Washington and Oregon."

Holly reached over Maria's arm and hit **PgDn**. "I grew up in Honduras. El Progreso. My parents were missionaries."

"Dad and Anna went there the year my mom died. They got really sick when they came back. Grandpa, Grandma, and I took care of them." Maria continued to scan, but Holly scrolled down faster than she could read. She just got snippets. **Honduras is Spillover Site.**

"Bat flu," Holly said, hitting **PgDn** again.

"Bat flew? What the hell was Holly talking about? "What?"

"A local fruit bat is the likely reservoir for Influenza pandemic."

Maria skimmed the screen. "That's why we're immune?"

"Don't know if you are immune, but deaths in Honduras are the lowest reported per capita in the world." Holly had hit the end of the article. All that was left were stupid troller ads advertising celebrities who had plastic surgery and other questionable content.

"Are you saying we have a sixty percent chance of getting it? Or that sixty percent of us will survive?"

Holly frowned. "Not how it works. Sorry. We may be dealing with different strain, a mutated virus, or just been lucky so far. Nothing much we can do except wait the 28 days. Let's figure out what to do about Anna."

Maria clicked back to the labor links. After several sighs from Holly, she slid to the side. "Here, you must read faster."

Maria knew from her own recent experience that there was no lack of information about pregnancy and childbirth, but much of it contradicted the rest. The main things to stop early labor were rest and hydration. Drinking lots of water and lying on the left side of the body. Well, none of that could hurt. Also, red raspberry tea was supposed to be good for morning sickness, preventing miscarriage, and easing labor and delivery. "You have any red raspberry tea?"

Holly shook her head as she scrawled notes in a composition book. "There's a market in town might have some. It's got a small health foods section."

After a bit it all seemed the same, Maria stopped reading and let her eyes close. Her thoughts drifted. Working with Holly to find answers was almost fun. And easier than dealing with unanswerable questions like whether or not to marry James. She pushed the thought from her mind and tried to feel the baby, make sense of her body, feel her breath. She focused on the fullness under her ribcage and relaxed.

Holly hand on her arm startled her awake. "Hey there, sorry to interrupt your nap, but I've got what I need."

Maria shook off the sleepies. "Let's go."

"Need me to drive?"

Maria shook her head. "I'm fine. Think the nap did me some good."

When they got back to Grandpa's, Holly sent him into town to look for raspberry tea.

Maria saw Holly hesitate at the door to Anna's room. Why would she want to go back in there? "I'll go in and talk to her. She's never been good with medical personnel."

"How is she with authors?" Holly smiled.

"You write religious fiction?"

"No. Quite irreligious."

"Probably stick with the former-nurse face with her." Maria impulsively hugged Holly. "Thanks. I'm glad you're here."

"Me, too." Holly chuckled. "Mostly."

Maria took a deep breath and went in to tell Anna what they'd found out.

Over the rest of the day, the contractions gradually slowed and finally stopped. Grandpa had found some of the raspberry tea, but it had taken him half a day. He didn't say how far he'd driven, only that he could go pretty fast with no cops on the road.

Somewhere around midnight, Anna fell into an uninterrupted sleep. Maria's head had been nodding for hours. She stood, checked that Anna had plenty of water and tea, then dragged herself down the hall. She had to check on Dad and Abi before she crashed. She tapped on the door to her father's room.

"Come in," James soft deep voice floated through the door.

Inside, her father lay on his bed, eyes closed. Maria's eyes jumped to her father's chest. It rose and fell softly.

James sat in the big cushy armchair reading a book. He slid a bookmark in and closed it. "How's Anna?"

"She's all right. Asleep for now." Then she noticed that a bed had been brought in for Abi. She was curled up in it, her arms wrapped around a giant bear.

"Your Grandpa's with Noah. After a while we'll switch. Whoever has Noah gets to sleep when he does. I swear that kid sleeps more during the day than at night. But he's pretty damn cute." He placed his hand gently on her belly. "I don't mind."

Maria's relief stole over her as exhaustion kicked back in. "James. Thanks for helping take care of my family." She kissed him on the forehead and turned to go.

He caught her arm. "I know you need sleep. But give me a real kiss at least."

"Sorry, James." She knelt down; her lips met his. Her arms wrapped around his solidness. She felt more muscle on him than what she was used to.

"Don't worry about it, Ria." His warm hand cupped her face as he kissed her forehead. "You could sleep here." He opened his arms.

Maria knew she should get to a bed. Here, she was going to wake up whenever James moved, Abi coughed, or her father groaned. But the warmth and comfort conspired with her tired body to keep her where she was. "Maybe for a bit." She sat sideways on his lap, snuggling herself in as his arms cradled her. She let her eyes fall closed. "I love you, James."

"Then marry me, silly."

Had he really said that or was her mind conspiring against her?

In the middle of the night, Grandpa came in for a shift to watch her father and Maria awoke. James helped her to her feet. Once she was in bed, James left. But a few minutes later, he came back in carrying Noah, asleep in his arms. "If he wakes up in here, he won't get scared that he's alone. And we won't have to get up and take care of him."

"Good call." Maria pulled back the covers and let James back up to her with little Noah on the other side. She relaxed into his warmth and released her stubborn waking self.

\* \* \*

Samuel woke coughing. He levered himself up on his elbow to drink some water, and a sharp pain stabbed in his side. The water felt good and the coughing settled down. His throat hurt and his nose was running. Anna was sleeping crossways in the recliner. He relaxed back into the pillows to catch his breath.

There was a knock on the door and it swung open. James slid through the door balancing a tray of food in his hands. Coffee sloshed over the rim of a monstrous moose head mug.

Samuel shook his head and lay back. "Thanks," he croaked. "Don't think I can eat."

James shushed him. "You'll want this." He waved the mug under Samuel's nose and set it on the table beside the bed. "Let me help you sit up."

The cinnamon scent tugged at Samuel's memory. He allowed James to adjust him using minimal muscles of his own. "Thanks." His voice came out gruffer than he intended. He tried to catch James' eyes, but the young man kept staring at the food on the tray. There was a momentary glimpse as he placed the hot cup in Samuel's hands, but only enough to ensure it didn't get dropped. Samuel held it to his nose again. Apples, cinnamon, and a kick—Grandpa's legendary apple brandy. "Brandy?" he rasped.

"You can smell the alcohol?" James asked.

"James. Please, look at me."

James raised his head slowly, his eyes full of regret and tension.

"The accident was not your fault. It was an accident. I should have given you more training."

"I did it. Almost killed Maria. The baby. You."

"I'm not dead. And if something kills me, it's gonna be old age or this damn virus. Okay?"

James nodded, but his eyes dropped back down staring at the floor.

"You are the father of my first grand-kid. I need you to not dwell on this. I need you to move on, help Maria. Help me."

James eyes met his with strength. "I'll work on that, Mr. Herman."

"That's all I can ask." Samuel smiled at him. "You're gonna be a great father, James."

"Thanks."

"Ria said you've finished clearing away the tree?"

"Yeah. Nearly done."

"Thanks."

"Grandpa and Holly fixed the roof."

"Yeah, I heard." Samuel made a hammering motion.

"Right." James face relaxed into a smile. "I'd like to split the wood. I've done that before."

"There ought to be an ax, a sledge, and some wedges somewhere in the garage downstairs."

"I'll look after you eat."

"Deal."

# CHAPTER THIRTEEN

THE DAYS DRAGGED BY FOR Maria. Everyone kept going through their routines. Maria, James, Grandpa, and Holly kept food on the table, kept the house warm. It took the four of them to make Anna take it easy.

Anna refused to completely give up caring for her kids, but spent a good part of her day at her husband's bedside.

Abi's cough and fever had gradually faded, but she still slept a lot. She didn't seem to have any desire to talk or do much of anything else. Maria managed to get her and Noah outside, but once outside, Abi would stay wherever Maria helped her sit.

James finished sawing the vengeful tree into short rounds. When he needed a break from nursing, he went out and split wood.

Maria needed to get out by herself, too. So, after her morning shift at her father's bedside, she went for a walk. The cool afternoon air, moist and quiet, left her calm and thoughtful as she meandered down to the creek. Its rushing water kept an accompaniment to her thoughts. How long had it been since she'd had some quiet alone time? James hadn't been asking her to marry him, but he, too, had been quiet, overwhelmed. To her, it seemed like the least important thing to be thinking about. Most important was the health of the family.

How long since the Bat Flu had hit? She wasn't even sure what day it was. They'd left Portland on Halloween, arrived here on the second of November. The big storm was on the third. Dad got hurt on the fourth and then Grandpa and Holly on the sixth? Everything else was a blur. She pulled out her cell phone to check the date, but it was dead. How long had she been carrying around a dead cell phone? She hurried back to the house.

The digital clock in the kitchen with the thermometer said it was November 30th. She grabbed the calendar off the wall and slid into Grandma's writing desk. Anna was sitting in Grandpa's recliner, staring at her bemusedly.

"Thanksgiving was two days ago," Maria said.

Anna sighed and stared out over the lake.

If the pandemic was contagious 28 days, how long until they were safe? Her fingers were shaking as she picked up a marker and started making Xs through each of the dates since they'd found Grandpa and Holly. Or rather since Grandpa and Holly had found them. If Abi was infected and contagious, anybody who was going to get sick should have already done so. She counted to

25.

James and Grandpa hustled in. Grandpa slammed the door behind him; rubbing his hands together, he backed up toward the fireplace's flames. James followed him in and came over to Maria.

"Three more days and we're in the clear." Maria glanced from one to another, excited for the first time in a month. "If Abi had the Bat Flu and anyone else was going to get infected, they already would have."

Anna's tired face lit up. "Well, we'll just have to have a late Thanksgiving."

Grandpa slapped his hand on the table. "I know where a turkey is languishing in a freezer. Maria, you want to take a trip? James? You want to join us?"

"We should do it on Thursday." Maria stood. "Thanksgiving should be on a Thursday."

"What does it matter?" James asked.

"Anna, we should wait until you're up and around," Maria said. "And give us time to plan a feast."

"Okay. And Sam, too. And Abi." Anna's face blanked. Like she shut herself down. In a small voice she continued, "Maybe we should do it now."

Maria's brain filled in Anna's unspoken words. While we're all still here. "Okay. We'll plan it for Thursday, December fifth. Let's go get a turkey."

*   *   *

Maria helped Abi set the table for Thanksgiving dinner. Grandpa and James had extended the table with two extra leaves inserted to make room for the crowd. Maria remembered the old green table cloth and watching Grandma grab it in the middle and flip flip it was folded neatly. She hadn't learned that one yet.

Maria recited all the rules Grandma had taught her while showing them to her little sister. Abi still hadn't spoken, but the white clamminess of her skin had been replaced by her more normal pinkish hue. Her eyes glowed brighter, still hazy, but not lethargic. The strangeness of her silence stilled some of the joy of her survival, but not much.

"Thanks, Sissy."

Abi rewarded Maria with a big smile. Her mouth moved like she wanted to speak, but all that came out was air. "Can you make any sounds, Abi?"

Again her mouth moved, her tongue clicking against her teeth. Abi's eyes showed frustration.

"Does it hurt?"

Abi shook her head, her hands gripped into little fists. And a sound came out. Squeaky, but clear. The volume rose, and Abi's smile grew.

Maria's face cracked. The joy flowing from Abi's triumph warmed Maria. She had an idea. "Can you finish, Abi?"

Abi nodded, plunking down the silverware mostly where Maria had shown her.

Maria tousled her hair and went in search of something to write with. In Grandma's writing desk, she found scratch paper and crayons Grandma had gotten Maria long before Abi came. She hurried back. Abi had finished the table settings.

Maria wrote her own name on the paper in broad strokes and handed it to Abi. "Here. Can you write your name?"

Abi pursed her lips, took the crayon and placed it to paper. The long shaky strokes were jagged, resembling the M-A-R-I-A.

"No. Your name." Maria watched her sister struggle. "Abi. A-B-I." But it looked the same as before. Her sister was copying to please her. She gave Abi a big hug from behind. "I love you, little sis." Abi's arms did not return the embrace.

Maria's thoughts twisted and fell. Abi, her eyes looking glazed, handed her the paper. "It's wonderful." She hugged the little girl again and felt her hands wrapped around to participate this time. "What's wrong, Abigail?"

Abigail's smooth brow contracted like she was thinking, but no words came out. Her face twisted up. Another squeak came out.

"It's okay, Abigail. You're getting better."

Abi gave a her a glare worthy of her mother's daughter and sat down with a pout.

Maria tousled her hair and returned to the kitchen to help. The kitchen was a hubbub. Maria escaped with the stuffing as Grandpa brought the potatoes and gravy in.

"Holly's making the turkey presentable," he said.

In minutes they were all sitting around the giant table. All the food spread out. Other than her father in the wheelchair, it seemed a perfect Thanksgiving. And they had a lot to be thankful for.

"This looks great," James said. "And it smells delicious."

"It's been a while since we've had a feast here," Grandpa piped up. "And the first time in a long time we've had a Native American guest. You're family now. What tribe are you from, James?" Grandpa asked as he handed James the gravy boat.

"Numu," James answered, shooting a glance at Maria.

Grandpa's eyebrows rose. "Don't know that name."

"The Spaniards called us Payuchi," James explained. "Paiute was what white men called us. Numu are the northern tribes."

She chuckled. "Don't worry, James, Grandpa always wanted to be Native. Built a dugout canoe when he was younger."

"Damn thing hardly floats," Grandpa grumbled as Holly brought in the turkey.

"My people lived in the desert," James said, turning back to his plate. "No canoes."

Maria stared from one to the other, feeling awkward.

"No canoes in the desert," Grandpa said. "Right."

"I'm hungry. Tukanna means food," James said.

"Tukanna," Grandpa said tentatively. "Let's eat."

James smile twitched at the edges. How badly had Grandpa butchered the language? "Yeah. Let's eat."

Grandpa stood up and turned on the weird electric slicer. "The turkey might be a bit freezer burnt," he warned as he cut into it. "Gotta get ourselves some poults. Wild turkey, and I don't mean the whiskey, is something so much better than this raised in a box."

Anna rolled her eyes. "And where are you going to find baby turkeys, Grandpa?"

Grandpa stared at her as if she had questioned his manhood.

"You just wait and see, little mama. This time next year, I'll have you some turkey that will melt your taste buds."

"We better get vegetables to go along with it," Anna said.

"Gotta clear the field first," Grandpa said. "Been thinking about doing that for quite a spell. Hey, it'll keep us in shape. Samuel? You think you'll be up to giving a hand by spring?"

Maria's father nodded. "Sure as hell hope so."

Anna's face spun, trying to look angry, but Maria saw her anger melt. All Anna said was, "Watch your language, Sam."

A knock at the door froze everyone. Maria's heart pounded. Everyone she knew was here.

"Well, who the hell is that? The Park Ranger?" Grandpa shoved his chair back. "Pretty piss-poor timing, if you ask me."

Maria's father grimaced as he tried to unlock the stops on the wheelchair.

"I'll come with you," Anna said, grabbing the rifle leaning against the wall next to the cabinet.

Grandpa's nod to her was appreciative. He pulled on his belt with the revolver attached.

Maria glanced at the other faces at the table. She saw her own fears reflected. She'd accepted the fact that they were alone.

"Get ready to run," her father barked quietly. "Out the side door."

Maria's feet hit the floor, and she helped her father with the brake. He rolled the wheelchair back and forth, jockeying to get out from behind the table.

The doorbell rang as Anna and Grandpa disappeared around the hall.

"Didn't think the damn doorbell still worked," Grandpa said.

Maria heard the door open, and a sharp intake of breath.

Then Anna's voice, "Oh, my God."

"Somebody help me move this God-damned chair," Samuel ordered. "James? Help?"

The young man pushed him toward the front door. Maria's feet flew as she ran ahead.

Anna was hugging someone, a gray-headed, gray-bearded man with a bandage on his neck. He turned to Maria and she stopped breathing.

"Holy shit," Maria blurted. Uncle Brad turned toward her; she saw pain held in check. "Dad!" Maria hollered. "It's Uncle Brad!"

When Brad saw her father, he nodded an acknowledgment, but still didn't speak. He pointed his throat and rasped slowly, "Hurts to talk."

"Welcome to our Thanksgiving feast."

Brad's smile eclipsed the pain in his eyes. "Congratulations," he whispered with a grimace.

\* \* \*

Maria finished rinsing the last serving dish and handed it to Grandpa who fit it expertly in the dishwasher.

"That it?" he asked. "Let's go join the others."

The joy in the living room was as warming as the popping fire. Abi stared at the flames and Noah played with the cat on the floor. As Maria sank into Grandma's recliner, James came through the doorway with another armload of dry firewood.

Uncle Brad sat next to her father, writing notes on a tablet for him to read.

Samuel stopped Brad's hand on the tablet. "It's okay, Brad. Tell me later. I'm so glad you're here." His face glowed in the warmth of the fire and the friendship. "Really is Thanksgiving." He lifted a glass of Grandpa's brandy. "I'd like to make a toast."

"Whoa," Grandpa crowed, "then I need a glass."

In a minute everyone had a glass. Grandpa poured Maria's half full with a twinkle in his eye. "Glad you thought of Thanksgiving."

"To friends and family," her father said, raising his glass again. He drank. Then coughed. And then drank. And coughed. Brandy spewed from his lips as his coughing grew out of control.

Maria rushed to him, but Anna shoved her aside. "Sam. Breathe. Somebody get some water. NOW."

Maria gritted her teeth. She heard Anna say please as she ran to the kitchen for a glass.

When she returned, her father had quit coughing, but tears ran from his closed eyes.

"Water?" Maria offered.

His eyes opened. Anna took the glass and held it to his lips. He sipped. "Well. That hurt. Sorry to be a downer."

"Next time," Grandpa said gruffly, "take some more cough medicine instead of wasting my brandy."

Maria could see the same twinkle for her father, who smiled back weakly. It was nice to see the two of them enjoying each other's company.

"You want to lie down, Samuel?" Anna asked. He nodded and rolled the wheelchair toward the bedroom.

Uncle Brad watched the kids, his mouth locked tight.

Maria walked to him and set her hand on his shoulder. "You okay, Uncle Brad?"

He shrugged and took a sip of his brandy and patted her hand.

"Grandpa? Can we set up a place for Uncle Brad to sleep?"

"Makes sense to use my old bedroom. Holly and I can head home tonight."

Uncle Brad looked like he would complain, but then it was like all the tension fell out of him and he slumped and shrugged.

Grandpa looked thoughtful. "Maybe set him up in the old Moir place in a few days. Getting kind of crowded here."

Maria sat down next to a sleepy James. She snuggled against his comfortable warmth. Her eyes were quickly drooping. Turkey as a sleep aid. She let them fall closed as she listened to the low rumblings of conversation interrupted occasionally by silence and the snap and crackle of the fire.

Another knock resounded on the door. Maria jerked up, fully alert.

"What the hell is this, Grand Central Station?" Grandpa picked up the ancient double-barreled shotgun leaning against the pile of firewood. "Haven't had this many visitors since I had the party to compare my Apple Brandy batches in 97." He pointed at the gun rack by the main door.

Everyone except Holly moved toward the hall. She scooted the children toward the bedrooms as Anna came out and pulled them into the far bedroom. James grabbed the rifle by the fire as Brad pulled out a deadly looking pistol. Even Maria had grabbed Grandma's old 22 single-shot rifle.

They moved to where they could see the door, but could also duck for cover.

Grandpa glanced through the peephole and motioned for Maria to open the door while he held his shotgun at shoulder height. She swung it open.

"What can I do to help you fellows?" Grandpa asked.

Brad stepped into firing stance behind him with some sort of pistol. It looked big and dangerous to Maria. She pushed the rifle in her hands through the gap between the door and the frame.

It was the boys from the panel truck, no guns visible. The short blond swallowed and glanced at the taller one. Their eyes were big as saucers.

The shorter one talked like he had before. "Uh, we were thinking we might be able to offer a hand. Looks like you got some folk not up to prepping for winter. I'm Dave. He's Rafe." He hooked his head at his partner.

Maria saw a couple dogs bouncing around in the seats of the truck parked at the top of the driveway. She shook her head at Grandpa. No. She glanced as Anna wheeled her father toward them.

"Thanks, Dave, I think we've got it all under control here. Why don't you run along?"

Maria stepped out from behind the door. Both young men smiled really nice, but Maria thought their hygiene choices needed improvement. A chill came over her when she met eyes with the taller, quiet one.

"Well," Dave said directly to Maria. "If you need a hand around the place, we're over at the lodge." They walked back to the truck and climbed in, waving as the engine turned over and the truck backed up the driveway.

As the truck turned back onto the road with a little spit of gravel, Grandpa shut the door. "Well, what do you think? Trouble?"

Her father nodded as did Brad. "I don't know. I think they were expecting some womenfolk and maybe one able-bodied adult male. Means they've been watching us. Maybe we ought to keep an eye on them."

Brad nodded again. He pointed at himself. Then held up his rifle with the scope.

"So far," Samuel offered, "no harm, no foul. But something about them doesn't seem right."

"I don't like them," Maria said in a low voice. "Especially the tall one. Rafe. Can't tell you why."

Grandpa returned the shotgun to its place. "Those are the kind of hunches you don't want to ignore."

Brad wrote something on his notepad and handed it to her father.

"Going for a walk?" Her father chuckled. "Dress warm. We could use some fresh meat. But something less stringy than those boys would be preferable."

When Brad left the house, Maria saw her father slump. Like he had to show himself tough for Brad's sake. She understood that. She was trying to be tough for his sake.

# CHAPTER FOURTEEN

THE NEXT EVENING SAMUEL SAT up and sipped at a mix of Grandpa's apple brandy with honey and lemon juice. Holly pulled the stethoscope away from his chest as Maria looked on.

"Can I have some time to talk to Holly alone?" Samuel asked. Maria's face showed fear as she glanced from him to Holly. She didn't want to leave. He smiled at her. "A few minutes, please?"

Maria nodded. "I'll go check on Abi." She left, shutting the door behind her.

Samuel listened as her footsteps moved down the hall. "How long do I have?"

Holly shrugged. "How long do you want?"

"The virus kills in a matter of weeks."

"You don't have the virus."

"What do you mean, I don't have the virus?"

"I don't know. You might have it. Your fever seems more like an infection. That's why I gave you antibiotics. I'm pretty sure Abi has the virus. Enough of her symptoms match what the reports said. But she's going to survive. Not sure she'll be affected. What you've got is a bad cold, coupled with your other injuries. I need to keep you immobile. Then your body has a chance of taking care of itself."

"When I die—"

"If you die, you mean."

"When. Can you please not tell anyone what you just told me?"

"That you don't have the bat flu? You want me to lie? Why?"

"You're a writer, right? You lie for a living. Or at least avoid the truth. I don't want James feeling guilty. I don't want Maria blaming him."

Holly's eyebrow rose. "I'm not sure your lie will be worse than the truth."

"Haven't they all been through enough?"

"You take care of yourself." Holly patted his shoulder and stood. "And I'll never have to tell anyone anything. I need to check on your wife."

"Thanks, Holly."

She left, the shut door gently behind her.

Samuel closed his eyes and took a deep breath, testing himself for pain. His lungs still tugged sharply when he breathed that deep. There was a knock at the door. It opened again.

Brad entered and sat across from him, haggard and cold. Brad's eyes begged him as he handed him a sheet of paper. He stared at the words his former best friend had written. Brad scribbled as Samuel read.

Pam made me promise, if the kids died, I would put her out of her misery. When you came. The kids were dead. Pam was passed out, nearly dead. When you left, I shot her.

Brad tore off the next sheet of paper from the notebook and handed it to Samuel. He grabbed the first sheet of paper wrote on it again.

I was going to shoot myself. But I heard a sound. Like a cat. But we don't have a cat.

Brad dumped the metal trash can's contents out on the floor and pulled out a lighter.

"Oh, God, Brad—" Samuel had no words of comfort. He read the next note as Brad lit the corner of the first sheet. When it flamed, he dropped it in.

Lianna was alive, crouched on her bed, mewing, hoarse from no water.

"I'm so sorry, Brad. If I had known."

Brad shook his head and handed him the next sheet.

Picked her up, she was shaking, so weak. Took her downstairs and heated some broth. Spooned it to her. Didn't seem to know me. But she wasn't dead.

Brad handed Samuel another sheet, took the last one and repeated the process.

She fell asleep in my arms. Died the next day. Tried to kill myself. Fucked up.

Samuel stared at his friend as he motioned shooting himself under the chin with his fingers. The words continued.

Lay on the bed. Woke up. Lots of blood. But I didn't die. Lay there waiting. Waited a long time.

Fire. Flame. Ashes. The smoke stung Samuel's eyes. He glanced around to see if there was a smoke detector to set off. There was, but the battery clip hung loose and empty. He stared at the next sheet.

I don't get it. Should have died. I deserved to.

Tears flowed from Brad's eyes. Samuel's too.

I needed water. Once I got up, I felt like death had rejected me.

Brad took the slip and dropped it into the can, but didn't bother lighting it on fire.

I buried Pam & the girls. Sat in the house for days. Followed you.

"I'm sorry," Samuel held his arms open as his best friend collapsed into them, his ruined throat scratching out sobs. Eventually, Brad turned away. He slipped his lighter in his pocket.

"Thanks," Brad said, his voice only a whisper. Then he walked out.

Samuel stared after him, his brain spinning. How had he gotten so lucky? And Brad so unlucky? He let the softness of the hospital bed accept his exhausted body.

\*    \*    \*

Maria knocked gently on her father's door.

"Come in," his gravelly voice called.

"Hey, Dad. How are you?"

A smile broke his exhausted face. "Been better."

"I think we all have. It's weird how easy I had it and I thought it was hard."

"There is something you should know, Ria. I didn't leave you," her father spoke again. "I moved out of the house I shared with your mother."

"Daddy—" Maria said. He was trying to make peace with the past. For once in her life she didn't want him to.

"Please. We fought so mu—" He gasped for breath. "I didn't want to hurt you. Or your mom. I didn't want to hurt."

"Dad, it's all—"

He reached for her hand. "No. It's not all right. I don't know if I'll get the chance to say this again. I'm sorry we never went to Disneyland. I'm sorry I left you home when I went on the Mission trip with Anna."

Maria snorted snot and tears. She snagged a Kleenex from the box on the nightstand and blew her nose as she laughed again.

"What's so funny?"

"Dad. That's it. Holly thinks that's why the pandemic is not killing us. Because you went to Central America with Anna. People in Honduras are less susceptible than elsewhere. She thinks we must have all gotten exposed to an earlier version of this virus that you two brought back, a less toxic one. All of us. Less likely for the kids."

"Oh, my God, what does that mean since Abi is adopted?"

"Holly says she's past the point where the disease would have killed her. She must have got some natural immunity. Or she's a lucky survivor. So if you hadn't gone, we might all be dead. No baby in Anna's belly or mine."

"What about the secondary strain?"

Maria shrugged. "We don't know." She rested her head on

her father's chest. "I'm sorry for being a beast to Anna. I'm going to try to make it up to her. We've got to stick together. If any of us are going to make it."

"But Abi? Is she going to get better?" His voice caught. "She seems gone." He stifled a sob.

"She's not gone. Just—" Maria searched for the word. "She's subdued. We don't know. Try not to cry. It makes you cough."

Her father smiled warmly as tears flowed down his face.

"You're right. She'll be fine. She's alive."

"Oh, Daddy." Maria held him and wept; silent tears dripped onto her father's shirt. Her head hurt; her heart hurt. When his breath softened, she carefully extricated herself from his arms. She stayed a while watching him, until Anna came to relieve her.

As Maria passed the front door, Uncle Brad came in.

"Raining out there again?"

"Buckets," he hissed.

She lifted his wet coat from his shoulders.

He grimaced and smiled. "Thanks," he mouthed.

Since he'd arrived, Uncle Brad had been gone almost all day every day. Maria figured he still needed time to deal with his demons. Her father had given her an idea of what he was up against. No specifics, but she knew the way his family had left the planet had been painful.

"Holly take a look at your bandage recently?"

He nodded and shrugged indifferently, pulling out his notebook.

Maria smiled. "I'm glad. Some of Anna's elixir, turkey soup, on the stove. Probably still warm. Help yourself." She took the notebook and wrote. The panel truck boys?

Brad shrugged again. Seem to be gone this time.

"Okay, Uncle Brad. Go get some food. I'll put your coat by the fire."

He tousled her hair like he did when she was a kid. Then he

trudged down the hall. Everyone seemed too old.

\* \* \*

Maria trudged down toward the lake. How many days since she'd made the last trip, when everyone had been okay? Maybe she could go cry again and things would be better, or easier to face.

Dad and Abi were both doing so badly, she couldn't think of anything else. If she and James hadn't come along, none of this would have happened. Her logical brain interceded. They would still both be sick. They'd be out here in the wilderness, but he wouldn't be dealing with both the Flu and the battered body. And she and James would be alone together somewhere. As much as she needed space from people, she need people nearby to have space away from.

An explosion of motion in the brush, a flurry of wings, flew at her face. She stepped off the path. Her foot sunk in a mushy, boggy hole, instantly soaking through her tennis shoe. "Dammit." She jerked her foot out of the hole, but her shoe stayed behind. She choked back tears and collapsed cross-legged on the trail, digging into the mush with her hands to pull the drenched and muddy shoe from the ground.

It served her right for never bothering to tie or untie her shoes, always just forcing her feet in and out of them. If she was going to survive out here, she was going to have to pay more attention to what was going on around her.

She worked at the knotted laces, unwilling to give up despite the difficulty. Her fingertips burned by the time she got them loose. Tying it tight enough to prevent a repeat, she was tempted to leave it at that, but instead focused on the other shoe. Despite the pain, she attacked the dry knot with ferocity. When she had it tied firmly on her foot, she realized the dampness of the trail had soaked up through her underwear. She sat there for a moment before pushing to her feet with a sigh. She was beginning to feel pregnant, like her body was working hard enough on something to not give her all the energy she was used to having.

She swiped her dirty hands on her jeans and continued her walk down to the lake, now accompanied by a squishing with every other step. Maybe she was noisy enough to not get startled by another bird.

When she got out to the log jam, she pulled her shoes and socks off and set them on a stump. The sun was out, not very warm. At least the wind wasn't blowing cold. The wet shoe might dry a bit. She stepped carefully from log to log out toward the water, watching for the spurs of lost limbs that might tear the soles of her feet, waiting to see if the log sank before she put her full weight onto it.

The late afternoon sun glowed through the cloud cover and reflected off the relative calm of the lake. A bald eagle circled over near Canoe Creek. "What are you thinking?" she asked the bird. She settled on a big log worn smooth by years of sun and water. "It's quiet." She stared at her feet and a shiver ran up her spine. Really too cold to be out here barefooted on the logs.

Maria remembered coming out here when Dad and Anna had first gotten together. Neighbor kids had come down and built forts in the driftwood with her. Sometimes the cousins came, but that was rare as they lived back east. Everything had been simple.

It had been magical then. Could she find that magic again? No. She couldn't find it. Magic wouldn't bring back her mother, save her father, cure little Abi. How could she survive without either of them?

The tears came. She let them flow, hugging her legs, holding her blue-cold toes. The sun fell behind the hills, but continued to shine that strange pre-twilight glow off the windows of the Lodge and the other homes across the lake. The Quinault River burbled in the distance where it met Canoe Creek.

With the sun gone from the sky it wasn't long before she was shivering. She dried her eyes on her sleeve and stood. If she splashed some cold water on her face, perhaps her crying might go unnoticed. She carefully stepped forward on to the next big log. She skipped to the next log. The tears had done her good, lightened the load. Nothing had changed, but the peace of the lake calmed her.

A few more logs, and the cold water would feel good on her face. The next log rolled, she slid downward, cold water slicing into her pants, shocking. She grasped at the logs. Her brain flashed, crushed or drowned. The logs were closing back in. She ducked under water; she'd have to get out from down and under.

She kicked out with her legs to push herself toward deeper water. Branches snagged her clothes. In panic she kicked harder, shoving her feet into the muddy lake bottom. Her head jammed into the hard underside of the log. Stars flashed inside her eyelids. Grabbing the branches she jerked herself forward, but the branches came toward her, spinning with the log.

I can't die here. They need them. James and the baby... Her thoughts brought her back from the edge she flipped to face sunward, reaching in between the branches, letting her feet rise to find the logs and push her in the direction of open water. From the darkness of the now murky water, she could see stabs of light. But the grit storm kicked up by her feet stung her eyes She closed them and dragged herself under the bottoms of the logs, pushing with her feet and pulling with her hands. The logs rolled, but she made headway. Then a rush of cold water on her head shocked her, she opened her eyes and her mouth. Inflow from the snow fed river. Light. No more logs overhead. Though her mouth was full of water, she had managed to not swallow it, but she needed to breathe. She stroked strongly toward the light and exploded into the air, gasp for breath before sinking under again.

The next time her head came into the air, she treaded water. It was icy and she had to get out. This was a good way to die, but she wasn't ready for that yet. She was out passed the drop off so standing up and getting back on the logs was not going to work here. She swam along toward the shore looking for a stable jam of logs to climb out on.

A shiver ran through her, but the adrenaline of surviving would keep her going. She dog-paddled along, cursing herself for her carelessness. Not good future mom behavior in the apocalypse. Her feet hit grasses growing out of the bottom of the lake, so she stopped and let her body go vertical. She could touch the top of the mud. She kicked some more until she could stand. Then she slogged forward through the water, looking for a good sturdy mess of logs to crawl out on.

Her chattering teeth decided her on the next log with a root base attached. She grasped a root, floating her body up; she heaved her leg onto the log and rolled onto its broad girth. Her breath gasped out. Where was the calm she'd found a few minutes before? Her heart pounded.

"Are you okay?"

Maria rolled to her knees and confronted the newcomer jumping across the logs. Don. No. Dave. Another shiver shook her body. She didn't like him, but if he was coming to her rescue... "Stop," she yelled. "Slow down or you're going in."

He slowed, stopped, the log he stood on dipped and he looked panicked as he stepped backward onto the last one and pulled his now soaked foot out of the water.

"These logs will roll. You get stuck under them, they move back together and you're dead. What the hell are you doing here?"

The look on his face went from panic to guilt before that faded into blankness, but she'd seen it. He'd been watching her. Another shiver slithered down her spine. Where were her shoes? She glanced back to where she had been. If he had bad intentions, could she get across the logs faster than he could?

Maria reached automatically for her cell phone. Not in her pocket. Had she had it or was it at the bottom of the lake? "Go back where you came from!"

"I'm trying to help you."

"I'm fine. If my Uncle Brad sees you, he's going to come after you."

"And you wouldn't like that?"

"I wouldn't really care, but you and your friend might."

"Yeah. Me and my friend. What's your name?"

"None of your business."

"Well, Ms. Nunoyerbizness, you're not very polite to your potential rescuer."

"I'm going back home. And if you know what's good for you, you'll go your way."

He didn't leave, but he also didn't continue forward. She turned away. Don't look back, just get across the driftwood. She walked to the end of the log she was on, feeling too tired to be moving yet, but she was wired. Not going to be the deer in the headlights. She hopped across to another solid-looking long log and stepped carefully, but quickly down its length, snagging a walking stick from a pile of smaller drift. The next step across she pushed onto the log she wanted to step onto before putting her weight on it. She found a good excuse to jump at an angle that would let her see if he had left. He hadn't. He was still there watching her, but hadn't moved closer.

When she got back to her shoes, she sunk down on the log and glanced back. He was moving now, back the way he'd come. Her breath escaped. She pulled the one dry sock and shoe on one chilly foot and the damp ones on the other. She worked her way carefully, willing herself to not look back at him until she had made it back into the brush. Then she looked. He had disappeared. For a moment she wondered if he'd dunked himself and was even now drowning under the logs. No. She wasn't that lucky and didn't really wish that on anyone, not even a peeping tom.

Maria hurried back up the trail, watching her footsteps carefully. Escaping death and injury had so far been a matter more of luck than attention. She resisted the urge to look back to see if he was following her.

By the time she got back to the house the chill of the water had her shaking. She came in the back door and hurried to the shower, dumped her clothes in the hamper and cranked up the heat. Under the water the tears came again. Should she tell anyone? And what would she say? That she'd been stupid? She could let it go. He would have tried to save her. But he'd been spying on her. She vowed not to go down to the lake alone and to not be stupid. Like that had ever helped.

Was he just interested in her? No. She had James. Steady, stable James. And that guy gave her the creeps. Trust your instincts, girl. When the tears had been washed away and she no longer felt cold, she shoved the knob on the shower in and scrubbed herself dry before wrapping the towel around her and slipping down the hall to the room she shared with James.

# CHAPTER FIFTEEN

THE DAYS PASSED IN A hazy blur for Maria. Her father seemed to be getting weaker by the day. Abi had regressed to her zombified state from before Thanksgiving. She would follow directions, but if left alone, she would sit staring at the wall or the sky or the fire. Another bout of contractions had Anna out of commission again. Maria had convinced her to remain on her side next to her sick husband.

It meant more work for the rest of them. Grandpa and Holly and James had helped set Brad up in the Moir place, but he did not spend much time there. Instead he busied himself with helping James and Grandpa get the corner of the roof patched and more wood cut. In the short gaps between rains they started dropping the small alders in the field, step one in returning it to Grandpa's vision of a plowable field.

One morning Brad stormed into the house; he pulled Maria toward the door. "Let's go," he mouthed with a soft wheezing sound.

"I don't understand."

He started to write on his pad. Panel

"Panel truck boys?"

He nodded and scribbled. Missing guns & ammo.

"Wouldn't it be better to take Grandpa or James?" Maria asked.

Brad frowned and shook his head. Not here. Scavenging more meds for Holly. Scare boys.

Maria shrugged. "Okay." At the door she grabbed Grandma's .22 again.

Brad took it from her hands. He picked up a sighted rifle with a clip, checked that the clip was full and handed it to her. He picked up his rifle and squeezed her shoulder gently then motioned to the door.

What the hell? I'm not going to kill anybody. Uncle Brad wouldn't put her in danger. Would he? She followed him to the truck. She opened the door, but he shook his head, his finger to his lips. He headed up the trail to the road.

About five minutes walk down the road, he pulled her over to the side, pointed up the embankment and set off, ferns swishing behind him.

The climb was steep, but he wound back and forth working his way slowly upward. When they reached the top, Brad handed a small pair of camouflage binoculars to Maria.

The two young men and their dogs were lounging around the campfire, drinking beer and smoking something. Pot, probably from the crappy roll job on their joint.

She scanned the camp. "Shit." A spotter scope pointed in the direction of the house. Through the trees she could see the log jam on the lake. "Bastards are watching us." She scanned the rest of the camp. Two rifles leaned against the truck. "Guns against the truck," she whispered.

Brad put his finger to his lips, then two fingers to his eyes.

Be quiet and watch. Maria clicked the safety off and lay down on the top of the hill where she could rest the rifle.

Brad held his rifle in his right hand and pulled a revolver out of a shoulder holster. He nodded at Maria and slipped quietly down through the trees.

Maria's hands were sweaty on the rifle. She'd never shot anything but cans before. Could she shoot another human being? Hell of a way to find out. She stared into the sight at Rafe, the taller one, then slid her view over to Dave at the fire. But it wasn't Dave. Damn. Where's Dave? She pulled the binocs to her eyes and scanned the surrounding area. Nothing. She wanted to alert Brad, but that would blow his cover and give the boys time to get to their guns. Breathe.

Brad was in their camp coming at them from behind that truck. He set something black inside the open door. Then the dogs were up and growling at the end of their leashes. He pulled his revolver and shot the dirt in front of the nearest dog, sending it yipping backward. He re-holstered the revolver, keeping his rifle pointed in between the men—not really threatening either of them. Brad pointed at the road. "Go," she heard him croak. He aimed his rifle first at one and then the other.

"Dave?" Rafe, the bigger, quiet one hollered.

Brad spun on the other guy. Through the binocs she saw him realize that the other guy was not who he thought it was. "Thought there was only two of you."

"Jerry was sick," Rafe said with a grin.

Jerry nodded his head. His hair and beard was really similar to Dave's..

Brad still had his rifle pointed at the boys. "Go." He said again. A bit louder. And a bit crazier.

"Son of a bitch." How close was Dave? Or was Rafe bluffing? They didn't know she was here. Play it cool. Maria was sweating. She couldn't shoot someone in cold blood.

"I don't think so." Dave shouted from behind a tree. His rifle pointed at Brad.

Maria's eye found the scope and she centered the cross hairs on Dave. Her fingers trembled. Shoot the guy with the gun. Dave was in her sight, but her finger wouldn't move. She shoved her hand in her pocket at pulled out the laser pointer. She pressed it against the rifle and pointed it at Dave.

"Look at your chest, Dave," she yelled. "Drop the gun or I'll shoot."

He wasn't putting it down. "Hello, Ms. Numovyerbizness." Dave yelled. "I've got your Uncle Brad covered with a rifle."

If he shot Uncle Brad, she knew she could kill him. But she

couldn't shoot first. If she shot and missed... Uncle Brad was dead for sure. "And he's got both your friends covered. And I've got you. Uncle Brad here lost all his family to the plague. Don't think he really cares if he dies or not. How about you, boys?"

"Dave?" Rafe hollered. "Let's get out of here. This guy is crazy."

Maria stared through the sight at Dave. She could see his jaw tense. He glanced down, then up at her. His rifle dropped. "All right. You let us go; we're gone. Whole planet for the taking. You're not fucking worth dying for."

Maria kept the laser pointed at Dave even as he raised his rifle over his head.

Brad stepped back behind a tree, but kept his gun pointed at them.

"Get in the van, Jerry," Dave growled. "Rafe, you're driving."

Maria dropped the laser, but kept Dave in the cross-hairs of the sight. He turned her stomach even from this distance. She had to trust that instinct. Bad news boys.

They piled in the van and it rolled away.

Her hands were shaking as she knelt to pick up the laser pointer. She let her legs carry her down the hill, but stuck to cover behind the trees.

When the van was almost around the corner, Brad stepped out from behind the tree, raised his rifle and fired. Once, twice. The two red taillights flashed out as plastic tinkled onto the road.

Well, they ought to think twice now.

Brad jogged up toward her. She hugged him.

"Thanks, Uncle Brad. You think they'll stay gone?"

He shrugged. "Don't know," his voice rasped out. He returned her hug. "Thanks."

The walk back to the house was silent except for their breathing. Maria bobbled from guilt to triumph and back. Had they just flouted the rule of law or supported it?

When they returned, Maria debriefed Grandpa and James on what had happened.

Grandpa face twisted into a grimace. "They'll stay away if they know what's good for them."

James' dark brows pulled together. He didn't look happy about what she and Uncle Brad had done. "Either that or they'll be pissed off enough to do something worse."

"James, I don't think they'll do that." Maria put her hand on his cheek. "They know we're equipped to take them out."

James' worried glare didn't waver. "They knew that before."

Brad nodded as he scribbled the notebook and it handed to James .

Maria leaned around Uncle Brad to read it.

I'll keep lookout. From my place I can see anyone coming.

"Okay," James agreed. "We take turns."

Brad wrote more and showing it to Grandpa and Maria. Others?    Less easy to scare off? Probably shouldn't just shoot them. He wheezed out a half-laugh.

"Nobody's out here to charge, try, or convict us." Grandpa did not smile. "Except ourselves. But we could put up signs. Plague free zone. Violators will be shot."

"You think that would work?" Maria asked.

"No," Brad hissed.

James stare stayed dark. "I could rig up some electronic warning devices, attach 'em to cell phones and solar power. If I could find some power."

Brad scratched on the pad.

Grandpa grinned. "That I can help with. The park put in some composting toilets with solar powered warmers. July Creek tourist stop and out on the park headquarters."

Brad handed the note around. Make the road impassable. Vehicles on the other side.

"Yes. We could do that." Grandpa nodded thoughtfully.

"Some dogs for us might be a good idea. I let the neighbor dogs loose, but they've been sniffing around, begging for food."

You have access to explosives? Dynamite?

Grandpa laughed loudly.

An angry scowl clenched Brad's face.

Grandpa put his hands up in mock defense. "No offense, Brad. The river washes out the road every few years where the North Shore Road meets the South Shore. I'm pretty sure those boys don't even know they can get here the back way. And over near 101, there's a culvert we could block easily, maybe tomorrow. Road'll be gone with the next heavy rain. No explosions to alert anyone. Nothing to make it look like anything more than Mother Nature having her way." He clapped James on the shoulder. "How about taking a break from cutting firewood to drop a stump into the creek?"

James' face stayed stony. "Sounds like fun."

\* \* \*

James, Grandpa and Brad had been gone from early morning until late at night the last three days. Maria sat in her father's room writing a letter to the unborn baby, trying to remember all the details she cared to share about how she and James had met. Her first computer-based graphic design classes. He was great with tech, or had been before he dropped out to take care of his mom. And he'd been patient with her frustration. Her hand felt crampy; she could have written it all on a keyboard, but that wasn't personal enough. She set aside the notebook and pen. Letting her eyes fall closed.

The door swung open and Anna stood, one hand gripping the door jamb and the other on the door knob. "Maria. Time."

If Anna's estimate of her due date was right, then she was only two weeks to term.

Holly came in to check on Anna, but Anna's response was immediate and vitriolic.

"I want her out. Now." For being exhausted, Anna managed to sit up quite well.

Holly took a deep breath, shrugged at Maria and left again.

Maria followed her as Anna lay back down.

As Holly reached the door, Anna spoke. "Maria. Stay. Please."

Maria turned to Holly, rolling her eyes, but sending her own request. She mouthed: Don't go so far. Then she turned back to Anna's pleading eyes. "I'll stay, Anna, but Holly can help you. All I've done is watch You-Tube videos on pregnancy."

"I need somebody in here I can trust," Anna blurted after the door closed.

"Anna. Really. Let it go. We got shit to do." Shit. Maria needed to watch her language around Anna. She left the room quickly afraid she'd say something worse and ruin all that they'd built.

Holly was outside, waiting.

"Thanks," Maria said. "I don't know what she's thinking, but I need you even if she doesn't."

"I'll be fine," Holly said. "Not as bad as some of the junkies I saw when I was in E.R."

Maria laughed. "Good." She slipped passed Holly to go to hers and James' bedroom.

Despite not thinking she could sleep, Maria napped while James sat outside the door to their rooms, promising to alert Maria if either Anna or her father called.

James came and got her when he started nodding off.

The contractions kept on steady for a day, low level, then steadied into regular contractions on the second day.

Maria didn't look forward to facing Anna again, but she also didn't want to wait too long before going in. Her father was down the hall behind one door, and Anna was behind this one. She pushed the door open and went through to check on Anna.

Anna's eyes were closed and her chest moved gently. Her face, even more pale than usual, was set off by the dark circles under her eyes. They'd been there for days, but had accentuated since her labor started. Maria knew from her research that labor usually got shorter for later babies. Why was Anna taking so long?

She checked that there was still water in the cup on the night stand. God, she wished she could go back. Back to before the end of the world, back to before she was pregnant. But what would she do different? She played it forward. Would she have made James use a condom? Would she be able to change anything about how the pandemic happened? No. Would she really rather be dead than being here? No. She let her breath out in a long sigh. Now, I sound like Anna. That heavy sigh was an indictment.

As if in response Anna stirred. "Sam?"

"Samuel's fine, Anna. It's me, Maria."

"Oh."

"Rest if you can." Tomorrow she'd probably be helping this woman deliver a baby. One way or another. Maria never wanted to be a nurse, but this brave new world didn't offer a lot of choices. Art design for video games was about as useful now as counting grains of sand.

She swept aside Anna's sweat-soaked hair from her face. "You can do this." Then she went back outside to find Holly. She found her sitting on the bridge over the creek, swinging her feet over the frigid waters.

"How long can this go on?"

"Days. But not usually. I'm hoping and praying her body figures out how to get his baby out. I certainly am not set up for Cesarean birth."

"Oh, God. No. Tell me no."

Holly shrugged. "I hope not, but it's always a possibility."

"You ever cut anybody?"

"Sliced my own finger open. Not surgically."

"What about painkillers and all that?"

"I've been collecting all the meds we could find as we checked out the houses."

"And do you have anything that can help?"

"I didn't have this in mind. I was thinking more of things that an old man and a slightly younger woman might need to get by."

Holly's brow creased. "Maybe BRad will bring something back this time. Not sure what though." She stood up, shook off the coat she'd been sitting on. Then she stared off over the lake, looking sad.

"Are you okay?" Maria asked.

"Okay as everybody else, I guess." Holly started walking back toward the house.

It reminded Maria of James' comment. "James says okay is the new excellent." Maria followed her.

Holly chuckled sourly as she stepped inside. "I suppose that's true. I was a nurse, but it made me want to allow people to die. Then I killed people in my stories. Now everybody is dead. I don't know what's next. Not a lot of call for either nurses or authors and I'm years overdue for a mid-life crisis. Who knows? Maybe midlife will be about your age for a while." Holly put her jacket on the hook and then took it back down.

"I hope not. I'd like to live a good long life with my family."

"Take care of yourself then." Holly pulled on her jacket. "I'm going to go check in with Tom."

"Thanks for talking," Maria said.

Holly nodded and left.

# CHAPTER SIXTEEN

MARIA STARED AT THE NOTEBOOK in her lap. Her message to her baby. But words wouldn't come. Brad had come back with some heftier painkillers and antibiotics. He promised her the panel truck boys were gone and that he hadn't shot them. All he told her was that he got his second phone back and some more guns. Still Maria couldn't shake the feeling that Brad might really have taken their lives without a gun.

Anna had been muttering prayers to herself every time the contractions rose and fell. "*Yea, though I walk through the valley of the shadow of death...*" Anna's air escaped with the words.

"Relax and breathe through it," Maria murmured. She took Anna's hand with a smile and placed it on her own slim wrist. "Squeeze if it hurts, Anna."

Anna's eyes clouded with pain. Her hand gripped Maria's wrist.

"I want to ask Holly for help."

"No," Anna gasped. "Not yet."

"Breathe, Anna. Breathe for the baby."

Anna closed her eyes and panted—whooshing short, sharp exhales. Her fingers dug into Maria's wrist.

A cry of pain joined the panting and on some level Maria realized the cry was hers. That article she'd read about helping the mother focus. She glanced around the room for an object. "Watch the clock," Maria said, trying to maintain a soft voice, but it still held an edge. "Look at the little hand spin."

Anna opened her eyes and focused like Maria told her to. As the pain contraction receded slowly, the pressure on her arm lessened. Anna's breath came slower. She released her grip on Maria's arm.

Maria rubbed the white imprint on her arm and the indentations from Anna's fingernails.

Anna gasped, staring at the marks she'd inflicted, "I'm so sorry, Maria."

"No worse than the pain I suffered from the boy cousins." The color returned. *This time it isn't me or Anna.*

"Noah?"

"He's been a little pill," Abi's said, "Abi's sitting with him. She's being real grown up, even if she's feeling sick."

"Can you go get them? Bring them in? While I'm between contractions, I'll put on my happy face."

Maria nodded and hustled off to get her siblings. "Abi? Noah? Mama wants to see you." She ushered them in, glancing at the clock. It had been two minutes since the last contraction. She needed to get them out before the next one. Maria could hardly handle Anna's pain. How could she expect the kids to? Noah shoved the door open and toddled over to his mother.

"Hey, big boy. What's wrong?" Anna patted his head.

"Wanna go outside." His pout was perfect.

Abi walked in slowly.

"Noah, pretty soon you can go out." Anna glanced up at Maria. "Maybe Maria can take you outside tomorrow."

"Yeah, Noah. We can go down by the lake."

"See deer poo-poo?"

Anna laughed out loud and Maria joined her.

Abi stood there. Not laughing. Maria knelt down and felt Abi's forehead. It felt normal, at least the fever had passed. "Give your mama a hug." Maria nudged her toward the bed and she bumped Noah aside. He moved to shove Abi back, but Maria swept him off his feet. Abi accepted the hug, laying her head on her mother.

"Okay, Kids out." Maria set Noah back on his feet and shooed him out. "You've got to let your mama bring you a new sister or brother.”

As Abi followed Noah out, Holly came in. She stood still, waiting by the door. She was neutral faced. Good thing she really was a nurse. She'd probably taken plenty of abuse. Then Anna saw her.

“I want THAT WOMAN out. I don't care if she is a nurse.”

“Anna,” Maria said, trying to keep her voice as soothing as she knew how. “We need--”

“I want her out!” Anna's voice shrilled.

Holly stepped back outside the room.

“Anna, shut up. You need her here. I need her here. I am not a doctor, nurse or much of anything. Holly was a nurse. I'll be damned before I let your pride get in the way of bringing my little sibling into the world. Nothing matters but the baby. Got it?”

Anna's mouth was a grim line. “Yes.”

Maria was surprised to see a sense of relief in her eyes. How often did Anna's sense of pride get in the way of doing something she knew she should? Maybe she and Anna were not so different. For once that thought didn't sting, Maria knelt and kissed Anna's sweaty forehead.

“What was that for?”

“Too many things to mention. I'm sorry, Anna.”

Pain flashed in Anna's eyes. Another contraction. A whimper escaped from her grimacing face. Then her eyeballs rolled up. Maria could only see white. Her face went slack and she slumped back, even as her body shook.

“Holly?!” Maria yelled. “I need you now.”

The door swung open. Holly came through the door, gloves on her hands.

Grandpa stood outside. “What can I do?”

“Make sure Dad's okay,” Maria said.

“I want ice,” Anna begged.

“Get ice,” Maria said. “Please check on Dad, first. Then stay close."

Grandpa gave her a salute.

Anna closed her eyes and leaned her head back.

Maria looked at Holly, hoping for some support. Holly shrugged. *Oh, god, she's powerless. I'm going to be here in a few months. How the hell I am I going to handle it?*

A soft knock, and the door opened. Grandpa stood, not quite coming in. "Here's the ice."

"Thanks, Grandpa," Maria said softly.

But he looked past her. "I love you, Anna." His voice was tight as he shut the door.

Anna's eyes snapped open and she stared at the door, bewildered. "Did he say...?"

"Yeah," Maria assured, resting her hand on Anna's shoulder, "he did."

"He's never said that."

"Well," Maria said, "when almost everyone you know is dead and you never told them how you felt..." She'd never gotten to say goodbye to her mother or to Grandma.

Holly nodded like she knew exactly what Maria meant.

Anna grabbed Maria's wrist, twisting, pulling her arm hair.

"Another one," Anna gasped.

"Breathe through it!" Maria barked. She wondered at who this person was that would bark at Anna and be obeyed.

Anna's breath came out in short bursts, "Ha, ha, ha."

When the contraction had crested and fallen, Maria wiped Anna's brow and offered her some of the ice.

Anna chewed the ice for a minute, letting her breath catch up with her. "This is nothing like the other kids. By this time I was done."

"I believe you." Maria kept her voice calm and soothing. "Like you told me, every birth is different. But you've got to do this, Anna."

"I want to push."

Maria looked to Holly for guidance. All she got was another indifferent shrug. "Okay. Let's try it."

Anna's face had some color and determination. "I want you to catch the baby, Ria."

"Okay. We'll see." Anna hadn't tried calling her Ria in years. "Right now, try to relax. Let your body do its job."

"I'm pushing. NOW."

Another contraction rose and fell. Maria scribbled the count on her notebook.

"How far am I dilated?"

"How the hell should I know?" Holly growled.

"Can you see the baby's head?"

"Shit!"

"What?" Maria and Anna asked in unison. Maria could tell it was bad. Holly's eyes were wide and her face as a white as a dinner plate.

"Breach," Holly whispered.

"Oh, shit!" Anna sighed.

"God dammit, I wish I had some drugs." Holly whipped off her gloves and threw them at the wall. "And a real doctor as long as we're wishing for the impossible."

Maria's hands rubbed Anna's shoulders. "What do we do, Holly?"

"The danger is the umbilical. Well, that and damage to the mother."

"I'm here."

"I know, Anna. Sorry, I have a shitty bedside manner. I'm a fucking novelist." She sat down in the chair next to Anna. "I'm going to turn the baby?"

"I want to push right now."

"Not until I tell you to," Holly ordered through gritted teeth.

Anna eyes rolled up again. She screamed, then grunted. She

squeezed Maria's arms.

Maria couldn't feel the fingers on her left hand. "Breathe, Anna. You can do this."

"Okay. Push," Holly said. "Now." Moments later Holly spoke again. "Okay, I can see both legs."

"Anna, the baby's a girl."

"Oh, God," Anna prayed. "Give me your grace tonight."

"Amen," Maria heard her own voice say. "Come on, grace."

"Come on, Grace." Anna's groans turned into howls. "Damn, it hurts."

In between contractions she sobbed quietly, accepting the ice Maria put in her mouth, but not communicating anything more.

Holly pulled Maria aside. "Okay, next time, when she pushes I need to work the baby around. The most dangerous point is if the cord is wrapped around the baby. I'm going to try to clear it. Keep Anna calm. It's going to hurt."

A gargled cry came from Anna and she spit out the ice and started hissing breaths. Maria went to her and wrapped her arms where Anna had something to pull on.

"Good job, Mama. You're gonna have a baby," Maria muttered whatever came into her head. Encouragement.

"All right," Holly urged. "Keep it up. She's mostly out."

Maria heard Anna's breathing slowing. "No. Don't stop. We can't stop pushing. Come on, Anna. You can do it. Bring baby Grace to us. Let her come out."

"MARIA," Holly's voice demanded help. "I need you now."

Anna wouldn't let go of Maria's arms. "NO, don't leave me."

"NOW," Holly yelled. "Or your sister's going to die."

Maria shoved Anna's arms away as her grip weakened. Holly guided Maria's hand down. "Put your hand here, now."

"NOW, Anna," Holly ordered. "Push. Push as much as you hate me. As soon as you're done here, I'll get the hell out of your space."

But Anna slumped back.

"God damn it, Anna," Maria's swearing had no effect. "Are you gonna let this baby die?"

"No," Anna whimpered.

"What?" Maria demanded. "Anna. Please. For Samuel. For Noah and Abi. For me. Dammit, Anna. Holy mother of God." Maria didn't know what else to do. Actually, she did. But she didn't want to.

Anna stared at her, a dazed glaze on her face.

Maria kept the pressure where Holly had said. "Do it for Jesse." Her voice broke. "And Rachel."

"How dare you?"

"Do it, now, Anna!" Maria screamed. "Don't lose another baby!" Tears ran down her face. "I want my sister."

Anna's face was pulled back against her teeth. All the times that Anna had looked like she would kill her were nothing like this.

"God!" Anna growled.

"Now," Maria said, "do it!"

"Good job, Anna," Holly soothed.

"You're doing it, Anna." The baby came. Maria's littlest sister was white and blue, no hint of any pink color. Her head was misshapen. Oh, God. Anna can't take losing another baby. Oh, God. If it's my fault.

Holly's fingers scooped into the baby's mouth. She turned the baby over and slapped her back, then she brought her ear down close.

Anna sobbed hysterically.

Maria stared.

"Come on, baby, breathe," Holly whispered. She placed her fingers on the baby's breastbone. "Help me, Maria. I'm going to start CPR."

"Come on, Grace." She reached for her sister. The baby's

stomach contracted and then she sneezed a slimy bubble. And her eyes came open, dark and searching. Her breath spread her chest, and a tiny whimper escaped.

"Baby Grace?" Anna begged.

"She's here. She's breathing." Maria whispered. "Thank God."

Holly had her stethoscope out, probing gently. "Need to keep her warm," she said, her fingers feeling for a pulse.

Maria grabbed the baby blanket from the top of the heating register. She wrapped it around baby, who stared up into her face.

Holly straightened. "Okay. Solid heartbeat. Don't know what else to do but give her to her mama."

Maria pulled her sister from Holly's hands and handed her to Anna.

"Oh, my Grace of God," Anna said as her shaky hands gently explored her dampened hair.

"You're so beautiful," Maria said. Her sister turned her head.

"That's your brave, big sister, little one," Anna said with a tearful smile to Maria. "She named you."

"No, you did. 'Give me your Grace.' I'm going to go tell Dad." Maria slipped into her father's room. Brad snored in the rocking chair. She knelt beside the bed and wrapped her arms around her father's chest. His ragged breath drew in and out. His arm reached for her and she moved so he could hold her hand.

"You're a father to a daughter again, Daddy."

His face broke into a weak smile.

"Her name's Grace, Anna says."

"Good." He said, his head collapsing back onto the pillow. "Love you, Ria."

"I love you, too, Daddy. We'll be back with your new baby real soon."

When Anna felt she could move, they bundled up baby Grace and Maria carried her into her father's room. Grandpa and

Holly helped Anna get into his bed. She snuggled up next to him and Maria set the baby on Anna's chest.

"She's lovely, Anna." Her father looked as exhausted as the rest of them and his voice was barely louder than Brad's.

"She is," Anna smiled, still glowing with the joy of having her baby in her arms. "Thank you all. I'm sorry for being such a bothersome patient, Holly, Maria."

Holly shrugged. "I'm used to rejection." She smiled. "Grace is a lovely baby. Congratulations." She turned and left the room with a smile for Maria and a gentle touch on her shoulder.

Grandpa knelt to kiss the baby and Anna. "You done good, Anna. I love you, Granddaughter. Never doubt that."

Anna nodded, tears running down her face.

"We'll leave you three to get acquainted." He kissed Maria on the forehead on his way out.

Anna smiled at Maria. Maria had never seen a smile so real from Anna directed at her. "I couldn't have done it without you. You didn't deserve to have to nurse me through it."

Maria smiled. "Well, give me a few months and you'll probably get some of it back."

"I'll be here for you, Ria. Thanks." Anna's eyes drooped.

"Get some sleep." Maria swept some hair from Anna's forehead. "Grace is lovely. Congratulations. Holler if you need anything." She kissed her father and gave him her best smile, then turned and left the room. Leaning against the wall outside, she finally allowed herself to feel the aches and pains of her own pregnant body. Tears ran down her face. She'd had no idea what hard work was until the world ended.

# CHAPTER SEVENTEEN

SAMUEL COUGHED, HIS HEAD SPUN. His stomach contracted. It felt like he was tearing in two. A cough again racked his body, and this time the fluid spewed forth from his throat—dark, blackened phlegm.

"Sam," Anna begged. "Are you okay?"

The pain twisted him forward, wrenching her from his view.

"Oh, God," Anna said

Samuel stared at the soiled sheets. "Anna, I—" Coughing shut off his words.

"Somebody get Holly," she screamed. Tears streamed down her face. "NOW!"

For a moment the coughing paused. He stared at his hands. Along with the dark phlegm, there were bright red drops as well. His head swam and his head fell toward his pillow. It took far too long. Then Anna's pretty face was over his.

She kissed his forehead. "try to relax. We'll get Holly here."

Samuel shook his head gently, surprised it didn't hurt. Coughing blood was a bad sign. That much he knew. He rolled to his back.

The door flew open. "Dad?" Maria rushed in with Abigail on her hip clinging over her slight belly.

Samuel tried to sit himself up, but Anna held him back.

"Don't move, Sam."

"Holly's on her way," Maria said. Her face told him she knew what the blood meant. Noah peeked out from behind her leg.

Samuel's heart twisted. *I won't get to see Maria's baby.* He held out his hands to his kids. Abi cocked her head to the side. Noah rushed to him and tried to clamber up. Maria boosted him into his arms with her knee as she and Abi joined the hug.

The physical pain had receded. He didn't think that was a good sign.

"Okay, kids," Anna said softly. "Give your father some room to breathe."

Sam saw Maria, her face tightened, trying to keep it together. For his sake? Or her own?

Another face appeared at the door. Brad.

"Sam. Old friend." Brad's voice scratched, "Stay." He'd hardly said two words out loud since he'd arrived.

Darkness teased at the edge of Samuel's vision. "My family."

"Will be fine."

Holly bustled in, pulling a stethoscope up to her ears. "Maria, can you get the kids out?"

Maria lifted Noah off him and set him on the ground. She guided them out, glancing back at him one more time as she went out the door.

Holly shoved aside his shirt and placed the cold metal to his chest. She listened carefully. "Breathe. Just breathe."

Holly shook her head, her jaw tight. "I don't know what I can do. Your lungs sound clogged. The coughing... I think the cough must have caused things to move. A broken bone might have caused injuries to internal organs."

"What can you do?" Anna begged.

Holly sighed. "I can make you comfortable, Samuel." She turned to Anna. "I don't know what else."

Samuel could see the exhaustion in both their eyes. He shook his head. "I don't hurt. Not right now."

"Okay, try to rest." Holly filled a medicine cup with a dark red liquid. "Drink some of this. It might stop the cough."

Samuel swallowed, gagging on the thick syrup. "Thanks," he gasped.

Beside him Grace began to fuss. He turned his head to look at his little bundle through the tears the cough had brought up.

New tears flowed as Anna nursed Grace, soothing her cries.

"I'll check back in a couple hours," Holly said.

"Thank you, Holly," Anna said.

Samuel smiled and nodded his agreement.

"You're welcome." The line of Holly's mouth softened into a smile. She exited.

"I love you, Samuel," Anna's hand caressed the curve of his face, the stubble of his beard.

"I love you," he said. It came out as a soft whisper. He rested his head on her shoulder, watching Grace nurse.

*   *   *

Maria woke in the middle of the night, James' arms wrapped warmly around her. She glanced at the clock. Three a.m. What time had she come to bed? When was Grace born? She realized she didn't know. Gently she moved James' arm aside. "Gonna check on Anna and Grace."

James mumbled something that sounded like an affirmative.

Maria knocked gently on the door. She waited for an answer. No sounds. She turned the knob carefully and pushed inward. The rocking chair was empty. Anna, Grace and her father were like she had left them. Maria moved closer. Anna's eyes were open. Staring at her. She'd been crying. Now she looked empty. Anna's hand caressed Maria's father's face. His eyes were closed. He was gone. There was no rise and fall to his chest.

Maria stood staring as tears fell. After a bit Anna motioned for her to come over. Maria sniffled back some tears and wiped her face with her pajama nightgown sleeve.

"He met Grace," Anna held her hands out to Maria.

Maria went to her, accepting her arms as she reached across to kiss her father's cold forehead and felt her baby sister's warmth against him.

"He loved you very much, Maria," Anna held her.

Maria felt her step-mom crying quietly as she sobbed.

\* \* \*

Grandpa closed the family bible. He nodded at Maria and Anna. Maria looked to Anna through her tears. Anna wiped her own and nodded. Together they shoved their spades into the fresh pile of dark dirt and tossed the soil onto the handmade coffin James, Brad and Grandpa had lovingly fashioned.

Grandpa held the bible across his chest, his arms hugging it close. There were tears on his cheeks as well. "By the sweat of your brow you will eat your food until you return to the ground, since from it you were taken; for dust you are and to dust you will return."

"Amen," Brad said from behind her. His gruff voice rasped softly, "Go with God, my friend."

Maria turned and handed her spade to James. Anna brought hers to Brad; he took it and pulled her into a quick hug.

Abigail tugged at Maria's maternity blouse, so she picked her up and carried her to the pile.

Anna helped Noah scoop some soil with a small garden trowel and drop it into the grave.

Maria did the same with Abi and then they stepped out of the way for James and Brad to do most of the heavy lifting. Abi no longer seemed ill, just resigned. The moments of bright flashes that had been a constant occurrence with Abi before she got sick had become rare. Maria hoped she'd grow out of it, but it least she was alive.

After a bit, Grandpa and Holly spelled them. Brad trotted off toward the garage. Maria wondered at her father's old best friend. They hadn't been close in years. He wasn't showing a lot of response to her father's death, but for that matter, neither was she.

James came over and wrapped her in his arms, pulling her close. He was hot and sweaty even in the winter cold, but she appreciated the closeness and warmth of his chest.

Brad returned with a rake. He handed it off to Holly in

exchange for the spade, digging into what remained of the pile of dirt. It would be all filled in soon. The cross was simple and rustic. Recycled wood from the old barn. Her father would have liked that.

"Ria?" James' soft voice rumbled near her ear. "Can we walk down by the crick?"

"The crick?" she teased.

The hint of a gentle smile played across his lips.

"Sure. I'll go let Anna know." She let go of James' warmth, but he held onto her hand and walked with her.

Anna held Grace in her arms while the two bigger ones, sat solemnly on either side of her. Odd to see them all so still. They probably had no idea what was wrong, but that something definitely was.

Anna looked up from Grace with a sad half smile on her face. She looked passed Anna to James and the smile grew slightly. Maria glanced over at James who had a similar smile. "We're going to head down to the creek, okay? Unless there's something we can do for you?"

"No. We'll be fine. Thank you both for all you've done."

"You're welcome." Maria's heart longed to reach out to her, but she didn't know how. "We'll be back soon."

"Take your time."

Maria would need to find away to reach out. "Come on, Ria."

She let James guide her as her thoughts collided. On top of the birthing exhaustion, Anna had lost her husband. Maria had lost a father, but it hadn't really hit her yet. And she'd already lost her mom. At least Anna had Grace and the kids. And me, Maria thought, without the usual surge of tension that thinking about Anna caused.

"Come back to me?"

"Sorry."

"No need to be sorry. We're all sorry enough, don't you

think?"

Maria nodded. That was certainly true. She followed him out onto the split log bridge. When she was a child, it had a guardrail, but now the only safety was keeping your own balance. She held onto James hand as he led her confidently across. "Where are you taking me?"

"A ways past the creek. There's a cool tree over here. Your grandfather calls it the old oak. Says there used to be a fire pit where they had family picnics."

A memory of a picnic with a bonfire took her back once again. She remembered s'mores and her father cooking two at a time, one almost perfect and one blackened. She'd gotten the golden brown one while he took the one that had caught fire.

"I want you to close your eyes for a minute."

"Not on the bridge."

"Now, we're across the bridge." He turned around in front of her and opened his arms.

She moved back into the warmth of his arms. "Okay," She let her eyes close and let herself feel her breath.

"Picture the fire pit as you remember it. Now picture us, our baby playing with Grace. All of us sitting around, watching the sparks flow up into the dark sky. Can you see it?"

"Hhhmmmm...." She could. Grandpa and Holly, Anna and the older kids, Brad and James.

"I'm there with my wife."

"Yes,"

"Maria, marry me."

She pushed him away, opening her eyes as she teetered back toward the non-existent hand rail of the bridge. The water burbled by underneath the mossy log. She collapsed into a cross legged sit, not caring about the moisture soaking through the seat of her pants. "No, I told you no."

James knelt down in the moss and duff off under the trees.

"Please."

Maria turned away, hoping that if she didn't look at him, she wouldn't cry again. No luck. Tears were welling up in her eyes. "Why? You're going to die. Or I am. Or we're just going to hate each other like most of the married couples I know. Then we'll have to get a divorce and there are no courts out here and then what do we do?"

"Ria. Honey."

"No. If we become a real family... Shit happens. My father. Your father. My mother..."

"Yeah." James reached for her hands; she let him take them, holding them in his big, warm hands. "That could happen. But it can happen even if we don't get married. I'll screw things up. So will you. But I want to be your husband. I want you to be my wife. Then when shit happens, we can forgive each other. Say we're sorry. Talk it out. Just like we're talking now. We don't have to shut each other out like so many couples do."

"But what if we do?"

"I will still love you." He pulled her hands to his lips and kissed them. "No matter what. I won't play favorites with our kids."

"Our kids," Maria sputtered, snot and tears and laughter all at once. "You going to have the rest of them?"

"I would if I could," James said.

His voice was so earnest, she believed he would. "I don't know if I want to have any more."

"Well, then playing favorites won't be a problem."

"It's not that freaking simple."

"What if it is? What if I say I love you, you say you love me, and we get married? Then we figure out how to make it work? Trust me, please. Marry me."

Maria swiped her sweatshirt sleeve across her dripping nose. "Okay.

"Yes."

"Yes, you'll marry me?"

"Yes, James, I'll marry you. I want to. I think I figured it out when Grandpa pointed the gun at you. Just took me a while to accept it."

\*    \*    \*

So instead of Christmas, they had a wedding. Maria stood with James' arms wrapped his hands to smile at them benevolently. Behind him the fire blazed. Anna stood nursing Grace next to Maria. Brad stood next to James. For once Noah stayed still, holding Abi's hand. Holly's grip on his shoulder might have added to his stillness. She smiled at Maria and nodded. Together they made a circle.

Abi stood solemn, her basket mostly empty of the fake leaves cut from Grandma's collection of Sunday comics. She had lit up momentarily when she had strewn them in the procession.

The ceremony had been simple. Stripped down for Maria, with enough of the churchy stuff to keep James happy. Made Anna happier, too. The only missing piece was the father walking her down the aisle. Maria let the tears fall; brides were supposed to cry. Her heart was full. Her father would always be with her. James had agreed to name the baby Sam whether boy or girl.

"By the traditions of humankind, I now pronounce you husband and wife. You may kiss each other." His smile broke into a grin.

Maria raised her face to James and he bent slightly to kiss her, pulling her up onto her tip-toes. Their lips met. Inside her belly, their baby kicked him.

*The story for these characters will be continued with a 15-year gap in the lives of the characters. At that point it will connect with folks from ALL IS SILENCE. I'm aiming to write that novel in 2018. Who do you think will appear from Lizzie's story? If you haven't read Lizzie's story, head to www.DesertedLands.com*

# Editorial Reviews

"Hardly the familiar post-apocalyptic novel of zombie attacks and desperate efforts to rebuild civilization--a personal story of a scared girl and the survivors she finds in the ruins of her world. Lizzie is hard-edged and gritty, vulnerable and kind. Her personality is so compelling that she grabs you by the heart and pulls you along until it's three in the morning and the story's over and you just want to read more." ~ **Don Sakers - *Analog Science Fiction***

"A post-apocalyptic world that is inwardly and outwardly consistent by paying attention to the details. Lizzie, the anti-hero is the tough chick with a heart of gold. She survives the pandemic apocalypse that wipes out 95 percent of the world's population [and] captures the reader by being so human that you can't help being sucked into her world.... like Rowling and Suzanne Collins, writes about young people, but engages a wider audience [in] what it is like to be young in this difficult world." ~ **Christopher Key, *Entertainment News NorthWest***

"A fast paced, adrenaline soaked novel. . . . Lizzie, or Crazy Lizzie to her friends, makes for a rather dark character. A former cutter who has occasional suicidal tendencies, she nonetheless manages to be very compelling. In fact, all the characters manage to be interesting. . . . Slater ramps up the action and suspense until you're flipping the pages almost too fast to read the words. . . . waiting (impatiently) for the sequel." ~ **Kayti Nika Raet, *Readers' Favorite.***

on top of journals, most scribbled with song lyrics or tattooed with intricate pencil and pen art of abstract shapes, calligraphic characters and rudimentary nudes. Some of the art had made it to the walls. She'd intended to plaster over the ugly blue and green paisley wallpaper, but had only gotten partway done.

Lizzie tucked the cigarette between her lips and pulled out a small burgundy velvet journal, Jayce's birthday gift for her. She held a pen over a blank page, not knowing what to write—how to honor her brother. Her mind flitted from memory to memory.

With pen in hand and only tears on the empty pages, Lizzie gave up. The cigarette she had forgotten to smoke had burned down. She ground the butt out onto one of Jerkwad's CDs she had adopted as an ashtray, wondering if her own cigarettes were more like second-hand smoke.

She could hear Jayce's voice offering to help her organize her room. She'd thrown Dante's *Inferno* at him. If she couldn't write for him, Lizzie could at least clean up a little. She shoved the journal and pen in her pocket and started in on the mess on the floor, piling clothes and stacking similar things. Everything called up thoughts of the past. She picked up a multi-colored shoe done in permanent marker and threw it at the closet. Enough cleaning.

Lizzie ran downstairs. Her hand caught the asylum sign, tearing it off the wall. She wadded it up, wishing she could go back to the past as easily as it came back to her.


*If you'd like to read more please go to*
***www.desertedlands.com*** *for links to purchase a copy of **All Is Silence** in Hardcover, Paperback or Ebook. You can also get information on recent publications, appearances, special prices, newsletter signups, T-shirts and more.*

the container, dropped one in her hand and put the container back on the shelf.

The pale face staring at her in the mirror reminded her of Mama. She'd never seen it before, but in the black circles and the sad, red eyes, she looked like Mama. Except for the piercings and the hair. Lizzie's buzz-cut had grown out to a boyish length. The frizzy pale pink at the tips faded to bleach blonde and dark at the roots. *I need more sleep.* The alarm woke her way too early.

Maybe she would sleep better in her own bed. She trudged past the sign that said "This way to the asylum" on her way upstairs. The house was bigger than most of the mobile homes and trailers she spent her childhood in, but still small for a family of four. A previous owner had converted the attic into a bedroom with enough space to stand upright if you were short. That's why it was Lizzie's room.

An eerily quiet noon day sun streaming in her window Lizzie woke from her dreamless sleep. No noise—alarms, angry voices, or TV—blared through the thin walls.

She grabbed the cell, checking the screen. The phone was working but Mama hadn't called. Jayce was gone. Dead. Her chest felt hollow, her eyes beaded with tears. "Jayce."

Lizzie wanted to call Mama, but it probably wouldn't do any good. *Trust the nurse, Lizzie.* Mama said she'd call. "But what if she forgets? Shit."

Her head no longer pounded. She felt more herself and even more alone. No people. Not even her cat, Gordito. He'd disappeared last summer—probably had gone away to die.

Out of habit her hand found her cigarettes—one left. She searched for a jacket to go outside and smoke. Mama and Jerkwad had tried to get her to quit, but had done a pretty half-assed job. They both smoked, but they insisted she do it outside by Jerkwad's illegal burn-barrel and use her own allowance. Screw it. She lit up and smoked on her bed.

The cigarette helped, but her restless nerves needed activity. Lizzie could clean up, but the amount of cleaning overwhelmed her. There were piles of laundry, candy wrappers, old CDs and cases strewn all over the floor. Sheets of paper lay in stacks and couch. Her phone flashed. MISSED CALL. "Damn." She thumbed the 'return call' and held it up to her ear. "Mama?"

"Lizzie?" Mama's voice was feather-light and tired.

"Yeah, Mama. Sorry, I missed your call. I was sleeping." Lizzie's explanation felt lame.

"Liz." Her voice broke off.

Lizzie could hear her crying. Her gut twisted and her throat tightened; she felt like she was going to throw up. "Jayce?"

Mama sobbed harder in response.

"No, Mama. I'm coming over there."

"NO!" Her mother's voice was steel. The sobs stopped. "You will not. You are not sick. I am. Doug is gone. Now Jason's gone. Dammit, I'm dying! Please. Lizzie, promise me you'll stay inside." Another sob escaped. "Promise."

"Okay, Mama." Tears fell. Lizzie heard a voice in the background.

"The nurse is here to give me meds, Lizzie. I'll call you, okay?"

"Yeah, Mama. Okay." The phone clicked.

Why hadn't she said *I love you*? Was it too much like goodbye? Or was she just withholding her love like her mother had done? Lizzie grabbed a plate, the closest thing to her, and hurled it against the wall. It left a dent, fell to the floor and shattered. She screamed. It gave her no release.

She headed to Mama's room, keeping her phone close. She collapsed onto the bed and pulled Mama's pillow into her arms. It smelled like her: spicy sweet perfume and a hint of her cigarettes. It had been a week, but Mama's scent had not faded.

Lizzie thought of little Jayce, his short blonde hair she'd dyed red for his first day of school, all the ketchup he put on everything, his annoying habit of having the right answer for everything and never getting into trouble for anything. Jerkwad loved to point out that Jayce was only her half-brother. But losing Jayce wasn't half the hurt; blood was blood. Sobs wracked her body. She lay there for a long time until the sobs faded.

Her head throbbed again. She slid from the warmth of the covers and stepped into slippers. She walked into the bathroom and opened the medicine cabinet, going straight for Mama's pills. She ignored the bottles with her own name, prescriptions meant to help her "get along better" in the "normal" world. Not much point in that anymore.

Mama's codeine would kick her headache quick. She opened

She crossed to the liquor cabinet and pulled out Jerkwad's favorite whiskey, the glass Canadian Club Reserve bottle he kept refilling from plastic ones. Lizzie pulled out the sticky cork, "Here's to you, Jerkwad." She tipped it back, her lips on the bottle. The whiskey burned going down, but there wasn't a lot in the bottle, so she took another swig.

If cell phones worked again, were things getting better? Lizzie spun through her contact list and stabbed a name at random. Jennifer. It rang and went to voicemail. "You know who I am. You know who you are. You know what to do."

"Jen. It's Lizzie. Call me."

Another stab; another message. The sound of voices, even if the people were gone, was like music.

Jayce's screaming-bird alarm clock woke her the next morning. Lizzie's head throbbed, her mouth so dry her tongue felt like sandpaper.

She rolled off the living room couch with thoughts of murdering her brother and his wake-the-dead clock. "Jason Ronald. Turn that thing—" Reality slammed back into place. Her brother was in the hospital with Mama. "Shit." She stumbled to her feet, clothes twisted from sleeping in them. Lizzie stalked the alarm clock to its nightstand, wrenched the cord out of the wall and dropped it on the floor.

Lizzie wobbled back to the couch. The whiskey bottle on the floor made her heart jump. Jerkwad's best. But he was dead. He would not be slapping her, or anyone else, for it.

Mama had rotten taste in men. She'd kicked Lizzie's father out when Lizzie was three, blaming drugs and the army. The only thing left was the CD and movie collection Mama kept. When she was old enough Lizzie claimed them and Mama hadn't objected.

Lizzie raised the whiskey bottle to swig the dregs, gagging as it hit her dry tongue. Her stomach threatened to empty its contents. She went to the bathroom, turned on the cold water, and splashed her face. Her head pounded and she knew from experience it would only get worse. She grabbed some ibuprofen from the medicine cabinet and swallowed a few.

She returned to the living room and flopped back on the

Lizzie stopped breathing.

Mama sniffed. "Doug's dead."

Lizzie sighed, her shoulders relaxed. Not Jayce. Just Jerkwad, Mama's boyfriend. "I'm sorry, Mama." She hoped it sounded sincere for her mother's sake.

"Are you okay? How's Jayce?"

"Jason's a trooper."

Mama hated Lizzie's nicknames for her little brother.

"I'm in his room," Mama's voice softened. "They didn't have enough empty beds. You have food? You're staying inside?"

"Yes, Mama." Lizzie gritted her teeth; she wasn't going to cry. "How are you?"

A cough exploded into the ear piece. "Other than too many years of smoking? Lizzie, burn the bedding. In Doug's barrel in the yard. Then come back in. Promise?"

"Okay. I will. I promise. Is *Jason* awake?" Jayce was eleven. Was he as freaked out as Lizzie?

"No. He's asleep, snoring. Can you hear?"

"Yeah." Lizzie laughed. Jayce could sleep through anything. She took a deep breath. "Mama. I'm sorry for all the things I said. All the times I was a bitch."

"Lizzie-girl. It's okay. I was your age once."

Lizzie didn't remember having a conversation where Mama forgave her for anything. "Mama?"

"Get some rest. We'll call you tomorrow. Sweet dreams, Lizzie."

"Mama, don't go. I—" She heard the phone click. "I love you, Mama," she whispered.

*Jayce is doing good and Jerkwad is dead.* Jerkwad always said she'd be out of the house at 18. *Well, I'm here, you're gone, and I'm not 18 for two months.* Was Lizzie a bad person for being happy?

Mama sounded horrible. What if they didn't come home? The cat lady next door never did.

She fidgeted with her cell. It still had the picture of Lizzie and her ex-boyfriend Chad at the water slides. They had stayed friends when she broke up with him at the beginning of the summer. And in September after school started, he was the first person she knew to die. Then the names of the dead started to flow from the school loudspeaker and down her Facebook feed, one by one, until classes were cancelled and the world finished falling to pieces.

## Chapter One

**"I HOPE YOU** ALL DIE!"

Those weren't the last words Lizzie had told her family, but they might as well have been. She couldn't remember what she said when Mama took Jayce and Jerkwad to the hospital, but it didn't matter anyway. They were gone, and all she could remember were the screaming fights and hateful words.

Lizzie stared out through the gap in the dust-encrusted living room blinds. The streets were empty. At first patrol cars had come by several times a day blaring, "STAY INDOORS. NO PHYSICAL CONTACT."

Now all was silent. Lizzie couldn't remember when she had last seen a patrol car.

The clock showed mid-afternoon, but the gray excuse for a day in the Pacific Northwest was fading. Lizzie hauled herself out of the threadbare recliner and trudged to Mama's bedroom. She snuggled under the covers wondering what she should eat for dinner. Mama had filled the freezer with pizzas before she left, but the same menu for a week was getting old.

Holes in the sheetrock beside the nightstand and the wires hanging out reminded her of the dead land-line. The day they went to St. Joseph's Hospital, Mama called to say Jason, Jayce to Lizzie, was in room 314. The next day the phone didn't work. At some point, fixing it  became tearing it out of the wall in frustration.

Cell systems had been overloaded since state officials declared the pandemic four weeks before. With the phones down and spotty Internet, Lizzie was alone and disconnected from what was happening. She wanted to go outside. Screw the quarantine.

AC/DC's "Highway to Hell" jerked Lizzie back to her surroundings. Her cell phone? When had it started working? She threw off the covers and followed the sound to the couch in the living room.  A picture of Mama  that Lizzie loved and Mama hated glowed on the screen.

"Mama?" Lizzie sat on the couch cradling the phone to her ear.

"Honey… I've been trying to call on both lines." Mama's voice teetered on the brink of hysteria.

*One generation passes away,*
*and another generation comes;*
*But the earth abides forever.*
**Ecclesiastes 1:4**

# PART I

# The End of the World as We Know It

# ALL IS
# SILENCE

## A DESERTED LANDS NOVEL

# ROBERT L. SLATER

## About the Author

Growing up in the Pacific Northwest in the small town of Hoquiam, Washington, Robert L. Slater wanted to be an astronaut or a rock star. At 42, he gave up those dreams to become a writer of science fiction and fantasy, where he can pretend to be both.

Like some of his characters, he has a propensity for speaking in lines from 80s movies, drinking Mountain Dew and eating pizza. He loves music as a listener, a zealous fan, a guitar player, and a singer/songwriter.

After more than 20 years as a schoolteacher, he is beginning to have a hint of insight into young-adulthood. He has been in that hood a long time!

In addition to his websites:
www.desertedlands.com and www.robslater.com,
Robert can also be found on various social media:
Twitter - @robertlslater
Wattpad - @robertlslater
Facebook - Robert L. Slater
Google+ - RobertLSlater1

## Acknowledgments

I'd like to thank my family first and foremost: Elena, Cail, Tanner, Daen, Sheridan, Ian and Miranda, Mom and Dad, James, Michael and Megan.

And all the usual suspects: Sam, Alex and all the rest at Village Books, the Heinlein Forum, my WATTPAD Followers,
My Google+ers, My Facebookians, My Twitterfans, and ALL MY STUDENTS!

My friends, fans, and critiquers: Amanda J. Hagarty, Andrea Kinnaman, Jesikah Sundin, Betsy Childs, James R. Wells, Brian Soneda, Christopher Key, Kayti Nika Raet, Donald Drummond, Mark Leslie, Virginia Herrick, Pam Beason, Joannah Miley, Selah J. Tay-Song, Michael Sarrow, Peter Rust, Jim Kling, Katie Kindland, Alberta Hendrickson, Dave Straub, Tina Shelton, James Hagarty, Alice Acheson, Tsena Paulsen, Janet Godsoe, John Seltzer, Kathy Brown, Hope Musick, Tonja Myers, Aubri Kellerman & Tamar Clarke. The Fanily: Eddi, Katie, Nicholas & William Vulic. Brian Lenius, Chris & Christine Perkins, Joe Collins, David Miller.

I am certain I have forgotten people. My apologies, and know that I appreciate your support.

# OUTWARD BOUND

## Science Fiction and Poetry

Robert L. Slater

ROCKET TEARS PRESS

Bellingham, Washington

OTHER WORKS
BY ROBERT L. SLATER

*All Is Silence* - Deserted Lands I
*Straight Into Darkness* - Deserted Lands II
*No Man's Land* - Deserted Lands III

*To all the teachers and librarians who supported my reading and writing, especially when I was out of bounds.*

*To my friends and family who supported me, but sometimes had to pull me back when I would go outward bound.*

*To my students who I hope will be inspired to take their own trips outward bound.*

# Beginnings

*A Deserted Lands Story*

THE  END, GEOFFREY TYPED. *YES. That'll do for a start.* The ancient Underwood felt solid under his fingertips. He glanced at the screen of his broken tablet to make sure the new USB interface worked and the words saved as clean as they appeared on the sheet of paper. His hands found their way back to the keys, their letters worn down by decades under his fingers.

> When Mother called, I was heading
> out in the alpine wilderness to
> measure transects for the citizen
> science project counting
> butterflies I ran for a National
> Parks partnership.
> A pandemic. The End of the World
> as We Know It.

Geoffrey paused, closing his eyes. First Person was not his favorite P.O.V. but for apocalyptic fiction, it seemed best. His hand found his coffee fortified with Gran Marnier and brought the cup to his lip. Still hot. It burned down his throat; heat and alcohol.

Funny how ideas popped out fully-formed when they were ready. He'd read the article about diseases having longer incubation periods. That would lead to greater risks of infections; Geoff had his story idea. End of the world as we know it. And who wouldn't be so unhappy about it? An

introverted scientist, recently single, might be happy not to have to worry so much about the human part of the equation.

> Despite her news, I went anyway.
> Just like Mother told me to, but
> I set up the transects and
> counted butterflies. The sky,
> clear and blue, welcomed me when
> I hit the end and marked it with
> the aluminum marker, I kept
> walking up the ridge, stepping
> only on rocks, away from
> humanity. My pack weighed me down
> with enough food for a couple
> days, but I knew what to eat in
> the wild and where there were
> stashes of food.

Geoffrey sighed. He'd been part of the butterfly project from the beginning, but then his hip started giving him trouble. The doctor suggested replacement, but pride would not let him get the surgery at 58. Not even retired. Well, now he was re-tired, tired over and over again.

> It had been almost two years since
> my boyfriend of 17 years, had
> moved on with his life and moved
> away with my truck. *God, I miss
> that truck.* But I didn't miss him
> and I wasn't certain about the rest
> of humanity.

The doorbell rang. The street front entrance to the apartment was the reason he could afford the writing retreat space, but it had its down side in a big city—solicitors. "Bloody Hell! If you're selling vacuum cleaners or salvation, I'll send you there." He jerked the door open. His glare cracked into a smile. His girlfriend stood ready to push the

doorbell again.

"Gwen, what are you doing here?"

His brain flashed through all the scenarios: *something had happened to the kids, the Ex, Gwen's mother, sister, nephews and niece? He'd won the Pulitzer Prize?* The November wind and rain whipped her dark hair.

"I wouldn't wreck your writer's weekend, Geoff." Gwen's pretty face had a stressed out scrunch.

*Not the Pulitzer then.* "I know. Come in." He reached for her. "It's cold."

"Don't touch me. Don't come near me." Her hands made quick 'stand aside' motions.

*Holy shit. What have I done now?* Geoffrey stepped out of the way.

Gwen entered. "You want a drink?"

"Yeah." She slumped into the couch.

*Damn.* Gwen never drank before five o'clock and it couldn't be past two. He glanced at the Gran Marnier and then went for the gin, her favorite. His hands knew what they were doing, ice, tonic. His brain spun. *Why was she here?* He tasted it. Nice. Strong, but nice. He poured a double shot, neat, into a glass for himself and carried them in on the hand-painted tray she'd bought him for an anniversary.

He sat across from her and set the drink down on the coffee table. "Well, what shall we drink to?"

She downed about half of it. "Geoff?"

"Okay." He did likewise. "Is it the kids?"

"No. Yes. They're fine. Celeste called. She's taking them to her folks. Probably on their way to the airport. Praying the flight isn't canceled."

Seemed like normal behavior for his ex. "GWEN! What the Hell is going on?"

"It hit." She finished the drink and set it down hard. "Your epidemic, plague, whatever the Hell you want to call it."

"My plague? It's just an idea for a novel, Gwen." He stared at her. She was shaken up. "You're not pranking me?"

She shook her head. Her eyes, big, brown and beautiful were wet, waiting for one wrong word from him to come

streaming.

Geoffrey waited. Words failed him. He wanted to kiss away the tears on her cheeks. *What would I have my characters say?* "It was simply a *what if?*; I didn't mean to be right." He drained the rest of his glass and set it down carefully.

"I know." She turned away into the couch, hiding her tears.

She'd come here on public transit and was already exposed. "Is it really happening? I've only been off the net for two days." *What if it's true? What then? I should talk to the kids. I don't think they want to talk to me, but why give weight to Celeste's accusations of imaginary neglect?* When Gwen was settled, he could call them.

"It's real. I guess it's been building for a month." Her body shook as she broke into loud sobs.

Geoffrey stared, helpless. *Go to her.*

"What are we going to do?" Gwen asked when the crying had subsided.

"What do you want to do?"

Gwen twisted herself to face him. Her eyes were red-rimmed, but thoughtful. Then a wicked little smile played across her face. "We could stay here and make love until we starve to death or die from the disease."

"Yes, we could do that." *God, Gwen was lovely. Why had this lady, twenty years his junior, fallen for him, a washed up British ex-pat writer? What had he done to deserve such happiness in what was turning out to be the last years of his life?*

"But we won't." She sat up, moving farther away from him and wiping the tears from her eyes. "You're still safe."

"Safe?" Geoffrey noted the bitterness in his reply. "Sorry. I doubt if anyone in any city is safe. The cabin in the woods I couldn't afford might have been a better idea. What info do they have about the infection?"

"They're saying 98% fatalities in Europe. The incubation period is a couple weeks, and then the symptoms start out as sniffles and progress. It's three weeks before you know you're really sick." She swiped at a tear, her eyes fearful,

"Geoffrey, I don't want to die."

"I don't want to die either, but what will life be like for the survivors? I've been living this fantasy. It won't be pretty. Shit. Probably neither of us will live. But you might make it; you're young, healthy, and fertile."

"You unfeeling bastard. I don't want to live without you."

Her anger stung. "Yes. I am an old, infertile, unhealthy, artistic lout, who has nothing to offer the end of the world."

"I'm going to go before I infect you." Gwen stood, strong now that she had made a decision. "I'm going to go to my mother's, then my sister's to see what I can do for her kids." She walked to the door.

He sighed and let the words fall from his mouth. "If we both survive and you really miss this old bastard, come find me. I might just stay here." He followed her to the door. "Maybe they'll find a cure."

She turned back to him, her lips trembling, and nodded. "I wish I could kiss you good-bye, but I might infect you."

Geoffrey nodded. But every muscle in his body wanted to reach out to her. His hand did. He stepped toward her. She backed against the wall.

"No, Geoff. I don't want to kill you."

He pulled her into his arms, kissing her forehead, caressing her hair. "I'm sorry. If I lived, but we never got to kiss or hold each other again, that would kill me."

Gwen pushed him away enough to look in his eyes. "You stupid, old man." Her smile belied the negativity in the words. "I love you." She lay her ear against his chest.

He slid his face down through her hair, down her face, scraping his stubble across her cheek until their lips met. "We can make love. Then you're going to take care of your family. And yourself. Go to your mother. Take care of her. Your sister. Her kids."

"But what about you?"

"I'm going to write. All I have to offer the future is words. I still need my writing weekend. Maybe we'll both live." He held her for a very, very long time. Then they stumbled to the bedroom and made love.

When she left, there were no more words. A kiss and that was it.

Then he sat in the dark nursing another neat double. The pain of the world ending was nothing compared to knowing he wouldn't likely see her again. Either it was the most selfish or least selfish thing he had ever done. He didn't know which.

Geoffrey sat back down to the sheet of paper he had started.

He pulled the manuscript sheet from the typewriter, enjoying the sound of the gears and cogs and rubber wheels straining to keep up. He fed another sheet into the Underwood and turned the platen knob until it was properly spaced. Then he typed.

**THE END**

**An eyewitness account**

**Geoffrey Smythe**

**I never meant to be right. Ever. And I never meant to tell the truth. I'm a writer.**

**Today, I will tell the truth. Then I will go out into the city and talk to people, tell their stories, and find someone, some way to publish and preserve it so that future generations might remember, if there are any.**

Geoffrey didn't think. He typed. His fingers flew.

*This story was written specifically to open this collection. I'm not sure if I'll return to Geoff and Gwen in the future. I have three other major story lines competing in my head for additional Deserted Lands Novels.*

*Author's Note: There really is a Cascades Butterfly Project through the National Park Service in partnership with other local organizations including my alma mater, WWU. Want to volunteer? http://www.butterfliesandmoths.org/project/CBP for more information.*

# Free to Fall

Free to fall
      Strangely
         Spinning
            Weightless in the womb
      In this darkness
             Sprinkled with suns
     In this lifeless space
Is found
    Our birthright
          We are free to fall
               Tumbling, turning
         Airless in this void
In this spaciousness
         Painted black
           In this goldfish bowl
        Is found
      My soul
And my direction
        I am free to fall
            Free to fly

"Free to Fall" appeared on the PBS' program, *Earthscape.*

# Outward Bound

**UNDER THE ENORMITY** OF THE gate an old man sat on a park bench, green grass underfoot. The circle of grass stood out against the dusty lunar regolith. He replaced his shoe as a little girl wandered away, deep in thought. A young man crossed to the bench, let his bag fall from his shoulder and sat down next to the old man. The bag settled into the grass. The old man eyed him quizzically and pulled a silver embossed flask from his pocket.

"You flashin' the gate, son?"

"Yeah," the young man replied  as the hum of the gate generators grew louder in the background. "And the name's, Bren, pop."

The old man chuckled, "Outward bound?"

Bren's mind returned to his surroundings. It took a moment for the man's question to penetrate. "Yeah, I guess. Uh huh."

"Where you headed?"

"I don't know, but I'm going."

"Your girl leave you?" the older man asked.

"It shows?" The young man bent and plucked a blade of grass from in front of the bench.

"Not too much. It's just that. . . Well, that's the same reason I went outward."

"Look, I don't really wanna talk, Mister–"

"Johnson. Call me Wayne."

"Wayne. I don't feel like talking."

"All right, just listen then. You got ten minutes to wait. Humor an old man."

"I'll try 'n' stay awake."

"Thanks." Wayne paused a moment, clearing his throat.

"Look at this." He stuck his left foot out and pulled off his shoe and began massaging a stump that should have been a foot. "I lost half my foot to stupidity almost 40 years ago. But I can feel it, like it's still there."

Bren looked up, regretting his curiosity. "Okay," he allowed, "What happened?"

"When they discovered flash-gate technology I was an engineer in the Lunar Free Corps. Not the first test group, but I went out soon after. Built more flash-gates than you could shake a stick at."

"I'm supposed to be impressed?"

The old man raised an eyebrow. "Thought you didn't wanna talk. Anyway, like I said, the reason I volunteered for hazardous duty? My girlfriend dearjohnned me. I moped around for a while till we got sent to our units. Then this woman in my group named Ashara appeared. With a quick wit, pretty smile and devilish eyes, I don't hafta tell you how quick I fell head over heels for her. When she walked into the briefing room my heart stopped."

Wayne stopped, took a pull off his flask, smacked his lips, then continued. "Ashara knew it right away. Whenever I got too close my brain would go into overdrive while my tongue struggled to keep up. I followed her around like a puppy and she treated me like a dog. It didn't last long. She had a wild streak. One night she dared me to go with her through the gate we'd just completed. It hadn't been tested but we'd never found out anything from the tests anyhow. I was stupid enough to take her up on it." He offered a drink to the young man.

Bren shrugged, then took it. He coughed, surprised. He'd expected something stronger than water.

"She flipped on the power and we saw a long, sandy beach with a green sky and a red ocean. She said, 'Follow me and you can have whatever you dream of.' Her eyes flashed and she headed through. I started after her, but paused, wondering if the reality would live up to the dream. She turned around and headed back for me. She took my hands and started pulling me in. A light flashed and an intense pain exploded in my left foot. I held her in

my arms, but half of her was missing. Our beach had disappeared, too. Her glittering eyes still looked at me. I gently lowered her to the ground as she started laughing. Then a wave of pain swept past those eyes and she spoke. 'If you were a man of action, we'd be on that beach now.' She coughed and spoke again, her sarcasm barely masking the pain, 'Take the path of least resistance, Wayne.' Then she died."

"That's it?"

"The service discharged me. Dereliction of duties plus the fact that they couldn't fix my foot. Won't take re-gen. I'll never see a clear sky out from under a dome. So watch out. Do what you hafta do. Don't go runnin' off on some half-crazed scheme thinkin' it's about love."

"I'll keep that in mind." The warning bell sounded. "Thanks for the story." The young man stood, slung his bag over his shoulder and headed for the platform.

"You're still going?" Wayne asked.

"Not for love," Bren answered.

"Bren! Wait!" A young woman's voice stopped his step.

"Stace?" he stood, not turning, and waited for her. "I gotta go. The gate opens in less than a minute." She carried a large bag similar to his own.

"You're going?" she queried as she popped in front of his face.

Wayne watched with amusement as Bren tried not to look happy to see her.

"I always planned to go someday," Bren explained.

"You got all your paperwork then?" she asked.

"Yeah."

"I'm sorry, Bren. You don't have to prove anything to me."

"I know." He looked at her for a moment before speaking again, "I'm not trying to."

"But you were only going because I wanted you to."

"Things have changed."

The old man could hear the words in Bren's head. *Is it love? Yes, it's love, but I'll be damned if I let her know that.*

"You mean you'd leave without me?" Stace asked.

Bren flashed her a determined smile. "I am leaving. Now." He took her in his arms and kissed her, neither too slow, nor too fast, but thorough.

She smiled, "Thanks for the kiss, but you're not getting away that easy."

Bren returned her smile, and they bounced arm and arm up the steps to the platform and toward the gate. They exchanged papers with the duty officer. As he motioned them forward, the young man turned and waved. Wayne saluted and the young couple stepped through. The safety plates rotated into place and the almost imperceptible hum ceased.

In the ensuing quiet a soft voice asked, "Wayne, you tellin' that boy more of your lies?"

"'Shara! Would you quit sneakin' up on me like that?"

"I'm not sneaking up on you." She wrapped her arms around his shoulders and squeezed. "You're just getting hard of hearing. You convinced him to do something crazy, didn't you?"

Wayne looked smug. "I tried to convince him not to, but you know how contrary young men are."

"Don't you mean all men?" Ashara asked with a twinkle in her eye. "You tell him the one about losing your foot plugging a vacuum hole in an unfinished tunnel on some far off planet?"

"No, I told him one about a flash-gate mishap."

"There's never been a flash-gate mishap. Where do you come up with these ideas? I know you've never been off Luna."

"I read a lot of books. You know those things they used to make from squashed trees, young lady." He winked at their old shared joke. "It's all I can do. Until they figure out how to get my body to accept a clone graft, we're stuck." Wayne paused and his eyes twinkled. "I just changed their lives, now. I ain't too old to go outward bound, am I?

Ashara kissed his cheek, "Wayne, you're never too old. Put your shoe on and let's go get a bite to eat."

"Outward Bound" appeared in *Continuum SF.*

*I wrote this story originally trying to capture a story with only dialogue. I had been reading Hemingway. I know. The first draft was 900 words and 90% dialogue. I added setting and characterization until it sold.*

# The Starrior

I hold the world in the palm of my hand
Unmolden clay prepared to form at my command
The fates control me I cannot break away
Destiny is waiting for me to take the stage

The stage is set, the curtain down, I am ready to make the scene
My blood is burning hot as life, the world is on its knees
A Quixotic lance is on my horse, it lies beside my heel
The sword of might is in my hands, a blade of cold, hard steel

It is forged from the blood of the enemies of man
Its power is the glory that I hold at my command
The odds are all against me, but fate is on my side
I must make my rendezvous with strength before I die

The river Styx is beckoning, it just seems to say
The ferryman is calling, come and meet your judgment day
But it's not my time to meet my maker, my destiny lies free
I must lead the men of earth against their greatest enemy

We must be the victor, this war must end in space
For our son's and daughters to attain their rightful place
I led my men to victory, we vanquished all the foes
A greater union in the stars will help all peoples grow

A thousand years have come and gone the violent times are past
Mankind's place among the stars is guaranteed at last
For a thousand years I haven't slept now comes my time to rest
My destiny is finished as I lay my head upon my breast

But I have left a message for a time of awesome need
If mankind's voices call from my slumber I will heed

"The Starrior" appeared in *Millennium SF&F.*
*Written as a high school student. Hopefully that's not too obvious.*

# In Formation

**2nd LT. DEAN O'NEILL** SNAPPED UP the fasteners on the composite vest and tugged the uniform into place. *Enough armor, now for some armament.* He hefted the .45 his grandfather had brought back from Nam. With a twinge of regret for its history, he laid it down and picked up his personal favorite, the Sig Sauer P426 rail-gun. As he checked the clip, Gramp's words came back to him: "In close quarters skill with the individual weapon is of greatest importance. A master with the saber can take out a squad with M-16s." He strapped the holster on his left side and inserted a riot stick for his weaker right hand. His link twittered. "Yes?"

His father's gray eyes and craggy face appeared in his visual cortex. "Dad."

"Dino. Finally sending you in, are they?" he growled. "It's about time."

"You know how important the training is," he admonished his father. "Besides it isn't the same as when you were in."

"That's what they keep trying to tell me. Retired. Harumph! I could whip any one of you punks into shape."

Dean heard his mother's placating voice in the background. "Is Mom there?"

"I'm here, honey. We're both so proud of you. Can you transfer to the home-phone? I want to see you."

Dean flipped the transfer key and crossed to the vid-cam. "There, Mom. Can you see?"

"So handsome. Grampa Johnson would be proud."

"Thanks. Look, Mom, Dad, I gotta go. The transport arrives at

0700 hours."

"We know, son," his Dad agreed.

"We love you."

"Love you two, too. Later. Phone off." The video faded as Dean slapped the door panel and slipped out into the early dawn. The cold January air chilled the sweat of nervousness.

He strode across the barracks area, pacing when he arrived at the mag-lev tram platform. Scattered thoughts chased through his brain like the movement in his stomach. A semblance of a quote from one of his humanities courses popped into his head. *Must've been drama.* "You never get rid of the butterflies; what you must do is make them fly in formation." He grinned to himself. *No problem.*

"Early as usual, O'Neil?"

"It's a big day, Captain." Dean glanced at the mag-lev tracks. With a deep breath and a straightening of his spine he tossed off the jitters. "But I'm ready, Sir."

The Captain chuckled, "At least as ready as you'll ever be. There's something about a trial by fire that'll let you know if this is really what you want to do."

Several other 2-Lites jogged up as the mag-lev tram streaked into view. The group assumed a formation. *Just like butterflies.* Dean chuckled at the thought. If they could read his mind he'd probably get his humor beaten out of him.

"Gentlemen," the captain began when they stood at attention, "today you'll begin to understand the purpose of your course of training. If you haven't done your homework, you might live to regret it. Good Luck. Debriefing 1700 hours. Dismissed."

Dean filed into the tram, his buddies beside him. He glanced back, trying to read the Captain's enigmatic smile.

As he stepped off the tram platform an overweight paper-shuffler greeted him with a grin. "This way, Captain."

Dean winced. Bad enough that he had to take orders from civilians without having to put up with this. He knew they noted his uniform with respect, but it rankled his sense of military hierarchy.

The genial gray-suited man led him down a hallway barely wider than his bulk. "Make sure you remember this route. If things get out of control, it's your only escape."

"Thanks. I don't expect to need it."

"It's nice to hear some confidence in this place, son. I like positive thinking. Here we are." He stopped before a non-descript door. "The Colonel is already in there. He'll brief you on your assignment." He slapped the door-pad and it slid aside. "Encode your palm-print before you leave."

Dean nodded, trying to see past the man's large form into the room.

"Good luck, Sir."

"Thank you." Dean stepped through the doorway and it closed solid behind him. For a moment fear pushed him back against the door, but then his eye caught on the Colonel and the stability of the uniform. He stole a glance at the rest of the room, and took a deep breath. All the homework in the world wouldn't have prepared him for this.

The Colonel, a tired-looking career man, extended his hand. "We're pretty informal here, Dean. I'm Colonel Parks, but I'd appreciate it if you'd call me Glenn. Welcome to the jungle."

Dean shook his hand firmly. "Thank you, Sir, I mean, Glenn." He tried nonchalantly smoothing his uniform. The feel of the weapons brought him comfort. "How do we start?"

"I'm not big on speeches, so I'll just introduce you."

Dean nodded.

"Privacy Off." The localized sound damper released a muttering hum of voices. Dean hadn't even realized it was on.

"Class!" the Colonel barked. "This is Mister O'Neil. He will be your student teacher for the next semester. You will treat him with the same respect that you treat me."

A few laughs broke out. "That ain't a lot," someone howled from the back of the room.

Dean scanned over the semi-dazed eyes. The few who watched him with more than subdued detachment glared in anger.

"Mister O'Neil? Do you have anything to say by way of introduction?"

Dean nodded, his throat now  dry. "I'd like to tell you a bit about myself." He heard his voice scratch out, too soft and awkward. He found his lecture voice and watched in amazement as he saw the students tune out.

As he recounted his reasons for wanting to become a teacher, they rang hollow in his ears. As his words wound down, he wondered if his choice had been a good one.

With a sigh he offered up the teachers' compulsory phrase, "Are there any questions?"

"In Formation" appeared in *Millennium SF&F, SBD SF&F,* and *Whispers in the Wind.*

*This story was written around the time I was getting ready to student teach. I had a more extended story in mind, but this is what came out. I don't feel this negative about the future of education in this country, but please support your local schools: students, teachers and support staff.*

# Highway Rider

The flatlands are burning in this land we've turned to hell
The world keeps on turnin' inside this fragile shell
We've got to get away from here before we start to rot
We've gotta get to somewhere else, this hell is all we've got

Off in the distance about to top the rise
The noise of tortured metal the smoke just fills the skies
I jump into the cockpit the mighty engine roars
The tires spin, the gravel flies, my foot is to the floor

Gasoline is life, it's the blood in my hands
It's the only ticket out of this cruel and battered land
My tank is full I cannot waste a single precious drop
The race is run, my time is done, if I can't make him stop

The law of the land means the fittest survive
The only thing I'm working for is tryin' to stay alive
Across the desert wasteland his fate he comes to meet
His car is getting closer burning through the blazing heat

I power brake and spin around and slow to catch my breath
The warrior is coming, running for his death
A deadly game of chicken means the fittest survive
The only thing I still can do is close my eyes and drive

Accelerate, my tires spin, my posi grips the road
The RPM's are runnin' up - about to overload
The nerves of steel come in play, the chaser now the chased
His fault he realizes now, his car a flaming waste

The smell of burning gasoline mixed with burning flesh
I slow my car to watch the scene and sigh a weary breath
I must escape this savage land, I cannot stand the pain
My son becoming just like me with all my work in vain

I leave the flaming hulk and drive into the setting sun
One day I'll make it out of here, today is not the one
Some think our lives are fixed, left to the hands of fate
But I believe I shall escape, I hope it's not too late

"Highway Rider" appeared in *Jackhammer.*
*Another high school one that was supposed to be a Hair Metal 80s song, but I*
*could never get music to go with it. Any retro-bands out there that want to give*
*it a try are welcome. Get my permission if you record it, please.*

# Shooting Star

"SAM!" ELLEN ADMONISHED, PULLING MY gaze up from the pair of legs and into the gentle face of the secretary. Thank God nylon rations had ended. As a teen I remembered women painting that line up the back of their legs. "We'd like to see Mr. Bancroft," I said, maintaining eye contact.

"He's waiting to see you, Mr. Slade."

I smiled my thanks and allowed myself one last glance at those shapely legs. Ellen elbowed me in the side and struck my war-issue .45.

"Ouch!"

"Be quiet. You hit me."

Ellen slid her hand inside my gun-metal gray double-breasted pinstripe suit. "I can't believe you're packing."

"He's an editor. I'm a writer. You're my agent. 'Nough said." I straightened my tie, tugged my suit down and strode into Bancroft's Office.

Mr. Bancroft glanced up at us from behind the gorgeous expanse of his spit-polished maple desk. Two chairs and a coat rack completed the furnishings, spare, but expensive. "There's no need for your agent," he explained, his voice warm and soothing.

Warning bells jangled. "You're an editor, right?"

"Of course."

"Then I want my agent here." My fingers stroked at the well-defined cleft in my chin.

"Very well, Sam," he lamented. "But she won't accompany you on the all-expense-paid workshop."

"She's only here to check out the contract."

"Here." Bancroft gestured expansively toward the desk. "This contract will make you one of the biggest rising stars in the Science Fiction firmament." He smiled, the wrinkled, soft face under his gray brows comforting.

The contract and pen looked lonesome on the huge desk--no typewriter, no manuscripts, no telephone. This guy took cleanliness to new heights. I glanced at the contract and saw the same smile reflected into an evil frown in the shiny desktop. It reminded me of the scene in *Damn Yankees* where Joe Boyd sells his soul to the Devil for a chance at the major leagues. Well, for the right contract. . . And I'd want to meet Lucifer in person, no sub-demons or motion picture producers.

I handed the contract to Ellen. Long ago I realized that my talent for business was inversely proportional to my talent as a writer.

Ellen whistled. "These rates're astronomical, Sam."

"Nothing but the best for our rising stars," Bancroft agreed.

"What's the catch?" I asked.

"The catch, Sam? No catch. Sign this and walk through that door," Bancroft gestured behind him. "Your transport waits on the roof."

"Ellen?"

She continued to scan the contract. "Have patience." Finally she shrugged. "I'd say it's too good to be true, but it's your funeral."

"I'll right, I'll sign." I whipped out my heavy contract signing pen and scrawled one of my more legible signatures.

"Welcome to the fastest moving corporation in the universe. On this journey you'll meet the best and brightest minds this planet has to offer." He held out his hand. It felt cold and clammy-the classic limp fish shake.

"Thanks for coming along, Ellen, I'll call when I can."

"Take care of yourself, Sam," she counseled.

"I always do," I grinned. "This way, Bancroft?"

"Yes, Sam, your chariot awaits." He punched a key on his desk and hydraulics opened the door.

I slipped through and looked down a long hallway, but something kept me from going down it. Paranoia, I guess. As the door closed behind me, I put my pen on the floor between the doorjamb and the door.

"Good Day, Miss Ellen," Bancroft acknowledged.

Maybe my paranoia filters needed adjustment. I bent to retrieve my pen.

"Bancroft, this door's locked," Ellen said.

"You're sure? Check it again."

"Yes, it's locked."

Sensing trouble, I pushed on the door. It didn't move.

"Well, Ellen," Bancroft murmured, "Perhaps we could use you." He laughed that sick sort of laugh you only hear in B movies. "Editors are always looking for something fresh."

I slammed my muscular bulk into the door. It didn't budge, my shoulder did. Grimacing in pain, I pulled on the knob and something in the door mechanism released. I shoved my way back into the room.

He had his hands all over her and his eyes shone like a used-car salesman on a Sunday. She fought back, clawing at his face, but it didn't seem to bother him.

"I don't think you'll be using her after all."

Bancroft turned, surprised.

Ellen grabbed the contract from him and skipped away.

"Let's go, Ellen," I suggested, trying the door. It didn't budge. I slammed on the door with my fist. It felt solid. I pulled my .45 carefully from its shoulder holster.

"What do you plan to do with that?" Bancroft inquired. He eyed me as the spider does the fly, wondering why fight the inevitable.

I flicked the safety off, pointed it at the door and pulled the trigger. The door took the slug like a spitwad on a chalkboard.

"I'm afraid its bulletproof and soundproof, Sam." His look of bemused disdain remained.

I turned the gun on him and pulled the trigger twice. The first slug blew his face off and revealed dark brown scales underneath.

The second knocked his head back. His head returned to vertical and his eyes attempted to focus on the silvery slugs imbedded in his face like a peas in mashed potatoes. He scraped at his hands. Like cheap rubber gloves, his skin came off in strips revealing wicked claws.

"Sam, be reasonable. You can see the stars. Distant planets. We'll take you there."

"If I go, I'll go my way."

His talons reached for me. I raised the gun.

Ellen screamed, "Why? What do you want with him?"

The monster that was Bancroft spun on Ellen. Its head cocked to one side. "Your species is advancing too fast. We would like this planet. His kind are providing to much motivation and ideas. We'd rather have him for dinner. But you're my appetizer."

My fingers worked the trigger involuntarily as the counterfeit human flesh sloughed off. His hard skull absorbed the blows as more hit. He turned his head and smiled predatorily. "You should've spent more time at the gun range, Sam."

The next slug hit his eye socket and the condescension disappeared. My finger clicked on the empty chamber. Bluish fluid oozed from his facial orifices as the body fell. It careened off the desk and landed solidly.

Ellen's hand grasped the gun. "You can stop now."

I glanced at her and nodded. She reached under the desktop and flipped a switch to unlock the door.

"You want to put that thing away?"

Dumbly, I slipped the gun back into its holster, but not before sliding in a full clip to replace the spent one. I opened the door, we strode out and I shut it behind me.

The secretary spun in her seat, smiling. "How was your meeting?"

"Excellent." No way she could hide reptile flesh under that skin. "Mr. Bancroft asked not to be disturbed. I'm afraid he's immersed in his slush pile."

Ellen and I strode to the door. I tried to maintain my calm as I opened it for her.

"Thank you, Sam."

We climbed into my Studebaker. I revved the engine and spun out into the busy midday traffic. Then my hands started to shake. "I think I want a drink."

"Me, too," Ellen agreed. "I don't get how you figured it out?"

I laughed, it felt good. "Simple. Writers' first rule: Never trust an editor with a perfectly clean desk."

"Shooting Star" appeared in *Millennium SF&F, Goblin Muse*, and *Chaos Theory: Tales Askew.*

*My first sale, inspired by Dean Wesley Smith, "Never trust an editor with a clean desk," at some workshop at a Worldcon in the 90s. I was going for the classic pulp fiction feel; I guess that makes it timeless. As long as there are editors...*

# Crossroads of Time

Time and space mean nothing here
There are no ties that bind
Life and love don't matter here
At the crossroads of time
      Here at the crossroads of time

Thoughts abound in words so hollow
How to light the fuse?
There are too many paths to follow
Which one will you choose?

Like the fields left in fallow
Preparing for the use
Human minds are oh so shallow
It's only life to lose

Man must always forge ahead into every future
No one gets a second chance their own world to suture
Man can always make a choice be it good or bad
Changes happen all the time better times we've had

Worlds in which Hitler lives, all roads lead to Rome
Worlds dead from holocaust; Is this all my home?
Each world had an Adam, Each world had an Eve
They did this all to themselves this we cannot grieve

There are so many paths to follow

At the crossroads we must choose
Thoughts abound in words so hollow
Now it's our lives to lose

Like the fields left in fallow
Now we must prepare
Human minds are oh so shallow
Life and loves we share

Mankind was not made to travel 'cross the sands of time
He'll put to death the age old thought
            . . . . a stitch in time saves nine
We must save our own world, there is no mass escape
Before we can help another
We must put ourselves in shape

*Inspired by Andre Norton's novel of the same name.*

# Only Human

**I RAN. MY** LONG LEGS gave me an advantage. Their smaller shapes followed me, pursuing like dogs. Without slowing I ducked into an alley, praying that it still connected with the aqueduct. It did. I raced down the cement slope, dry this time of year, and hopped the algae film that had been a decent water source.

The councils warned us about them--traveling in packs. I longed for the good old days, when the only thing you had to worry about on a night-time jog was tripping over a sleeping bum or a pair of amorous lovebirds in the park. I had a good block-length on them, and I'd make it as long as they didn't warn others. I know how well their telepathy works. Like my body, my mind raced, remembering. They chased me, but sixty years ago I had been their champion. The irony caused a weak chuckle. If those I tried to save kill me, no one will know my story. Traitor or hero? Who decides? Hannah, if you'd lived, how would things be different? Now, no one knows me.

I ran from them. Like I ran from my own kind after the explosion. They'd tried to kill me like they'd killed Hannah. So I went underground, slipping from town to town, playing many parts in traveling theatrical groups.

My luck held as I leapt up the wall and grasped the pipe nearly nine feet off the ground. I pulled myself over and dropped to the street on the other side. I hadn't figured I'd ever have a use for the Reservations, but the divider between these two rose high enough that they wouldn't be able to clear it. I'd have headed for the Reservation entrance to register a complaint, but I'd never heard of anyone getting anything done. Our own police forces had

their hands tied.

I trudged along the darkened street. This Rez's self-government concerned itself more with the self than the government. Burned out streetlights left my imagination to question what shapes lay in the gutters. Loud, raucous sounds intruded on the quiet night. A guitar spewed forth chords resembling music while a vocal line screamed over the top, not caring for tune or tone. Following the sounds to their source, I entered the bar. Not to put the vocalist out of his/her misery, but rather to wet my own vocal apparatus.

The long run left me tired, dry and a little shaken. I ordered a whiskey on the rocks and found a seat in the back where I could observe what remained of humanity. I glanced from face to face. The eyes betrayed the illusion of youth and vigor. We'd lost the luxury of dying out. They'd made us immune to cancer and its brethren, forever young, not needing to reproduce. Those who survived the first slew of suicides took to killing ourselves slowly.

I reached the bottom of the glass and signaled the barkeep. When the music started sounding appealing I decided I'd had enough. Leaving the bar, I walked, somewhat unsteady, back to the wall. Chemicals to convince me that life remained livable chorused through my senses. Pulling myself up I glanced around, but saw no one. I dropped to the other side giggling to myself as the alcohol warped my sense of propriety.

Though we had thought them all dead, they had risen again in enough force to stop World War III. Then they brought us Reservations—places for normal humans to go and be safe. Dubbed Homo Christus, they would take care of us. They searched for me, their patron saint. But I couldn't live with them any better than I could live with my own kind. And now their children's children chased us for fun, for sport. Not very Christ-like. But I suppose even children of angels have a need to rebel.

Strolling around the corner, I felt myself slammed into the wall. Panic held me for a moment, but left as I took in the size of my captors. Only human cops, their hands certainly not tied. The bigger goon grabbed me.

"Come on, you old wino." His partner got in my face. "You can sleep it off in the tank. Carl, hold him so I can ID him."

Carl shoved me against the wall and peeled back my eyelids. My eye burned as the retina scanner did its work. The feeling may be psychological, but it's always bothered.

"Get his hands," ordered the gabber. "We need prints. Orders are orders."

Fingerprints? I'd cemented the new personality when the retina scans came into common usage. What the Hell did they want prints for?

"Come on. You don't need my prints."

"'fraid we do. Don't make it hard on yourself."

I glanced around for an escape. None presented itself. Then Carl, strong and silent, grabbed my hands. Oh, well. No sense fighting these guys. "All right, take them." What good would it do probably? The fingerprint files that would give away my identity were lost. "Look, I live about a block from here--a secured compound. Don't make me sleep it off in the tank. I'll lose my job."

"Whattya think, Carl? He doesn't have a record."

Carl finally spoke, rather soft and gentle for such a big man. "Well, Mr. MacDonald? Are we going to see you again?"

"No," I said, trying to sound serious and sober.

They assisted me none-too-gently back to my apartment compound and even went so far as to deposit me at my own door. They waited until I'd opened it and gone in before they left.

No. They wouldn't be seeing me again. Time to move on. It wouldn't be safe tonight, but the packing could be done.

Old newspaper clippings went into the fire. I'd carried them with me far too long. And I could never burn away the memories of Hannah. She was of the first generation of Homo Christus. The day they brought her in remains vivid. She had no money and her parents wished to become her permanent legal guardians on the grounds that she presented a danger to herself and others.

I made the ultimate young lawyer's mistake. I fell in love with my client. When we shook hands, her touch had been electric. I

stared into her eyes and felt like I'd known her forever. We shared a love for the pre-virt movies and modern jazz. But it never would have worked. My intense aloofness couldn't handle someone reading my thoughts. She taught me to distort my thoughts and cover them so they'd be indecipherable, but I could never get over the fear that she could see inside me. Sometimes I don't think I know myself, not the real me. I've played so many parts, I don't know when I'm playing one for myself. And if I couldn't know myself, I didn't want anyone else to either.

*      *      *

The following morning everything I wanted to take waited by the door in two suitcases and a small trunk. I'd have to get a cab to pick them up. God, I longed for the freedom offered by a cars. The car laws had done more damage to personal rights than all the gun control laws in history. Oh well, I could walk where I needed to go this morning.

Locking the compound door behind me, I glanced across the street. There, lounging in the doorway, lay one of them, looking like an average human adolescent. But any human of that age would be sheltered and protected, not out on the street. So I knew he or she, gender is difficult to tell without clues, was Homo Christus. The eyes followed my movement. This one didn't have the look of the punks that chased me last night, but that didn't mean much. With their telepathy I didn't matter. I knew not all of their young got their kicks from hunting humans, but enough did to make me nervous. Their parents claimed they couldn't control them, but did they even try? Did they care what happened to us?

But if they had targeted me, why show their hand? They were smarter than that; their genes gave them no choice. So why? Unless they wanted me to realize that they were in control, that I had no power over them. I headed down the street. No reason to look back, the tingle on my neck told me I had acquired a tail.

I strolled nonchalantly toward the aqueduct, humming an old metal song from my youth to cover my thoughts. Let them think I lacked the sense to try something new. Besides my path lay in the

same direction. I spun around the corner glancing back to check my pursuit. I could see seven of them now, stalking toward me in that pubescent strut. I broke into a gentle jog. Reaching the theatre by the stage door, I didn't bother to relock or even shut it. My goal lay close at hand, but I wanted them right behind me. I took the stairs two at a time. When I reached the top, I opened the door to the roof, ignoring the warning that I'd trigger an alarm. It hadn't worked since before I arrived. Facing the door, I backed toward the edge. Stopping to sit on the ledge, glancing back to see the street six stories below, I waited.

They appeared sooner than I'd expected. Three of them came through the door. Where were the others? They moved in. I reached behind my back and grasped the pulley. For some reason I couldn't resist waiting till the last minute, when they might be able to catch me.

A blast of mental energy hit me. They rushed me. I kicked out, flailing at their smaller bodies. Using them to push off of, I jumped over the edge, swinging with the pulley as it engaged the line and my weight sent it spinning out over the chasm. The street below looked farther than six stories, but my grip remained tight. I couldn't help grinning back at them. So much for superior intelligence. Well, they could hardly be blamed for not knowing about the line we used to transport equipment for the theatre. My progress slowed as I hit the upswing in the line, moments before the platform appeared under my feet. Releasing the pulley, I waved across at them. After all, I meant them no harm. Then I spun neatly on my heel and hustled down the stairs from the landing to the roof. Inside the building I ambled to the elevator and slapped the button to open the door. It calmed me to know that it always waited at the top floor. As the door opened I glanced back to see if they'd managed to get across, and they grabbed me.

They'd outsmarted me. Or perhaps they'd simply tired of my silly games. They'd allowed me the close shave only to heighten the final capture. Three chased me to set me up for the rest of the pack. But how could they have known I'd pull this stunt? Unless

they could see through my primitive block.

They closed in around me, discarding all pretense of stealth. The leader, pulled away from the others and rose to his full height like a bully on a playground. I glared down at him, but my size gave him no worries. His eyes, in the first stage of metamorphosis to adulthood, stared up into mine.

My last chance lay in convincing them I meant no harm. With my comforting defense attorney face, I smiled at him. Now they'd torture me. I could deal with that. Mind games. Hell, I didn't know any human better at mind games. Maybe that's why they chased me. My block gave them more of a challenge. All I had to worry about was keeping my real identity secret. They could have everything else.

The leader glanced around at his gang. One by one, some nodded, while others answered his unspoken question with unspoken answers. Finally he turned to me and spoke, his attitude tough, "We know who you are. You are David Young. You will come with us." He auto-cuffed my wrists and we started walking.

Fifty years since I'd heard that name. The sound of it chilled me. What could they do? I knew the answer to that. They could take my freedom, keep me around like a favorite pet, a not-so-pretty bird in a perfectly safe gilded cage. All for doing the right thing, for trying to save a new species. And, of course, for trying to live out my life unchallenged. I could see the headline announcing my death. Like the obituary I'd once found for the first chimp in space. The world had mourned him and honored him, but they'd never given him the chance to go back to where he belonged, to his home in the jungle. He'd have died there like I nearly died in the streets of my jungle. I'd survived by never getting close to anybody, Homo Sapien or Homo Christus. Now how would I survive losing the freedom to die of my own free will or stupidity? At least Pocahontas' cage a had a key. Her early death brought her relief. I probably wouldn't die of old age for a couple hundred more years.

By the time we'd reached the bottom of the building, the three I'd left had arrived with transportation, an auto-cab. For all

their advancement, none of them would know the joy of driving a car. This cab was truly an automobile. Punch in a destination and sit back and the vehicle's computer does the rest.

To my surprise we didn't leave the Reservation. Instead we headed for the old manufacturing area, abandoned since the establishment of the Reservations. The auto-cab stopped in front of a warehouse, no different from those on either side. They didn't pull me out, but stepped aside to let me exit. The eight of them surrounded me in a loose circle as we walked toward the building. As the auto-cab moved off behind us, the door to the warehouse rolled up.

Inside minimal fluorescent lighting showed halls leading off away. We moved into the closest hall, our footsteps' echoes growing faint as we left behind the darkness of the warehouse.

They led me to an inside office, its windows soundproofed and layered over chicken wire. They shut and locked the door. After a few minutes the leader returned with a few blankets and a pillow. "Why am I here? What are you going to do to me?"

He stared at me, his mind tickling mine for information. Finally he shook his head, a little bemused. "I suggest you get some sleep. Food will be brought to you." He left.

I relaxed a little. At least my mind block seemed to work. They left me alone for two days, only bothering me with food and drink. The office had a bathroom and an old terminal. They'd locked out everything but library access, so I spent the time reading. Fiction and news. And pacing. Finally, on the third day they came for me. The whole honor guard of seven led me from the room and down into another huge warehouse. The walls existed in the distance as darkness.

A large transport vehicle parked in the middle of the warehouse. We walked to it and the leader motioned me up the steps to the nondescript door. I noted the tell-tales of telepathic communication. His eyes moved as if he was experiencing REM sleep while awake. The door slid back and he guided me in. The largest vid-wall I'd ever seen faced me. It contained more information on it than my mind could begin to catalog. In front of

the wall sat a desk with a chair turned to face the screen and one for the guest, me. The leader backed out of the room and the door shut. I tried to make sense of the data on the screen, but it changed too quickly.

Who was I waiting for? The chair swiveled and I glimpsed a figure sitting in it. The light of the wall revealed a darkened silhouette. My breathing sounded out of place and forced. Still the figure in the chair said nothing.

"All right," I complained to myself, "this is just a little too campy for me."

"I could never tell the line between theatrical and campy," said a familiar voice. "I would have thought the swing across on the rope a la Arnold Schwartzenegger was camp."

"Hannah?" The lights came up. There she sat looking exactly as she had the last time I saw her. I wanted to run to her but disbelief and uncertainty held me. "But you're dead."

"So are you." She had the same enigmatic look on her face that had captivated me throughout the trial. "I couldn't be sure you were still alive, but I've been trying to trace you for years. Why did you give up on me so easy?"

"Look, you died first," I joked.

It brought a smile to her face to match the stupid grin on mine. As I studied her more carefully, the years appeared around her eyes. The lines showed that belonging to a superior race didn't exempt one from time's ravages. "You're alive," I sputtered the obvious. "But why?"

"But why what? Why am I alive? Probably for the same reason you are. The attempt on my life wasn't immediately successful. I recovered, and my work continued."

"What work?" I asked, realizing that I had no clue what she had been doing since I'd last seen her.

"Ensuring the survival of my species. You remember me quoting the Bible to you? The meek shall inherit the earth? Do you remember what you said?"

I remembered. "The meek shall inherit shit." I laughed, fighting back tears. "And I didn't think you paid attention."

"On the contrary. You're the only human I ever trusted. That includes my parents."

"But what did that quote lead to?"

"It made me realize that I could not wait around for humanity to accept us, to help us. Someone had to start a defense. I traveled to every report that sounded like the discovery of one of us. I communicated with them, giving them the knowledge to hide their differences. I found some of us locked in asylums. We established a telepathic network. We lost a few, but our mortality rate dropped to a negligible amount. Once there were enough of us, taking control of the world was child's play. A good thing too, since we were children. I am one of the few first generation survivors."

So, my race had charged me with their betrayal, and the charge appeared valid.

"David... We... I owe you everything."

Her words fell on my ears like water pounding down from a waterfall. I sat down in the chair beside me as my thoughts and my body wobbled off balance. "Why didn't you tell me?"

"How could I? You were dead." She smiled chewing gently on her bottom lip. "You always believed in me, in what we were doing. I knew of your love." She breathed deeply. "And eventually I came to the conclusion that I loved you, too. At least to the extent that I am capable of it. I know you believe it could never work, but there it is anyhow." She paused before continuing more quietly, "Besides, the fact that I love you makes little difference now."

"What do you mean?"

"David, I'm dying. It took thirty years, but my killers' work appears to be a success, unfortunately they're not around to see it." She said that last with surprising vehemence. "You look surprised? I had them killed. They didn't suffer, though I was tempted. Those who attempted to kill you are also dead."

"Hannah, I'm not sure I know you."

"I'm not sure I know myself. But, I've got to make peace. In many ways, all the terribly important ones, we are the same as

you. We feel the same rage. We lose control when we're backed into a corner. We love. And we feel guilt and regret."

"Regret and guilt—" she paused as her eyes delved deep into me.

I pulled my gaze away. "How did you find me?"

"For all my alleged intellect, it escaped me until recently that with your fingerprints I'd eventually find you. If you still lived. I knew you didn't die in the explosion, but you could have died later."

"You instituted fingerprinting to find me?"

"All over the world."

"But why am I worth all that effort?"

"We still need your help. This planet and both of its sentient races need you. There is much we could accomplish, but I will not keep you in your gilded cage."

"Stop it. Don't read my mind."

Her face clouded. "Perhaps you should go. You'll be safe in this district for the moment, I have more than the usual Reservation control. Take the time you need. You're free to go. Or stay. I'll be here. On the premises. At least for a while. I'm close enough I can hear you if you think my name." She came around the desk, kneeling in front of my chair, almost as a worried adult to a confused child.

I stood. Her hand reached tentatively to touch me, but giving in to that contact would make my choice before I had time to think. Our eyes met for a moment. I wondered if I let her in could she make sense of the thoughts spinning in my head. I certainly couldn't. A glimmer of a smile played across her lips. "Please, Hannah, can't you shut it off and give me privacy?"

She shrugged. "I'll try. Promise me you'll return and tell me what you decide."

I nodded.

"If you leave, know that what protection I can offer you goes with you. If you stay..." Her voice faded and her eyes turned away.

I spun around trying hard not to show the tears that threatened to spill, trying hard not to think of anything. During my

exit from the building I saw no one. But the tickle on the back of my neck would not go away and the front door opened as I approached.

Wandering the streets helped to clear my thoughts. I strolled down avenues once thriving with workers, human workers, and I thought of what we'd lost. What I'd lost. The freedom to choose my own destiny.

For years I'd harbored resentment against those Homo Christus who had taken control. The voices from the past had sometimes even made sense. I'd somehow managed to separate Hannah from the rest; after all, she'd died. She couldn't be blamed for taking away our freedom. Now I'd discovered she not only helped bring down humanity, but almost single-handedly masterminded it. And at my bidding. I picked up a rock from the street and heaved it at the sky. I was angry enough to kill. Hadn't I hated them? Even more than I'd hated my own people. And myself.

What did I owe humanity? They'd tried to kill me and the one I loved. But another part of my race had kept me sane through all those years—the people I'd played packed houses to. Where were they now? All those people who I'd reached through a shared theatrical experience? Humanity has theatre because we can't read minds. We want to. At least we think we want to. But what we really need is to share in what others are feeling. Not thinking, but feeling.

Besides, what is humanity? Hannah was born to a human mother. What did that make her? I'd gone through this argument in my head uncountable times. The answer never changed. Hannah's mother's face entered my mind. How could someone be so loving and yet so cruel?

My random path had returned me to the warehouse. And I realized my decision had been made. I walked, a spring in my step, unsurprised that the door opened in front of me. I walked to her door and knocked. She opened it. I crossed to her, trying to read in her eyes what thoughts spun through her head. She remained unreadable, but I didn't care. She met me halfway, her arms open.

The first contact reminded me of our first touch—a heightening of my senses.

We held each other, as both our bodies shook, finally feeling the pain of a loss we'd never admitted. Years of tears flowed free. And then I knew what she wished to accomplish. She wanted to build a bridge that would link, and separate, our two peoples, and give each person the choice she had just given me—the freedom that both races had taken from each other. I heard her joyous laughter inside my head and I joined in aloud.

Her voice echoed in my head, incredulous, David, you can hear me?

Yes. My arms held her tight. There is much to do. If we can share this, there is hope for us all.

"Only Human" appeared in *The Martian Wave*, July 2000. *Another novel concept that became a short story.*

# Gone

In my fear for my life

I don't lose sight of the machine that brought me here.

Then for one moment, an eternity,

I glance away and am lost.

The ship is gone.

The tether is gone.

The suit is gone.

And with them

All air and water that will keep me alive.

But I don't need them.

I am looking on endless time.

I am nothing next to the universe.

Yet that knowing makes me something.

Seeing such beauty and depth makes me

      something more and something less

         than what I thought I was.

*Written to submit to PBS' Earthscape.*

# Born of Human Kindness

"**YOU'RE NOT HUMAN**," JONES REPEATED for the third time, tossing his moon-suit on its rack.

The statement no longer ended in a question mark. Will glanced from face to face outside the airlock. The distrust took on different guises. The hate in Jones' eyes made Will want to crawl out of his skin and leave it behind. Seren's amusement eclipsed all; her skeptical smirk brighter than usual. The others quiet said more than Will wanted.

"I am too human," Will demanded. "Prove I'm not." He wondered again if the Board's plan had been in the company's best interest. Of course they hadn't asked him.

"No," said Jones thoughtfully. "You prove you are human."

The trial had begun yesterday and this parry of Jones's only added one more level. *Well, I've been trained for this.* "You want me to cut my hand and let the blood drip out?" Will asked, weighing the sarcasm to force Jones's hand.

Jones grinned. "That's a start. But I want a sample of it. We'll use the lab at school to test it."

The others glanced around. Talk of blood changed everything. They eyed Will, expecting him to back off.

Will made a show of nerves, before nodding. "Yeah, I'll do it. But I get to test you, too."

"Deal, wimp. Let's go. I've got extended access for my extra credit project in molecular reconstruction."

*Just my luck, my fifteen year old judge turns out to be a jerk and a full-fledged genius.*

Jones wasted no time when they got to the lab. He handed

Will a lancet and took one himself. He set out two plastic dishes to catch the blood and paused, the lancet above his index finger, glaring expectantly at Will.

*Here goes.* Will slashed the lancet across his palm.

Jones stared in surprise. He jabbed his finger, squeezing the tip to make the blood squirt and to demonstrate his pain threshold.

Will formed a fist. The blood fell slow, like condensation dripping in a cavern.

Smiling, Seren slapped a bandage over Will's palm. Will appraised her anew, nodding thanks for her kindness.

"Hey, Seren, what about me?" Jones complained.

"Get your own bandage."

Will asked, "You need a bandage for that pinprick?"

"I'll mop the floor with you, human or not." Jones shifted Will's dish to the microscope. Lifting a few drops onto a slide he slipped it in. With a soft grunt he adjusted the knobs. After a silence broken only by breathing, he slid the microscope away.

"Doesn't prove anything. We'll send it through the computer." Jones poured the rest into a vial and placed it carefully in the input carriage. "Record sample of blood from Will... What's your full name?"

"William Jenson Branford."

"William Jenson Branford. Date it January 12, 2046. Test for all known antibodies, proteins and amino acids. Is this blood human or synthesized?"

Will's name showed as the only sign of progress.

"Damn thing's slow," complained Jones. "Schools got outdated equipment. For once I-"

"Quit whining, Jones," Seren said. "It's the same equipment my dad uses at the hospital, just slower."

"Shut up, Seren. You're not so hot, just 'cause your daddy runs the hospital. I'll bet you-"

This time the computer interrupted, "Sample is human."

Jones slammed his hand down on the computer.

"Abuse of hardware will result in restrictions of access,

Theodore Jones. Warning logged at 12:45 p.m. January 12th, 2046. Witnesses: Serenity Wentworth, William Branford, Kylynn Dion--"

"Accepted," Jones growled and thumbed the ID pad.

"He's human, Jones," Seren said smiling. "At least as human as you and me. Well, maybe more than you."

Jones glared at everyone, but his eyes settled on Will. Will saw it wasn't over as Jones stalked out.

"He'll get over it, Will. He's just jealous that anybody beat him at GravBall. Especially somebody your size."

"And what do you think of me, Seren?" Will asked.

"I think you're cute."

Will's face grew warm and he felt a twist in his stomach. *Damnit, a bit too early for puberty.*

"Let's get out of here." Seren called to the others, "Anybody for some GravBall?"

A chorus of positive sounds drowned out Will's lonely "No."

"Not coming, Will?"

"Maybe later, Seren. I gotta check in. Mom's gonna be penc'd off at how late I am."

"Okay." She grinned at him. "Tomorrow? After school?"

"Yeah."

*       *       *

At home Will took the punishment without complaint. He felt his mother's curious gaze as he headed for the 'tique room. Being grounded from all electronics set him off, but today he was eager to cut down inputs. Dad's books and mom's old crafts adorning the walls comforted Will as he sank down into lotus position on the simulated bearskin rug.

Buddhism had been one of his first discoveries. Its calm helped him consider his predicament with detachment. He'd taken this assignment as a chance to move up the Corporation's stagnant hierarchy. So far it beat all others in novelty. Experiencing birth was particularly amazing. Implantation had terrified him, but it went perfect. She'd never had regression

therapy that might bring out the abduction. Will'd been careful not to be a problem once he discovered that possibility.

The current trials were the first challenge to his humanness. He'd stay clear of Jones until he could get on his good side. He still had at least ten years before he could implement the Plan. Kandrian law required voluntary submission. That forced Will and the other Kandrians scattered throughout humankind to wait.

It wasn't a long wait for them and Will sometimes regretted the shortness of this assignment. He wished humanity's life span offered a more leisurely approach, but that shortness of life made them more valuable to the company. If he, could pull this off he'd be the richest man in the Kandrian system. The initial advance alone would keep him high style. A knocking brought him out of his near trance.

"Will," his mom called, "wash up. Dinner's ready."

"My work is never done," he said aloud.

*       *       *

Jones's face didn't grace the hallowed halls of school that week, and he returned surprisingly conciliatory. Other than a challenge to a GravBall rematch sometime in the indefinite future, he returned to roguish animosity. Will forgot the blood incident until it returned to haunt him.

He arrived home from school to find his parents awaiting him. Their faces beamed with pride. What did I do now?

After dinner, they retired to the family room. Father poured wine for himself and Mom and a token amount for Will. "William, we're proud of you. You know that?"

"Yes, Dad."

"Now we're equally proud of ourselves. It seems that your blood has miraculous rejuvenative powers. Dr. Wentworth at the Medical Institute, I believe you know his daughter, has requested your cooperation. You have antibodies for things his computers don't recognize. Son-"

"Will," his mother interrupted, "we're still proud of your scholastic achievements, but in this we feel we had direct

contribution." She flashed a seductive smile at his father.

Damn, not too subtle. Now they'd apply for a second child.

"But, Mom, Dad. I don't wanna be poked like a lab rat."

"William Jenson Branford," his dad said, "you mustn't be uncharitable. This is a boon to all humanity. Your name will go down in history."

Right along with yours. "Can't we keep it anonymous?"

"Absolutely not. Besides, Doctor Wentworth promised it will be a short battery of tests."

"What about that Wentworth girl?" asked his mother, trying to keep him off guard, "She's very cute."

I'm not prepared for mom to marry me off. In this body I'm a prepubescent thirteen year old. God, give me strength.

"I'll think about it, okay?" He glanced from one to the other with all the gravity he could muster. "Wait, this combination of your gene structures is now mine, right?"

"Will, honey," Mother slid toward her classic condescending tone, "Of course it's up to you. We'd never make you do anything you didn't want to. Right, Dear?"

Dad nodded. They left, leaving Will to wonder what effect they'd tried to have on his psyche.

*       *       *

Will agreed after evaluating his options. For all the respect children hold in human society, they're often worse off than cattle, human chattel to their parents' whims.

Besides, the corporation had assured him that no human being or machine could detect his alienness.

Will wondered on the intelligence of his decision after the second week as a practical prisoner, Seren's nightly visits his only relief. He poured out his soul for her examination, revealing everything except his true self. She listened kindly, nodding appropriately. When he finished she waited, but he had nothing to say.

"So, why are you still here?" she asked, her voice playful.

"What can I do?"

"We can leave." Her slight smirk spread.

"But my parents... Your father--"

"Haven't listened to us." She grinned. "If we disappear maybe they'll take us seriously."

For all his thirteen years of human experience, he still didn't understand the alienness of the child he inhabited. When it comes to real choices, Will admitted, I let others make the key decisions. "You think it'll work?"

"I'm sure of it. You trust me, don't you?"

"Of course, Seren. You're the one person I trust. I know you act, first from certain knowledge of what is best for you, and secondly for those you care about. I understand enlightened self-interest."

Seren beamed. "I think that's the sweetest thing anybody's ever said to me." She pecked Will on the cheek. "Come on, I've got it all planned. Bring anything you can't live without."

Will glanced at his belongings. Nothing. "Let's go."

She grabbed his hand and pulled him through the door. "This new wing is deserted at night. But, Will, there're guards at the main building."

"Guards? Why?"

"Think." They slipped down the dim hallway. She slapped a door switch and shoved him inside. The light came on as she closed the door.

*A janitor's closet?* Cleansers assaulted his nose, but two moon-suits caught his eye, his and Seren's.

"Wait. Where are we going?"

"The gang's hideout. No one but kids knows about it. Our parents know it exists, but they think it's inside the city limits. Come on," she prompted, slipping into her suit. "We've gotta hurry. We're going out with the maintenance drone. It'll save us walking time."

In minutes they sat atop the drone, exiting the lock into the lunar night.

"Can you find it in the dark?" Will's voice trembled.

"Of course," Seren replied. "I've never tried, but... Look, we

could walk there with our eyes closed, right?"

"Yeah."

"With Earthrise soon, we'll have light. Quit worrying."

They stopped talking, alone in their thoughts. Will reached out and grasped Seren's gloved hand. When the robot stopped rolling, she pulled him to his feet.

"Look, the Earth crest."

Will gazed where she pointed. The Earth's glow shone on the horizon, spreading long shadows over the rocky terrain.

"You know where we are?"

"Yeah. Sorry I doubted."

Skipping, they bounced toward the hideout in three meter strides. The entrance had been a cave, but now appeared as another odd formation of rocks. They'd blown the "rock" from plastics, and laid it in place as protection for the air lock. They'd improved it regularly. Once a rough tumulus, no outside clues remained of the bubble from the moon's molten youth.

Inside, Seren and Will collapsed onto bunks. The heating system activated, humming as Will removed his helmet. Cold crisp air greeted his nostrils.

"Seren?"

"Yes."

"Thanks."

"What're friends for? You hungry?"

"No, tired."

"Sleep then. I'll check the pressurization alarm. Set the one in your suit, and leave your helmet closed."

"Think I'm stupid?"

"No, Will, I always thought you were smart... for a boy."

"G'night, Seren. And, Seren... Thanks."

"Shut up and sleep, Will Branford."

*          *          *

"But we weren't kidnapped," Will complained at the screen.

"Relax and eat your breakfast. This'll work out to our benefit. Don't you see--"

Will shushed her. "—performing tests on the male child, William 'Will' Branford, whose genetic structure could be an elixir to match the legendary fountain of youth. If you have information, please contact the Goddard City police."

"Damnit. My name's all over. What're we gonna do?"

"Wait. Let's see if they figure out it's not a kidnapping."

The media repeated the information hourly. The following day pleas from their parents appeared. By nightfall, the novelty of being fugitives wore off. As they waited for sleep, they agreed to turn themselves in the next morning.

In the night the pressure alarm went off. Scrambling into their helmets, adrenaline racing, Seren flipped on the lights and Will released a directional smoker to show the leak. The airlock door slid open and a small suited figure entered.

"Jones, you jerk!" screamed Seren. "Damn you!"

"Nice to see you too, Seren," Jones replied, pleasant for once. "I figured you'd be here. I brought some friends."

Three adult figures stepped out. Their reflective view screens left no clues to their identities.

"Thank you, Mr. Jones."

The tall figure nodded. "You've proven valuable. But I'm afraid we won't need more help."

"Nice place," said the other, in a softer commanding voice. "I think it'll do for tonight." They opened their palms to show palm guns. "Tomorrow we'll make a trip. My apologies, Mr. Jones, but I'm afraid we're breaking our bargain. You'll accompany us. You found us. We cannot afford to be found. Not till we're done with Mr. Branford."

"What?" whined Jones, his face shocked.

Will couldn't tear his eyes from the palm guns. One flip of the wrist and we're dead.

"Come children," the softer voice crooned, "The darts contain only tranquilizers. We don't wish to harm you."

The three children exchanged glances.

"Mr. Jones, get the smoker from William."

Jones did, but Will saw anger and hatred in his eyes, for once,

directed at someone else.

"I'm sorry, Will, Seren. I guess I didn't think this through." Jones's eyes met Seren's for a moment before he jumped, landing in front of the adults. With a twist of his hand the smoker exploded.

"Run, Seren, Will!" Jones yelled. "Get out!"

The three figures, camouflaged with smoke, stood between them and the lock.

"There," Jones continued, "into the airlock. Shut the inner door. They can't get out until it cycles. I'll drive their rover."

"Shut up, Jones," Seren growled.

Will glanced around wildly for Seren, but couldn't see anything but smoke. Had she gotten out with Jones? Where they leaving him? An arm spun Will around. Seren put her finger to her mask and pulled Will under the bunks.

The lock chimed and the door opened, sucking out enough smoke for Will to see. The adults shoved each other into the lock. The door slid closed and Seren moved, shoving hard off the bunk and sailing toward the lock. She spun and landed crazily, grabbing for the control panel. She ripped off the cover and pulled wires as sparks flew and the lights blacked.

"Will?" Seren called. "You all right?"

"I'm fine."

"Seren?" Jones's voice screamed. "Will? I'm outside, but the lock isn't opening. Are they inside? What happened? Answer me."

"If you'd shut up I would," Seren retorted. "We're fine. The door mechanism's ripped out. A minute ago I'd've killed you, Jones. Now I'd kiss you. Can you drive their rover?"

An explosion of expletives erupted inside their helmets. "How long can you stay in there?" growled the once soft voice.

"Don't know if I can drive it," Jones said nervously.

"Try, 'cause we're not going anywhere until they're out of the lock."

Seren clicked the light on.

Will stared, shaking his head, his suit-light wavering. "How'd you guys do that?"

"Learned it from you," laughed Jones.

"Yeah," agreed Seren, "Your famous GravBall gambit. Now get the power back or it's going to get cold."

"Bad news," Jones complained. "It's code locked. I don't think I can hack it."

"Then go, Jones. It'll take a while to get back."

"I'm going to get help," he paused, to catch his breathing. "And Seren, Will. I'm sorry."

"Go Jones," Will said, slapping off his and Seren's suit radios. They leaned face-plates together. "Can you hear me?"

"Yes," answered Seren, her mouth exaggerating the movement of her words. "Talk slow."

"The lock has manual controls!"

"How long will it take them to get in?" Seren asked.

"Not as long as it'll take Jones to get help." Will's brain raced. Jones and Seren had saved him and finally he would take action.

"Then what do we do?"

"Call for help."

"But we don't have transmitting equipment."

"Yes, we do." The green oxygen light blinked on Will's faceplate. They ripped their helmets off.

"What are you talking about, Will Branford?" she asked. "We don't have anything other than suit radios and they won't broadcast that far."

"Remember that holographic thing I built for my science project?" Will said, busying himself with a crate under one of the bunks. "Here it is. It's a transmitter using an unused frequency."

"What good is it?"

"I can talk to my people."

"Whattaya mean?"

"Jones was right. I am an alien spy."

"Will, start making sense. You didn't lose enough oxygen to go groundhog on me."

"I can't explain right now. I know what I'm doing."

"But I don't know what *I'm* doing," Seren complained. "What can I do to get them to contact the local authorities? He arranged

the array."

Will punched a key and spoke in Kandrian. After a few minutes another voice emerged from the machine, agitated, and a little higher pitched. After a few more minutes, Will shifted back into English.

"That's what I'm telling you. I know it's early, but I've got a signed contract."

The other voice answered in English. "It's in order?"

"Would I mess this up?" Will's voiced rang with annoyance. "This is my big break. The Corporation's biggest break." He grinned at Seren, who stared back at him in amazement. "Now broadcast me on all bands. I want to announce the specifics of the deal before the competition."

"This is highly irregular. I'll have to get approval."

"Just do it. Now!" demanded Will, his childish voice cracking into his higher register. "My head's on the block here. Another corporation is closing a deal as we speak. Switch me!"

"I'm registering a formal complaint."

"Fine. Do it!"

"You're broadcasting on all frequencies."

"Hello humanity, I'm William Branford. I'm located on the moon at 47 degrees longitude and 23 degrees latitude. People are searching for me. I'm being sought for my amazing gene structure, but the fact is that I am not human, but a genetically developed host. My race, The Kandria, wish to make an offer to humanity. We wish to purchase rights to distribute humanity's treasures, your monumental quantities of entertainment output. I have a contract offering you free agency in this enormous economic opportunity. It is signed by me, a representative of the Jundvin Corporation, and is binding in our system. Seren Wentworth will act as assignee for humanity. Seren, please sign the docu-"

"Transmission canceled. You little fool. You'll pay for this. You'll spend the rest of your life human."

"I know," Will snuck a glance at Seren. She grinned back at him. "That's the stupidest business deal I've ever-"

A gruffer voice exploded, "Lij'bran'widan, you're fired! If I

come into contact with you I'll rip that human flesh off your bones like it was shedding time. This isn't over."

Will punched the transmit button off and spun to face Seren. "I'm sorry I lied to you."

"You never lied to me."

"But I'm not human."

"No, Will, you're human. It's more how you act than who your parents are. Now, tell me what you did."

"I cut into the Corporation's profits. Now, I need to write that contract or humanity is going to lose control of its assets."

"What assets?"

"Everything humanity has created for entertainment, your religions, video, histories—"

"What would your people want with that?"

"My people are bored. They're starved for information. Your virtual reality toys will allow them to become something with a purpose—"

"But what's wrong with the contract?"

"When a race declares free agency it means each piece of merchandise is dealt with individually. Tracing ownership cuts into profits." He couldn't stop grinning like a groundhog. "But I don't care about profits anymore. And I'm certainly not bored. Maybe you're right. Maybe I am human."

*Written as a group challenge from a Kristine Kathryn Rusch & Dean Westley Smith workshop at Rustycon in Tacoma, I think. I remember them asking, "How many of you want to be published?" Write everyday. Finish a story or a chapter a week. Send them out when they are done. That's the secret to getting published. We all left agreeing to go home and write a story with "YOU'RE NOT HUMAN," as the opening line.*

# Children of the Sky

A shooting star in the morning light
Descends to Terra with a desperate might
With a crack of lightning, the flame and smoke
Clears away from the giant's hulk

At the lake of the leopard in the thin plains air
The natives watch the enigma that awaits them there
The silver winged devils maw opens wide
And the man in white, enthroned inside

An angel or a devil, a man or a beast
The peasants stare in awe, has he come in peace?
As he exits the beast the sunlight catches his hair
The golden halo of light brings the people aware

With his shield removed, the sky man in white
Speaks into a stick as our minds alight
We hear his voice inside us and we understand
Our minds are open, beckoning to this hallowed man

We feel no fear of this man from the sky
He is here to enlighten our awakening minds
To fill our thoughts to grow and prosper
To find the path we need to follow

A thousand suns have passed
The silver-haired man's die is cast
He leaves his seeds as he returns to afar
The light of curiosity and yearning for the stars

He enters the silver temple, the flames beneath alight

The sky is like the sun on this, his final night
The temple shudders then rises on a pillar of fire
Then the night explodes and the false sun flies higher

Over the horizon and into the night
The aurora fades with a return of light
The sky man's legacy lingers with each rising of the sun
The great stone temples will remind us of the one

For fifty father's sons his memory won't die
To inspire and to guide us, the children of the sky
A starman's children will never lose their father
Whose children of the sky will someday inherit the stars

*One more written at good old Hoquiam High School. Probably in Geometry. Sorry, Mr. Gregory. I have used some of the geometry in figuring things out some of the science in the fiction.*

# Regression Therapy

"SHE'S GONE AND IT'S MY fault. I should be with her. We were going to go together, like in the movies," Paul said, taking the coffee from the old man and scratching the cat in his lap. "I was born in '76. I know, hard to believe, I'm that old."

"Hard to believe I'm this old." The old drifter laughed, settled his bones back on the ground and leaned up against his worn army-issue backpack.

"January 2000," Paul continued, "I'm hiking in the Olympic Mountains, in Washington, the other Washington, out on the *wet* coast. Almost through college and didn't know what I wanted. Anything but a forty hour a week job like other wage slaves.

"Didn't help that my girlfriend expected to get married and start having kids as soon as I finished. So I was hiking in the woods alone, wishing for something to take me away. I climbed to the top of this small peak, Mt. Hoquiam. It's got a glacier lake nestled in between it and another peak. Beautiful, calm, cold. I love snow camping, the serenity takes me away. I'm laying down on a snow drift watching the sunset and I fall asleep. Next thing I know I'm on an alien spaceship.

"I'm thinking, no one's gonna believe I've been kidnapped by aliens." Paul glanced at the man across the fire. *Is that what I'll look like?*

The man's wrinkled hands reached out for some heat from the fire.

"I'm trying to figure out if it's a practical joke." Paul chuckled. "Problem was only God could pull off a joke like this one. Or Rod Serling. I always wished something like that would happen to me.

Like Twilight Zone, or The Outer Limits or one of those Star Trek episodes where they pick up someone from another time.

"I woke in a bedroom-sized cell. One corner had a desk. The material looked like metal, but warmed to the touch, like plastic or wood. No grain or pattern and no connectors or seams. The ceiling glowed at the same level at all times. There was a pad attached to the floor. Looked like everything else, but softened with body heat. None of it moved.

"I found a pen and notebook with a Woolworth's price tag for 29 cents. Who's heard of aliens shopping at Woolworth's? Great ad campaign. How long has it been since a 200 sheet notebook sold for 29 cents? Maybe they bought in bulk."

"I was calm, considering my situation. Figured they could've killed me any time. Then I saw them. Little green men. I wouldn't believe my own eyes. Straight from a B-movie. Found out why everything was attached. Woke up one morning floating in the middle of the room. My response to weightlessness lacked finesse. I vomited. Well, they towed me to the bed mat and did something that kept me there. I hardly noticed them till they'd left. When I woke up, down had returned and the cell showed no signs of space sickness.

"Eventually they spoke to me, English, sort of. Their nouns came through clear, but the verbs had no logic. You had to ignore the verbs and try to guess what they meant. The first one came in by himself and asks me, "You buy happy." It took him a minute to say that. Told him I was fine. Then he says, "You weigh meat?" Threw me for a loop, until he showed me the plate and called the stuff on it meat. He wanted to know if I liked it.

"I named them Eins, Zwie, Drei and so on. according to which one called on me most often. They showed me their ship. A hallway connected my cell to a computer room. They took me in and seemed to want me to use it. When I started punching keys they got excited and left.

"Pretty quick I figured out enough to receive television transmissions. I watched the news. Never thought I'd be happy to see Dan Rather. Eins showed me that punching certain

combinations got the stuff they pass off as food. So I tried to get myself something decent, then, Dan Rather, the newscaster, is in my face. The screen floated in front of my eyes and moved with me. Interfaced direct to my optic nerve, so their biology's similar.

"Figured I was a rat in a maze, but the food improved, and I found I didn't miss anybody. I took prodigious notes. They found me notebooks with a price tag from Wal Mart. Is that a step up? I wondered how many people had run this maze.

"Their computer reminded me of a Chinese type setting machine, you know 3,000+ pictographs. Keys in a circular bank so each as accessible as another. They left me alone, sometimes a whole group watched me, as I puzzled out combinations.

"After about four months they started bringing aboard others. Lois Anderson, store clerk, age 48, came first. We didn't get along well. She worried about missing "Days of Our Wives," or some such shlock. They kept her aboard for a while, because my computer time increased. I found out the hard way that if I didn't go near the computer, people disappeared quick.

"They abducted Candace Butler, All-American Girl, ex-cheerleader, and beauty pageant entrant. Not too bright. She thought we'd been chosen to start the human race over again. Who was I to dissuade her? We spent three days and nights in bed. Then she disappeared. They carried me into the computer room.

"After three years and 17 people they got it right. Helena was worth the wait. I can still hear Mom say, 'How come you spend all your time with machines? When are you going to find a nice girl?' Mom'd be impressed with Helena.

"Unfortunately, she didn't want to be there. I knew how to send her back, but didn't tell her. I knew she'd come around.

"But she wouldn't eat. I tried to tell her that they wouldn't pay any attention. I was afraid to spend time out of the computer room, because they'd send her home. But how could I ignore her suffering? I felt plenty guilty.

"I spent every spare moment at her bedside to convince her life wouldn't be so bad. I wanted to tell her, but I couldn't.

"But as she got sicker I couldn't keep quiet. I finally told her. First I said I loved her. She smiled like she already knew. Then I told her I'd always known how to send her back. She didn't take it well. Moved a lot quicker than I expected for someone who hadn't eaten in weeks. Thought she was gonna kill me. Ripped out patches of hair. Gave me a black eye. I escaped to the computer room. Wasn't like I could lock the door, but she didn't come after me. I worked some, but mostly I thought. How could I have considered doing this to her? If I really love her like I said I did, then how could I treat her like I was some kind of kidnapper, or at least an accomplice?

"After a couple hours at the computer I decided to apologize and send her back. When I got to her room, she didn't answer my knock. My first thought was she'd killed herself. I barreled into the room to find her sleeping--a half-eaten plate of food lying on her bedding. She lay there snoring gently. I went back to work on the computer.

"I woke the next day, went to check on her and she was gone. I wandered through the rooms we had access to, still not finding her. Found her in the computer room. She offered me a deal, very business-like. She didn't apologize for my battering, though I think she wanted to. She agreed to give it a month. If at that time she wanted to go, I'd stop working and she'd be gone in a few days. If she decided to stay it'd be on a day by day basis. Her biggest problem with the whole thing seemed to be that the captivity was involuntary. We spent the next couple days reacclimating her body to food. She continued to sleep a lot, but when she wasn't asleep I showed her the puzzles that kept me going.

"The deadline passed without mention. She was the perfect woman for me. She liked to be alone, too. And seemed to sense when I wanted company. I got to understand her moods. We talked about great novels, the meaning of life and what kind of people we wanted to be. To allay the aliens fears that I'd stop my research, we practically lived in the computer room. One of us hit keys while the other wrote. It became our courtship.

"She loved languages and the arts as much as I love things

mechanical and electronic. She taught me to ballroom dance when we stumbled on a music library. We discussed high math. I approach it from a standard, learned approach while she came at it from an artist's point of view. Oh, and she read and liked Heinlein though she didn't appreciate Job to the extent I did. Probably 'cause she saw no point in religion as a idea. Me, I'm a seeker, not really expecting to find an answer, but always looking.

"Anyway, we went to the moon. They manufactured suits for Helena and I so we could visit the surface.

"Helena and I spent many hours debating the reason for our capture. First we figured that we were additions to an already extensive collection, like Columbus' return with Native Americans. So perhaps they would be leaving soon and taking us with them. They must realize mankind's limited life span. But after several years with no change in shipboard activity this conclusion wavered. They continued to collect and collate data. How much longer would this mission to seek out new life and new civilizations last? The series didn't show any signs of getting canceled.

"At first learning their language went swimmingly, but after getting down the words for food, entertainment and sanitary expectations, it bogged down. We both worked to teach them earth languages, but they couldn't get down the concept of verbs. Their vocal chords or whatever they use are wonderfully imitative, but they can't make any sense out of doing things.

"The collection of earth nouns we shared made rudimentary communication possible, but little else. For two years I had tried to discover where they came from. I read astronomy texts from Galileo onward. When I reached Clyde Tombaugh, they abducted a young astronomer named Aaron Gillis.

"Aaron immediately pinpointed their system as Tau Ceti. He begged me to let him stay, but he wasn't an optimal companion. Aaron babbled constantly to himself if no one else was around and to anyone else who happened to be unfortunate enough to be within hearing distance.

"They abducted Helena next. She seemed perfect because of

who she followed.

"She tried to discover their earliest entry into our system. The mother ship and the moonbase seemed undateable, but we discovered a collection of works that gave some clues. These books weren't in their information base. Real solid books, some literally solid as rock: stone tablets, scrolls and parchment. Must've been easier for them to work in the past when they were considered gods. Did they pilot Ezekiel's wheel?

"Our first communication breakthrough occurred when their second generation appeared. The process started eight years after Helena arrived. The others took turns regressing to the point of childhood. We assumed it was how they extended their lines, because the new ones had different personalities. The process was astounding. Like putting life on frame-by-frame rewind and then hitting play again.

"The first regressed one began to understand earth languages! Once she showed this capacity, they all regressed. Helena selected Esperanto for its simplicity. Of course, I had to learn it, too. High school Latin finally did me good.

"We learned more about their regressions. They weren't supposed to lose data in their brains, only their attitudes toward that data. Then they'd be able to reinterpret the information without preconceived notions. They'd have full knowledge of their language but no basis for its use. We discovered it was a medical and scientific choice set up to assist the mission. Every twenty years new viewpoints would surface. With this, their research could be unbiased.

"Finally they asked the big question. It was incredibly simple to have taken 20 years of a dozen lives to ask. "Can you help us get home?"

"Over the years enough of their original knowledge was lost so they could no longer read their own language. Everything they did became a ritual, religious process. They'd lost the ability to pilot their mothership other than for short trips. We'd been riding in a faster-than-light ship for twenty years with beings who'd forgotten how to operate it. Their regression, once their greatest

strength had become their greatest weakness. Sadly, we had to tell them we didn't know how to help.

"Helena figured out a plan. If they'd regress her, maybe she could learn their language. She understood their speech patterns. Each noun implied a verb and a different noun was required for each different action. So the word for ball would be different depending on if you were hitting, catching or throwing it. Combining her new information and my aptitude with machines, we thought perhaps we could discover how their ship worked.

"She started the regression. I watched her get younger and younger. We broke off relations when her breasts began to disappear and her pubic hair started falling out. She stopped at about 12 years old. She remembered everything, but she didn't have the emotions to deal with it. I wondered if she could ever love this old man?

"They said after we helped them solve their problem they'd regress me, too. Then they'd take us back to Earth as young people. What a second chance! To return to an Earth that is our own future with knowledge of hidden centuries.

"Once Helena knew their written language, their machinery proved simple to understand.

"She rediscovered feelings for me over the next year. Though it was difficult to take "I love you," seriously coming from a thirteen year old entering puberty.

"As I learned how to operate their ship, I taught them. We worked side by side with the machinery designed for them. Their natural perspective helped immensely.

"We took a dry run around Pluto, sliding by the other planets on the trip. Our solar system is incredibly beautiful.

"They regressed me. Helena and I joked about her being the older woman. I felt incredible. We helped them gather data and gave them first-hand information on what it's like being human. They said we'd always be welcome on their ship. I was living a school boy fantasy--An older woman who loved me, a chance to return to Earth young with all that I had learned.

"But Helena started talking about forever. How we could go

with them and raise kids to be real space explorers. Everything we could see. I wanted to go, but I couldn't. If I went I would never get to change my mind. I mean what if I stopped loving her? Or she me? So I tried to talk her into staying, but it was no use. She knew what she wanted and I was a tool for her to get it. Children and the stars and good old Paul to keep her company.

They brought me back. Same spot they picked me up. It's been ten years. Now I know I made a mistake. I can't look at a woman, no matter how gorgeous, or brilliant, or joyful and not think of her.

"My life before the regression was like a movie I'd seen. But as my emotions matured I learned how much she meant to me and what I'd lost. Adolescence wins again.

"I've been looking for them. I've tracked UFO sightings and contacted Aaron. He's meeting me in Albuquerque. I can put up with his babbling for the chance to find Helena. I'd like to visit her family, but what would I say? If I told them I'd seen her they'd think I killed her. I have no alibi. I'm a non-person, wandering around with false ID's. Nobody'd believe I'm 62. Maybe someday I'll find them and her. I mean, I'm young, at least in body. There's time. Or maybe I can outlive my broken heart."

Paul glanced up. The sun had set behind the freeway overpass. The old man lay sleeping against his bedroll. The coffee cup sat cold in Paul's hand, untouched. The cat purred gently in his lap and stretched.

"You believe me don't you, Doc?" The cat narrowed his eyes as if to show his skepticism. "You're probably some alien life form, too." Paul laughed. "Smarter than the rest of us no doubt."

Paul set the cat down, fished the can of hot stew out of the fire and placed the tin coffee cup on one of the hot stones. He swallowed the food mechanically, tossed down the black coffee and shouldered his pack. The cat had settled into the sleeping old man's lap. Paul sighed. *Someday maybe I'll be that content*. He strode out from under the overpass. The night sky shone bright and clear and his eyes absorbed every detail as he headed southwest.

"Regression Therapy" appeared in *Aoife's Kiss* & *Wild Child*.
*First draft was first person, diary. It didn't work.*
*This works better, I think.*

# Rocket Tears - January 28

I remember the day quite clear
As if it were yesterday
A day that had dawned bright and clear,
Soon would be torn away
I walked into a room, full and hushed,
Stunned into silence and sorrow
Their spirits were broken and crushed
As the blast took away our tomorrow

Smoke clouds of billowing white;
Next few moments flash by in a blur
We see the fire as the engines ignite,
Then the unthinkable occurs
I see the flash and then hear the sound
As it replays again on the screen
There I stand and ask why
As she crashes down into the sea

There I stood and I cried. . . rocket tears
Sorrowful tears in my eyes
As rain from the skies
Obscures the clouds and our fears

Five years later on that January day,
I drove to see a new life arrive
The clouds have now drifted away
And now we once again strive

The birth of a baby brings hope
A renewal of life and of dreams
As for death use the pain for our growth,
See what the future reveals

From death there will come life again
As the phoenix arose from the fire
Please don't let our dreams fade
With the flames of the funeral pyre
Tell the story to daughters and sons
Of the lives that people have given
In the dream of pursuing the sun
They'll remain in our memories living

Here I stand and I cry. . . rocket tears
Hopeful tears in my eyes
As rain from the skies
Obscures the clouds and the years

*Written for my daughter, Sheridan M. M. Slater and in honor and memory of the Challenger Seven, the Columbia Seven and everyone else who has sacrificed for our future in space.*

# One Tin Soldier

Jerzy Milosz looked from his wife's disapproving face to his flashing com.

"Answer it. I know you're going to." Ayita returned to their picnic lunch.

"We got him," Bill blurted. "It's really him. Shall we put him in the holding cell? It's not very secure."

Milosz nodded, no words coming. He'd waited his whole adult life for this. "Sedate him. Strap him to the bed. Post a guard." Milosz barked. "We'll convene the trial right away." He switched the com off.

Jerzy felt a tug at his sleeve. "Yes, Rafal. What is it?"

"You gonna help me build the fort, Daddy?"

"Daddy's busy. Tomorrow night." The little face clouded. "Tomorrow, Raffy-boy, I promise. I'll be home before bedtime."

He turned to see his wife scowl. "Ayita, they found him... After this... Then I'll take a vacation."

"Jerzy, leave vengeance with God. Your parents will still be dead. What about your wife and child?"

"Ayita, I'm going. We'll talk when I get home." He stepped onto the slidewalk and walked to increase his speed. *Does God care?*

Minutes later he stepped off the slidewalk and the Justice compound's doors opened. His eyes found Bill and another ranger with an old man in between them. "Bill?"

"He was out in the open." Bill and the other Ranger stood the old man up.

The strange bearded figure before him had killed his parents.

Milosz took in the ancient glasses and the soldier's uniform hanging like rags on a scarecrow. All he felt was disgust. "You will pay." The words shot like knives.

The old man stared back, a befuddled look clouding his face, as the Rangers led him away.

*    *    *

Milosz paced outside the cell. When the door opened he practically pounced on the psychiatrist.

"No good. He can't remember what he's done. He doesn't remember the war, hardly remembers Earth." The psych turned and walked away. "He's not fit to stand trial."

"What?" roared Milosz, following. "You're telling me that murderer can't remember killing anyone, so we can't try him?"

The psych continued walking. "The laws on Brierwold that you helped set up protect our people, but they also protect him. In his condition he won't stand trial."

Milosz grabbed the psych, "But these are war crimes!"

The psych gently removed Milosz' hands. "In what war?"

"I don't care what you call it. When a soldier massacres a civilians and then blows up the evidence... It's a crime."

"I've got all his existing memories on the mem-corder. There are only two of significance. He's signed a release. Experience them if you wish." The psychiatrist motioned him into his office and pointed to a chair. "The most recent memory isn't even from this century."

"What about the other ninety years?" Milosz sat in the chair. It reclined and a metallic device slid into place near his brain stem.

"Gone. You'll feel a little tingle. It hurts less if you relax."

Milosz breathed deeply to calm his pulse. The tingle came and the psych faded from sight.

*    *    *

Milosz became the old man.

He faded into the brush, absentmindedly pulling off a casshon thorn and shoving it into his belt next to his sidearm. He slunk back into a favorite spot. Hidden beneath one of the dead casshon vines, he spied Rangers through a gap. He grinned as they passed. When their noise died out, he crawled, scooting along on his elbows. He paused at the edge of the brush-free zone, and watched children playing. Pulling the hand-sized thorn from his belt he bit off the tip and sucked out the warm, sweet liquid.

It would make a fine wine to trade for the things he needed to survive. He found the specific vine easily. Odd that he'd missed it before. Perhaps, this year weather changes had altered its flavor. He broke off another, and took a quick suck to assure himself of its quality. He pulled thorns from the vine and dropped them in his knapsack. Either the vine took too much attention, or his hearing had faded too far. He didn't hear the Rangers' feet in the undergrowth.

Hands clamped around his arms. The time for action passed.

"Come with us, old man."

He'd lost the game. He stood at attention as they stripped him of his weapon, then marched, head held high. As he entered the schoolyard tears perched precariously on the lips of his eyelids, not daring to make the final leap. The children stopped playing. Had they ever seen a man like him? Carefully trimmed beard, glasses. They led him into town. He listened to the children laughing happily as they continued their play.

The Ranger's hands bit into his biceps as they shoved him through a doorway. Then they waited. A man came in, his gaze flared—hating, vengeful.

Words flew, but the meant nothing. He only felt the anger. *What did I do to you?*

They guided him into a cell. Its stark gray walls closed in. The one small window interwoven with metal echoed the walls' uniformity. How many years since he'd been inside a building? His winter cave's walls enclosed, but their strength, untouched by human hands, comforted him.

His captors closed the door. He paced. *I'm too old to run*. They stood outside the door. Where they waiting for him to attempt escape?

*   *   *

The walls melted from view and Milosz stared into the psych's calm face.

"Are you comfortable?" he asked. "We can do the earlier memory in a different session."

"No," Milosz said, "Let's do it now."

As his vision faded, his saw his own angry face staring untrusting and hateful. Then a new vision drowned out his thoughts and his volition.

*Just out of basic and they send me to Kosovo. Straight into the middle of a terrorist civil war.* United Nations peace-keepers hadn't kept the peace. The same questions whispered from everyone's lips: Why are we here? Who do we fight?

Raucous laughter rolled out of a pub as the fresh-faced young recruit continued his patrol. The smell of a gentle fall rain floated on the air. His ear-implant hummed, "Greenboy, check in."

"All's quiet. I'm just reaching the corner of--" The grass next to the sidewalk exploded outward plastering him with clumps of wet dirt. Something exploded behind him. He dropped to his face. A scream broke the air. He spun searching out the sound's source. The bomb behind him had caught a young woman in its violence, she lay at an odd angle, her white dress splattered with mud and blood. A small boy bent over her.

As he watched, a pipe-grenade landed a few meters from the child; its fuse burnt low. The child turned and moved toward it. *Not enough time to throw the bomb away.* He scrambled to his feet, ran, stumbled toward the child. He dove and knocked the child down, covering him with his body.

The bomb exploded. The world, suddenly quiet, retreated from the chaos. The young soldier rolled off the boy, wobbled to

his feet. The child looked uninjured; he screamed, but no sound came forth.

*I'm deaf. Better than being dead.*

The child pointed at him, eyes wide.

He looked. His camouflage fatigues clung to his right side, black with blood. *Odd, I don't feel anything.* He collapsed to his knees as the world returned with a vengeance. His surroundings spun, enclosing him.

*       *       *

The darkness faded and his head cleared. Milosz' own heart beat fast to provide blood to his phantom injury. *That kid was Rafal's age. My mother died like that.* "That's it? Nothing in between?"

"Nothing, but thirty years of tramping through the brush." The psych sighed. "There's nothing we can do. I'm sorry."

Milosz' mind raced. "If I can restore his mental capacities? What then?"

"If he can be made cognizant of his crimes, we can proceed." The psych paused. "How do you intend to do that?"

"We'll rejuve him."

"Only at his request."

"I'll get it. Thank you, Doctor."

"Be careful not to let revenge carry you away, Mr. Prosecutor."

Milosz brushed past the psychiatrist. He nodded at the guard and jammed his thumb on the door's seal. The door swung open. He inspected the prisoner. The clean gray coverall fit smartly, but in spite of the clean clothes, the beard and glasses left him an anachronism.

The old soldier eyed him with interest. He motioned toward the other seat. "Will you sit?"

"Thank you," Milosz replied stiffly.

The prisoner pulled off his glasses and polished them on his sleeve. "Of what am I accused?" he asked quietly.

"You massacred civilians who came to parley with you."

"Someone you loved was one of them. I can see it in your eyes."

"Yes, my father was their leader," Milosz answered, surprised at his own transparency. "But you killed my mother as well. You don't remember?"

The soldier's eyes narrowed and he gazed out the window.

"Can you convince me you're not a murderer?"

The old man shook his head.

"Tell me what you can remember." Milosz studied the face in front of him. He could see the lines of strength in the jaw as the muscles shifted.

The soldier sat silently, his eyes flitting across the wall. After a long, deep breath, the eyes rose to meet Milosz full on. The soldier began to speak, quietly and deliberately. "I can recall my childhood. 'Til I enlisted in the peace-keepers at 18. I got caught in an explosion. Then I'm here. The stars are different and people are chasing me. Been a long time. Anything I've done since then has been for survival. I did what I had to, but as far as I know I haven't killed anyone. I don't even know how many years I've been here, twenty, maybe thirty."

"Thirty-eight years?"

"Could be," shrugged the old man. "Kept track for a while, but converting to earth time made it seem kinda pointless."

"What else can you tell me about your time here?

"I never stole anything. When I needed something, I always paid for it somehow."

"Yes," agreed Milosz, "I've tasted your casshon wine. Its quality is famous." *I promised Ayita we'd make casshon wine this year.* "That's not what we're here for."

"Memories come in flashes, sometimes in the day, but usually in dreams. Can you tell me what I've done?"

"Your military record states you enlisted in 1998." Milosz received a nod. "Two weeks out of basic you were wounded in Kosovo saving a young boy. That's all you remember?"

"Yes." A sudden agitation animated his skinny face. "How did I get here? This isn't Earth."

"No, this is Brierwood. Do you know what year this is?" Milosz got no response but cloudy confusion. "2094 on Earth. Would you like to know what happened in the fifty-eight years between 1998 and your arrival on this planet in 2056?" For a moment he thought he saw a spark of life. *Pursue that spark.* "Would you like your life back? Not just the memories, but youth, as well?"

"What's the catch?" The old man's eyes bore into Milosz'. "What do you get out of it?"

*Time for a lie or the truth? The truth.* "If you recover your memory, you're fit to stand trial for war crimes. If not they'll send you back to Earth. There's a veteran's hospital on the moon."

"Where I can sit around with all the other loony old soldiers? No. I need to know the truth." The old man paused, then continued slowly, "I don't remember what it's like to be around people. Or why I'm running or hiding... Getting caught was almost a relief; even knowing that I'm accused of crimes is more than I remember. Half a lifetime. Isn't that long enough to not know who you are or why you're hiding? Can remembering be any worse?"

Milosz wondered. Not remembering would be pleasant. "Will you give me permission to start the rejuvenation process?" He could hardly conceal his anticipation.

"Yes. Do it." The soldier turned away.

\*   \*   \*

Milosz sat hooked into the mem-corder chair next to the old soldier. The psych dimmed the lights and the present faded.

He stared into the distance with the soldier's eyes. Nothing but marshland and water as far as he could see.

*Special Forces training at my age? Maybe they're right. Chest deep in a African swamp with two hours of sleep in the last 48. No, I'm not crazy.*

"Come on, old man."

The term had acquired a hint of respect over the last few days. By the end of training he'd relish the jibes. At 42, finishing the training and becoming one of the World Nations Special Forces,

would be quite an accomplishment to tack onto his distinguished career.

"Watch out, Sonny Boy," he croaked at Gibson, one of the youngest. "I'll beat you back and put your bottle on the warmer and your teddy bear on your sleeping bag." Good-natured laughter broke out behind them and lifted their spirits out of the dismal swamp.

The sheer monotony of pushing back swamp grass caused his mind to wander. He thought of the final confrontation at the airport. "Last straw," she'd said, but he'd heard that before. *She's right. My daughter's third birthday is important.* Especially considering he'd missed the others. He lit a candle for her that night at the base.

Then the letter from his wife arrived. Dearjohnned in the bush. *Dammit anyway, this is what I do. I promised her I wouldn't go off like this.* He answered his own unspoken thought, *I've said that before.*

All his life he'd been a soldier. He'd read every war book he could get his hands on. He recalled days like this one, tromping through backwoods swamps, paint guns slung over shoulders, surviving on adrenaline. *But we had more food then.*

A scream erupted behind him, and cut off in a gargle as he spun. Where Gibson had been his hat floated, air bubbles surfacing.

"Croc. Gibson's down." He scanned the surface, saw a man out of the corner of his eye, yelled, "Jones, catch." Tossing the rifle, he dove under the water, not waiting to see if the gun reached its target. The murky mud made sight impossible. He felt motion in the water, grabbed and felt hard hide scrape his hand. Something hit him in the stomach. His mouth opened and lost precious air as his arms locked around it. Spinning now, the thing grabbed back. Gibson! He seized the strap on Gibson's pack and pulled himself toward the crocodile. The croc's mouth held Gibson. Whipping out his belt knife he banged the beast's head with its butt as he dug his legs in. The spin stopped as his lungs burned; reversing the knife he hacked at the tough flesh, hunting

for the eye socket. There. It slid in up to the hilt. He twisted the knife toward the brain. The croc bucked, throwing him off. He needed air, but which way was up? He kicked at what he thought was the bottom. Arms grabbed him and dragged him to the surface. Gasping, air flooded back into his grateful lungs.

"Gibson?" One of the men asked.

The soldier shrugged.

"Look. Over here." Jones pulled at something.

In moments they had Gibson out of the water cradled between four men.

The squad looked to the old man for guidance. "Command, this is squad C. Man down. Croc attack."

"Is he alive?" one of the younger soldier's asked. Gibson's body, shredded from thigh to stomach, lay open. Exposed intestines and blood mixed among strands of ripped fatigues.

Jones hands were on Gibson's neck and his face over his mouth. "He's not breathing, but he's got a pulse. We need to start CPR. Get him to solid ground."

The squad carried him to a mud slick and laid him down.

Jones went to work, but his activity seemed to only increase blood flow. Helping hands tried to staunch the bleeding with psuedaskin, but it didn't help.

After a few minutes the soldier spoke. "Let him be. Damnit!"

"I thought crocs didn't attack like that," complained Jones.

"Maybe it had a bad day." He grasped Gibson's hand. For a moment it seemed to move and return the grip. He'd probably imagined it. *Death firsthand never gets any easier. And if it did? What then? I am too old.*

*   *   *

The psych removed the mem-corder from the old man's head and coiled it up. As he retracted his own hardware Milosz stared at the soldier. He'd hated him for years. But living through the old soldier's memories, he'd begun to know him. The image of the devil fighter, or the romantic Robin Hood figure, didn't fit this

strong, quiet and unassuming man.

The soldier wiped at his eyes as if he'd had real tears. "That was a hard time. I don't know what happens next, but I have a life now. Almost too much to handle."

Milosz nodded. "I'm sorry. If I could simply pick out what I needed I would."

"No apologies." The old man smiled, his jaw working against the emotion in his voice, "Besides it wouldn't be fair without putting it in the context of a life, would it?"

Milosz found himself returning the smile. The soldier's expression triggered a memory that raced across his consciousness. He's seen that look before, but he couldn't bring it back. "Shall we head to the infirmary? Don't forget that I've promised you your youth."

"I haven't forgotten." They walked on. "Three more years tomorrow, eh? You'll be there?"

"I'll be there." Guilt flashed as Milosz realized how much he'd been enjoying these memory trips. *I should be home making my own memories. And Ayita's. And Raffy's.*

Milosz glanced at his watch. In three hours he'd be done with this session. He'd taken the afternoon off to surprise Ayita and Rafal. He nodded to the psych.

An expanse of stars opened to his view. In between 1hem dark shapes floated. *Mars campaign of 2042.* Milosz thought as he faded from his own life.

He cleared his throat, felt the throat mike hum and spoke, "All right, close up those ranks." He punched his jets and moved into position at the head of the pyramid. Behind him, on each point of the pyramid, were his three hand-picked lieutenants. He trusted his life with them. "We're going in. Targeting on. Enemy in range 30 seconds." He felt great. The Renewal left him feeling half his age.

The enemy appeared as a long line, spreading out into a claw formation. A beam hit him and knocked him off point. He spun wildly. Lights and sounds bounced off the inside of his fishbowl

helmet. He felt the suit contract on his thigh to staunch the flow of blood. With a wrenching halt the suit froze, automatically counteracting the spin.

"Captain, MedEvac, monitoring your signals. Doesn't look good. I'm going to bring you in."

"Negative , MedEvac. No time. I'll come in on my own power when we're finished here."

"Captain, you don't come in you may lose that leg."

"MedEvac, roger, out." He pumped his jets and headed into the fracas. He neared the melee. They were outnumbered, but they wouldn't be out-fought.

He let out a battle cry. His answer echoed in fifteen tongues with a hundred voices. The pain kicked in. He tongued the switch for neo-morphine and kept fighting. His chest panel took a direct hit. The helmet blacked out seconds before he did.

Milosz followed the soldier into the hall, picked up the guard and headed for the cell. Something in soldier's manner, his proud walk tugged at his mind. He struggled to pin it down.

*   *   *

The old soldier pulled himself to a sitting position on the examination table. He scrutinized Milosz.

Milosz glanced away, trying to swallow the lump in his throat. "How do you feel?" He didn't want to admit he couldn't uphold his end of the bargain.

"Look. Your eyes are giving you away again. Give it to me clean. They've done every test they could. What's the diagnosis?"

"The renewal the military gave you in 2041 affected everything but your brain," Milosz explained. "Those were the early days. Great idea and it'll double your life expectancy, but still... A dead end. This rejuvenation can't counteract what they did. The only thing showing any signs of rejuve is your brain."

"That's why I can remember things?" the old soldier asked.

"Right."

"I'm even starting to remember not remembering. But you can't do anything about my body?"

"No."

"Then I'm dying." He waved off Milosz' attempt to interrupt. "Don't tell me it might be some time. I feel it."

"It still may be years. The life extension techniques they used worked well, except on the mind. We've taken care of that."

"I'll live long enough to finish your trial."

Milosz, suddenly remembering his position, spun in his chair, surprise etched in his face.

The old man explained. "I still need to know what happened. I'm sure you do too. I trust in your honor that you tried to keep your promise. Let's set up that mem-corder. I'll give you every memory I've got."

*We're getting close*, thought Milosz, as the familiar vista of twisting vines appeared. *We're on Brierwold*.

The now middle-aged soldier, a Colonel due to the field command, paced in front of his tent, his last patrol overdue by half an hour. *How many would return this time?* He'd lost 45 of his 90 men to attacks of attrition. *What the Hell was the W. N. thinking?* One frontier world, a company should be plenty. They were the best-equipped soldiers he'd served with, but they fought a foe that would die rather than give up their homes.

It wasn't like this world contained anything special. The name said it all--Brierwold, forest of briars. Two continents lay near the equator and everywhere under 3000 feet of elevation vegetation covered the land. It contained no intelligent life, but masses of insects and plant-life. After twenty years these farmers had fought back the briars and were holding their own. Then the verdict came down from system courts. Tolerating squatters would set a bad precedent.

So they sent in a company of Marines to clean things up. A show of force and those colonists would fall into line. They hadn't considered the tenacity of these people from countries that had been pushed around for hundreds of years: Irish, Amerindian, and

Poles.

They put him in command, a last grab at glory, but it hadn't gone well. The last order he'd received, already a year old, told him not to expect reinforcements. Two more worlds had opened up. The anti-squatters weren't screaming so loudly. But he still had a job. He was damn well going to do it.

A rumble from the direction of the settlement brought him out of his reverie. It didn't sound like troops; it sounded like a riot. He rushed into the tent, climbed in his PersArmor suit, strapped it up, checked the weapon's levels, grabbed a side arm and headed toward the noise.

He met them on the camp perimeter, a mob. Some carried weapons from his men, some axes, shovels, makeshift bows, clubs and knives. He strode up to the leader of the throng.

"You must disperse," the suit amplified his voice.

Roars of displeasure rose from the crowd, but the leader waved them down. He matched the soldier's stance and looked him in the eye with self-assured pride. "You're all that's left of your pretty battalion. Do you surrender or do we kill you, too?"

Milosz' heart skipped a beat. It was as if he was looking in the mirror. He saw his own rage and intransigence echoed in those eyes. The scene faded out.

The psych was bent over him. "Milosz. You all right?"

"I don't know." He sat up and the psych removed his wire. "My father- I need to go home." He stumbled from the room.

Milosz hopped onto the slide and continued to walk dazedly forward. His father's hatred stunned him. The few memories he had left of his father were all pleasant: planting together, long walks, games of catch. He didn't recognize the man from the mem-corder as his father. *How can I make it fit?*

He fell into Ayita's arms. As soon as they held him something let go inside. Tears flowed and sobs racked his body. At some point Rafal's smaller arms wrapped around both of them.

Later that evening, Milosz sat outside staring at the stars. He picked out the yellow sun of Earth. He'd never seen Earth.

Ayita offered him some casshon wine. "Do you want to talk,

Jerzy?"

He accepted the wineglass. "I don't know." Her hands rubbed his back and neck, silently supporting. Tomorrow would be another day. He'd finish the session. Maybe by then he would know.

\*    \*    \*

The scene faded back in. Milosz tried to remain detached.

*All dead? It's not possible.* "What happens if you kill me? They'll only send more."

"Then we'll fight them." Yells of agreement and support echoed his words. "We will do what we must."

"How many of you wish to die today?" the soldier asked.

The crowd grew quiet, but the leader continued on confidently. "As many as it takes," And then slowly and deliberately, "Will you surrender?"

"No," answered the soldier.

The crowd charged. He tossed the mob aside one by one, as they rushed. For a moment they let up. The soldier saw their ploy. He alone stood, surrounded by dozens of the settlers toting his men's guns. *They don't know how to use them.*

An explosion knocked him to his knees. The readings on the control panel flashed. A direct hit to his propulsion system. *They learned.* He started shooting with the side arm as covering fire. With his other hand he armed the perimeter bombs. He wasn't going down alone. The ground exploded in front of him. *It's me or them.* For just a moment after he pushed the detonator he saw the little boy in Kosovo bending over his mother. Then the foundation of the world broke loose. The ground shook, rolling him over onto his back. Screams broke the air then choked out. As the dirt settled over him he struggled, but he was stuck on his back, like a beetle in its shell. *I'm alive.* He rocked back and forth. Nothing worked, and he refused to shed the armor. Exhaustion hit and he slept.

When he woke, sound had stilled. He unstrapped the personal

armor and stood carefully. Night had fallen. The twin moons high in the sky lit the carnage in an eerie glow. Villagers lay around him, some buried, limbs at impossible angles, some nearly clean, laying as if they simply slept.

The horror of the scene finally broke through his stoicism. *No more. Too many dead.* He stumbled back towards the encampment, checked the company's medical sensors. The crowd hadn't lied. Every light save one was black. He set the self-destruct on the weapons lockers and armed the rest of the defense systems.

He piled a grav-sled high with provisions and supplies, then headed out away from the settlements and the camp. When he reached a safe distance he triggered the system. He didn't look back as the horizon lit up with the false sunrise.

The aurora faded and the present gradually intruded.


The two men sat silently in the darkness. The psych would return momentarily. The old man had back his memories, if not his youth. Milosz had his knowledge. Yes, the old soldier had once been the man who killed his parents, but he'd paid a terrible price--fifty years gone from his memories and then 40 spent in a dazed sort of half-life.

Milosz finally spoke, his voice a harsh whisper, "You're free to go. There's a transport headed for Earth, leaves next week." He crossed to the door, flipped the lights to low and left, leaving the door standing open.

Several hours later Milosz sat in his office and stared at the darkness of his com-screen. His ghosts from the mem-trips, his father's proud face and his own combined into one.

Bill burst into the office, "He's gone."

"Who's gone?" asked Milosz.

"The old soldier," the Ranger replied.

"Yes," replied Milosz, "I expected he'd go."

"But he... He's a dangerous man."

"I hardly think so. My report has been submitted to the

criminal court... along with my resignation."

Bill's eyes flashed. "Where is he?"

"If you must know where he is..." Milosz crossed to a terminal and hit some keys, pulling up a relief map of the area on the screen. "This is calibrated to his vital signs. We found a military implanted sensor during his physical. We can track the signal." He chuckled dryly, almost coughing. "We could have found him any time." He punched a few more keys and a small, steady green light appeared, moving slowly across the map.

"Why'd you do it. Why'd you free him?"

"Why did I free him? I didn't. I sentenced him to life."

The Ranger shrugged and exited.

*The war's over.* Milosz stared at the flashing light. *I hope you find peace, soldier.* He stood slowly and crossed back to his desk. Outside he could hear the children laughing in the school yard. *How many years have I wasted trying to bring peace to the dead with no thought for those alive*? He straightened out his desk for the last time. He glanced at the clock. He'd be home in daylight to kiss his wife and son. *I'll pick up some casshon wine and we'll watch the sunset.*

Sometime later, days, weeks, months, in the prosecutor's office the light flashed green to red and then faded.

# Afterword

23 June 2017

Dear Reader,

I wrote the afterword as a forward to the ebook. When I decided to release it as a printed ebook collection, I thought I'd do it as a flip book, like the the old Ace SF Doubles in the 70s. It has been a challenge to format, a challenge to get printed, but in the end I am proud of what is included here! As a bonus to you, I've also included *One Tin Soldier,* the first decent story I wrote that I didn't sell!

Cheers.


30 July 2013

Dear eReader,

First, thank you for purchasing my creative works. I've been writing short stories, songs, and poetry practically since I could place pen to paper. I've had my phases, song lyrics, plays, short fiction with interstitial poetry. I am a third generation writer. My mother released a book of poetry that included poems by her, my grandfather, myself and two of my children. I've released a CD of my own songs, Some of the Parts, and seen some of my plays performed.

I'd been reading Science Fiction and Fantasy since the golden age of 10, but hadn't considered writing it. At the age of 24 I read a Spider Robinson novel, *Time Pressure*, and I sat down the next day and wrote my first speculative fiction story. I started my first novel not long after and twenty years, 600+ rejections, 14 short fiction sales later I am finally releasing my debut novel, the third I have written and this collection, of many of my sold stories.

This last year has been one of synchronicity. In November I wrote 60,000 words for National Novel Writing Month

[NANOWRIMO], discovered the Speculative Fiction writers group at Village Books and was chosen as one of six writers for the Bellingham Herald's serial Science Fiction story, *Memories of Light*. I attended the Children's Literature Conference at WWU and the Chuckanut Writer's Conference. Cory Skerry, writer and reader for Tor.com, stalked me enough to decide I would be open to him inviting me to join the Bellingham Writer's Group which included fellow serialist, Amanda Hagarty. Amanda is now Editor for my debut novel: *All Is Silence*, to be released as an Advanced Reader Copy less than a year after I started writing it in November.

As I began to think of ways to develop buzz for my novel and learn the process of self-publishing, I decided creating an e-book of my published fiction would help both goals. Along the way I decided that it made sense to include some new fiction set in the Deserted Lands Universe, so here we are. I hope you enjoy these stories and poems written over the last thirty years. If you do, please, stop by and sign up for my mailing list at www.desertedlands.com or www.robslater.com.

Write on,